the final bullet

BOOK FOUR OF THE SYDNEY HARBOUR HOSPITAL SERIES

CHRIS TAYLOR

LCT Productions Pty Ltd
18364 Kamilaroi Highway, Narrabri NSW 2390

ISBN. 978-1-925119-30-5 (Paperback)

The Final Bullet is a work of fiction. Names, characters, places, brands, media and incidents either are the product of the author's imagination or are used fictitiously. Any resemblance to actual persons, living or dead, events, or locales, is entirely coincidental.

Published in the United States of America.

BOOKS BY CHRIS TAYLOR

THE SYDNEY HARBOUR HOSPITAL SERIES
(in order)

The Perfect Husband
The Body Thief
The Baby Snatchers
The Final Bullet
The Debt Collector
The Lab Test
The Stolen Identity
The Cliff Top Killer
The Likeable Fraudster

THE MUNRO FAMILY SERIES
(In order)

The Profiler
The Investigator
The Predator
The Betrayal
The Deception
The Negotiator
The Christmas Vigil
The Ransom
The Defendant
The Shooting
The Maker

Find out more about all of Chris Taylor's books, including the hugely popular Munro Family series by visiting her website at: www.christaylorauthor.com.au/about/books

DEDICATION

*This book is dedicated to all the current and former police officers
who serve our communities so bravely and so tirelessly, past and
present, and in particular, to Hayley Brown, Nicholas Kosseris,
Rebecca Bavister, Michael Kilfoyle and David Savage.
Your commitment and dedication is beyond question. The world
would be a scary place without you in it.*

And as always, to my wonderful husband, Linden. I love you.

Acknowledgments

As usual, no book comes into being without a lot of help and support by my friends and family. A world of thanks must go to my wonderful editor, Pat Thomas. Thank you for everything that you do to make my stories even more amazing than I could ever dare to dream. To Detective Superintendent Michael Kilfoyle, David Savage and to Senior Constable Rebecca Bavister, thank you for lending my story credibility. Any mistakes are wholly my own.

To Alisha and all of the staff at damonza.com, thank you for yet another fantastic cover. To my sister, Nicole Guihot and to my friend, Ally Thomson, thank you for your excellent editorial comments, proof reading skills and suggestions. I hope you like the final result.

To Amy Atwell and her dedicated staff at Author EMS who are so much more than book formatters. Amy, once again, thank you for your magic.

To the fantastic writer organizations such as

Romance Writers of Australia, Romance Writers of America and Romance Writers of New Zealand for all the help, support and encouragement they offer new and aspiring writers, including me.

To my readers, thank you for your support and love for my stories. Your encouragement and enjoyment make this journey all worthwhile.

And lastly, to my friends and family, especially my husband and children. Thank you for putting up with late dinners and even later conversations as I've emerged day after day from the sometimes scary but always enthralling world I've created on my computer.

PROLOGUE

Dear Diary,

The blackness inches ever closer until I feel all but consumed. Its icy fingers clutch at my heart. I silence my screams of pain and frustration with my fists pressed tightly against my mouth, lest I give myself away. The agony of it burns behind my eyes. Why can't she see? What can't she understand? I am falling...falling...falling...
I fear that I am lost...

The galvanized iron walls of the shed surrounded him in the darkness, suffocating him. The sun had long since called it a day, but still the heat in the air hung heavy and unrelenting. He sucked in a breath that scorched his lungs. Tears burned a path down his cheeks. He stared a little desperately at the gun in his hands. *How had it had gotten there?*

He thought of his years in the police service, the countless scenes of horror he'd been forced to witness: wives and mothers hacked to pieces with machetes; children deliberately drowned in the bath. Men who had committed unspeakable atrocities and were allowed to walk free on technicalities. The wrongness of it all left him angry and frustrated, the feelings made worse by the knowledge that those in charge of the legal system were often willing to look the other way. As long as it wasn't *their* wife or child, *their* loved one rotting in a grave. They preferred to focus their energies on more pleasant matters, like choosing a new national flag.

Another wave of anger and desperation flooded through him and he tightened his grip on the gun. It was loaded with a single bullet. He was an excellent shot. He would only need one.

"Dad? Are you out here?"

The sound of his young son startled him. He froze, his finger hovering over the trigger.

"Dad?"

The voice had drawn closer. The boy would be upon him any minute. The shed door scraped open. He leaped to his feet. He couldn't have his son find him like this. He stumbled across to the gun cabinet.

"Dad! There you are! What are you doing in here?"

The boy held a flashlight. The strong yellow beam cut a swathe across the man's face. He held up one hand to shield his eyes against the glare and then turned back to the gun cabinet.

"What are you doing with the gun?" his boy asked curiously, coming up beside him.

Panic swelled in his gut. "I-I'm cleaning it, buddy."

"In the dark?"

He stared down at his son and was filled with a sudden surge of pride. The boy might be young, but he was clever beyond his years. He'd go far in life. The thought filled the man with gratitude.

"Yeah, I just finished," he lied. "I was about to lock it back in the cabinet and come inside. What are you doing out here? It's way past your bedtime."

The light from the boy's flashlight puddled on the dirt floor. His son stared up at him in the dimness, his expression solemn. "I wanted to kiss you good night."

The innocent comment ripped into the man's chest. An agony of pain and desperation filled him, surging through his heart. Moments earlier, he'd been sucking on the barrel of a revolver. Now, his five-year-old watched him with love and admiration glinting in his eyes, waiting for a bedtime kiss.

He couldn't do it. He couldn't do it to his family. As much as he craved an escape from the darkness and the pain, he couldn't do it. He couldn't pull the trigger. The knowledge was like a band of steel around his chest. He bit back hard on a sob.

"What's the matter, Dad? Are you all right?"

Squeezing his eyes shut, he bit down on his tongue until he tasted blood. Slowly, he opened his eyes and nodded.

"Yes, son. Of course. I'm... I'm fine."

CHAPTER 1

Ava Wolfe pulled back the white lace curtains that covered the window of her mother's bedroom and smiled at her sister.

"It's the most beautiful day, Sammie! The clouds have drifted away and the sun is shining! Everything smells so fresh and new. It's the perfect day for you to get married." She turned and her smile widened. Samantha stood before her, dressed in a bridal gown. Tears of joy clogged Ava's throat.

"Oh, my goodness, Sammie! You look beautiful! The most beautiful bride in the world."

Samantha Wolfe laughed softly. "The world? Really, Ava?" she chided gently. "Today I'd settle for the most beautiful bride in Sydney."

Ava joined in her sister's laughter and enveloped her in a gentle hug, mindful of the exquisite white satin-and-lace concoction beneath her hands. Hundreds of tiny pearls and sequins had been hand sewn into the bodice. The dress gleamed and sparkled under the light, almost as brilliant as the dazzle in Samantha's eyes.

Ava's heartstrings tightened. She couldn't help but feel the tiniest bit envious of her baby sister. Ava had put a year of effort into her last relationship before deciding to end it. Now, she wondered if she'd ever find Mr Right. She'd give just about anything to look and feel like Samantha, who was deliriously happy and about to marry the man of her dreams.

Despite a mountain of obstacles, including a mother who'd undergone a kidney transplant and a brother who was now warming his butt in jail, Samantha and Rohan had come out on top and were a true testament to the old adage that love conquered all. They'd only been engaged a little over three months—at their age, neither of them had wanted to wait.

Ava knew the feeling. At nearly thirty-six, she was a year older than her sister and also had plenty of experience being on her own. It wasn't like she *wanted* to be single. She'd dated numerous men and had given each of them a fair chance—she was sure she had. She'd given twelve months of her life to her latest, Ian. She'd hoped they'd grow closer, that time would prove he was the one.

But that hadn't worked out. Instead, she'd come to realize no amount of time would change who they were. He simply wasn't the man for her. She'd let him down gently and had broken off their relationship, all the while trying not to feel bitter about the time she'd wasted.

Her mother disagreed with her on that score. As far as Enid Wolfe was concerned, no life experience was wasted, even when it came to dating the wrong man. 'It helps you become more discerning the next time, honey,' her mom had wisely counseled. 'You learn from your mistakes.' Ava could only hope her mother was right and that she'd have the opportunity to find out.

"How are we doing for time?" Samantha murmured, putting on her earrings.

The luminous pearls had been worn by their mother on her wedding day. The thought reminded Ava of their loss. She swallowed a tiny sigh of disappointment that their father hadn't lived long enough to walk his daughters down the aisle.

Recalling Sam's question, Ava glanced at her watch. "All good. We have an hour before the limo arrives."

"Where's Jessie?" Samantha asked, referring to Ava's identical twin sister.

"Downstairs, putting the finishing touches to Mom's hair."

A frown marred the smooth skin of Samantha's brow and concern darkened the color of her eyes. "How's she doing?"

"Mom?"

"Yes. It's been a madhouse with all the preparations for the wedding. I haven't even had time to bless myself and it feels like ages since Mom and I had a good talk."

"She's fine. She still gets tired if she overdoes it and the antirejection drugs take their toll, but considering she wouldn't even be here without the transplant, we have nothing to complain about."

"Of course not. It's bad enough that Dad isn't here to see me get married. I can't imagine not having Mom by my side, too."

Ava moved closer and adjusted the matching pearl necklace around the bride's neck. "We're lucky it didn't come to that."

A shadow moved across Samantha's face and Ava was immediately concerned. "What is it, Sammie? You're not having second thoughts, are you?"

"No, of course not. Rohan's all I ever dreamed of in a husband, and more. I... I was just thinking about Alistair."

Ava's lips compressed and her mood sobered. The thought of their brilliant older brother, serving a five-year prison sentence for human tissue trafficking, filled her with sadness. He'd told them prior to his hearing date that he was prepared to accept responsibility for what he'd done and that he was sorry for the pain he'd caused the family.

It was just like Alistair to spare them all the difficulty of a trial by pleading guilty. It still shocked Ava to know that he'd been harvesting human organs and tissue without donor or family consent. She understood one of the reasons he'd done what he did was because their mother had been on a transplant list for years and would have died if she didn't receive a donor kidney in time, but Ava still struggled to accept his actions and Samantha and Jessie did, too.

But now wasn't the time to dwell on their

wayward brother, or the reasons for his absence. Forcing a smile, she picked up the gauzy veil that lay spread across the bed.

"Let's put this on," she said, moving to stand in front of her sister. "The photographer's already downstairs. He's waiting for you to make an appearance."

Sam nodded and gave Ava a tiny smile. "Yes. If we don't get a move on, it'll be time to leave, and after the chunk of money we've agreed to pay the photographer, Rohan will kill me if we don't get some decent beforehand shots. He said he wanted a minute-by-minute photographic account."

Ava smiled back at her. She arranged the veil over the intricate curls woven around Sam's head, relieved to see her sister's mood improving. It wasn't right for a bride to have even the slightest of dark feelings on her wedding day and if Ava had anything to do with it, it would be nothing but smiles from that moment on.

Leaning forward, she kissed Sam on the cheek. "There. All done."

"What do you think? How does it look?" Sam asked, fiddling with the satin-bound ends.

"Beautiful. Almost as beautiful as you."

Sam threw her another smile, this one full of love and gratitude. "Thank you, Ava. You're very sweet to say so."

Ava shrugged. "It's true. Besides, it's your wedding day, little sister. It's the least I can do."

"Ouch!" Sam smiled.

Ava gave her a quick hug, once again mindful

of her sister's gown and veil. "I'm kidding. You've never looked more beautiful. Rohan's a lucky man."

"We both got lucky," Sam replied softly. "I've never met a nicer guy, with such a kind and generous heart."

"And sexy to boot," Ava added with a laugh. "What more could you want?"

Sam winked. "Now you see why I want to put a ring on it."

"On that note, we'd better get moving. Mom and Jessie will be wondering where we are."

Linking her arm with her sister's, Ava led the bride toward the bedroom door. Sam halted suddenly and squeezed Ava's arm.

"Ava... You're okay with Ian attending the wedding, aren't you?" she asked, a little anxiously.

Ava sighed at the thought of seeing her ex. Though it had been a fortnight since she'd told him it was over, his wedding invitation had already been delivered, along with the others. She'd hoped he'd do the polite thing and decline, but he hadn't seen fit to do so. Still, she'd only be around him a few hours and it wasn't like she'd have to sit with him. As the maid of honor, she was assigned the bridal table.

"I'll be fine, Sam. Don't worry about it. You just enjoy becoming Mrs. Rohan Coleridge."

Samantha smiled back at her and together they walked down the stairs.

———————

The beautiful strains of *Pachelbel's Canon in D,* played by a piano and violin, reached Ava's ears as she slowly walked down the aisle. Clutching her bouquet of pink and white roses, she nodded greetings to friends and family members who filled the church. As she arrived to take her place beside her twin and Sam's best friend, Hannah Langdon, she glanced across at the men who stood shoulder to shoulder, opposite them.

Tall and handsome in his black tux, Rohan looked slightly apprehensive as he waited for his bride. Ava bit back a grin. She could imagine he was only one of millions of men since time began who'd been nervous at this point in the proceedings. Her gaze slid past him and locked on the man by his side.

Every bit as tall and broad-shouldered, Rohan's best man, Lachlan Coleridge, looked enough like Rohan that he had to be closely related. Rohan had several siblings—four brothers and three sisters, if she recalled rightly. Most of them had been present at the engagement party, but his best man had missed it.

At the time, Samantha had offered the explanation that the second oldest Coleridge sibling had been caught up at work. Ava had wondered what could be more important than attending his brother's engagement party, but she'd shrugged it off and had helped celebrate the upcoming nuptials in style. She winced, recalling the headache she'd woken with the next morning. She hadn't had a shot of Tequila since.

Her gaze drifted across Lachlan's chest and

moved lower. His crisp, pleated, white dinner shirt was tucked neatly into a slim waistband. His suit pants hugged long legs. Shiny, black boots and a black bowtie completed the ensemble and she couldn't help but think he wore a tux well.

She glanced at his face and was mortified to see that he was staring at her. A single dark eyebrow was raised in silent query, a teasing smile graced his lips. She blushed hotly and silently cursed beneath her breath. *How embarrassing to be caught openly staring at him!* She'd been ogling him like he was a dish full of salted caramel ice cream and she'd just been handed a spoon.

Keeping her gaze fixed steadfastly on the floor, she barely managed to turn with the rest of the crowd when Samantha made her appearance. Beaming with love and pride, the bride made her way slowly down the aisle on their mother's arm. Though Enid's kidney transplant had been more than six months earlier, she was still a little frail. Ava had no doubt her mother leaned on Samantha as much as Sam took support from their mom.

Ava had moved in with her mother after the surgery. That was another reason things had fallen apart with Ian; he hadn't understood why she needed to be close to her mother or that her mother needed her help.

'Why can't Jessie move in with her?' he'd whined when she'd told him about her plans. 'Or Samantha? It's not like she's married, yet.'

Ava had given up trying to explain how important it was for her to care for her mother in her hour of need. The family had lost their father when Ava and Jessie were barely three. Sam had been even younger, a baby of fourteen months and she had no recollection of their dad. Ava's memories were hazy, too, but she remembered the feeling of safety, security and love that always enveloped them whenever her dad had been around. Alistair was eight years older than the twins and it had fallen to him to help fill in the gaps.

With four young children depending upon her, Enid had gone out to work. She'd held down two and three jobs at a time in order to make ends meet. Their mom had gone without and had put her children's needs before her own. Now, years later, and after the transplant, her mother needed help and Ava had been determined to do everything she could to see that she provided it.

As Samantha reached the altar, Rohan stepped forward. Their mother kissed Sam on the cheek and then relinquished her hold. Rohan took his bride by the hand and together, they made their vows. Ava stared at the two of them, at the unadulterated love that shone from their eyes, and her heart clenched with emotion. She wiped away tears of happiness and couldn't help but wonder if she'd ever find a man who looked at her like that.

She risked a glance in the best man's direction. He threw her a sardonic smile and then turned away to hand over the rings. Moments later, it was over and the crowd broke into applause. Ava followed suit.

"Congratulations, Sammie!" she whispered and pressed a kiss against her sister's glowing cheek before turning to Rohan.

He wrapped her in an enthusiastic hug and she found herself hugging him back. Despite the fact he was instrumental in sending her brother to jail, she'd learned to forgive him for his part in the awful situation and had accepted that he'd only been doing his job. Alistair had made his own choices. He deserved the punishment.

She'd barely stepped away from Rohan when another broad chest took his place. Her gaze moved slowly upward until she met the best man's smiling face.

"Hi, I'm Lachlan Coleridge. You must be Ava."

He'd stated it with confidence and for a moment, she considered pretending to be her twin. After all, they were identical and as far as she was aware, he hadn't met either of them before. Jessie didn't wear glasses like Ava did, but her contact lenses, worn in honor of the wedding, erased that difference. Jessie now wore her hair a little shorter and with highlights, but Rohan's brother wouldn't know that.

And then Ava dismissed the idea as silly. *What did it matter if he knew who she was?* She ought to be flattered he'd taken the time to find out which twin she was. Not everyone did.

"Yes, I am."

"It's nice to finally meet you," he said.

She raised a curious eyebrow. "It wasn't me who missed the engagement party."

He grimaced. "Yeah, I was bummed about that.

I was involved in a complex covert operation. The timing was all wrong."

She nodded. "You're a police officer, too?"

"Yes, a detective, like Rohan, but I'm not stationed in the city."

"Where do you work?"

"Out west."

She frowned. "Out west, like Campbelltown?"

He laughed. "No, not western Sydney. I mean, right out west. Moree. It's a small country town in the north west of New South Wales. There *is* life west of the Blue Mountains, you know."

Her frown deepened. He might be sinfully good-looking with his dark auburn hair and teasing green eyes, but that didn't give him the right to poke fun at her. He didn't even know her.

"Really? Life beyond the Blue Mountains? And here I thought everyone turned their cars around when they reached Katoomba and headed back to Sydney. Who'd have guessed?" Her sarcasm matched his own.

His grin widened and he winked at her. "Touché, Ms Wolfe."

His gaze held hers and grew in intensity. Her breath caught. She couldn't look away. Her pulse skipped a beat and then galloped away. She swallowed against a sudden rush of nerves.

"Ladies and gentlemen, I give you Mr and Mrs Rohan and Samantha Coleridge."

The priest's announcement broke into Ava's dazed thoughts and she dragged her gaze away from the man who'd held her attention for far too long. Joining in with the second round of applause, she watched Samantha and her new husband walk back down the aisle.

"Shall we?"

Lachlan's deep voice caressed her senses and she shivered under the impact. Stirrings of desire tightened her belly. Swallowing hard, she accepted his proffered arm and walked slowly after her sister.

Through the thickness of his jacket she felt the taut muscles of his arm. His cologne smelled expensive and its spicy scent tickled her nose. She breathed it in and tried to concentrate on the path in front of her, taking care because of her five-inch heels. It wouldn't do to trip over the hem of her floor-length dress.

No sooner had the thought taken hold, than Ava's shoe caught in her skirt. She gasped and stumbled forward and would have fallen if not for Lachlan's steely hold.

"Careful," he murmured, steadying her.

Heat stole up her neck and swept across her cheeks. She was grateful for the curtain of dark hair that half-covered her face.

"Don't be embarrassed," he continued, embarrassing her even more. "We can't all be graceful gazelles."

Indignation shot right through her and she swung around to face him with narrowed eyes. "Why you...you—"

His easy laughter slid over her. "Hey, I'm teasing you, babe. Lighten up."

Babe? Had he just called her babe? His brother might have just married her sister, but this man was way too cheeky. This was something she was neither used to, nor comfortable with.

As a psychiatrist with a busy city practice, she made it a priority to never let down her guard. No matter how distraught and emotional her patients became, she was the strong one, the rock to whom they all turned. She didn't have the freedom to lose control, to show her emotions. She was there to help them through a crisis, not contribute to it.

She was relieved when they made it outside without further incident. She disengaged her arm. "Thank you. I think I can handle it from here."

He quirked an eyebrow and grinned. "You're sure? Because those heels look deadly and the path's not exactly even."

"I'm sure." And with that, she turned away and lost herself in the crowd of wedding guests, wishing she could forget him as easily.

CHAPTER 2

Lachlan stared after Ava Wolfe and tamped down his desire. Hell, he was at his brother's wedding. How could he be walking around with a hard-on? He'd been erect from almost the moment he'd spied her. Even knowing how beautiful his new sister-in-law was hadn't prepared him for the impact of her feisty, older sibling.

The fire in Ava's eyes and the challenge in her voice excited him. It had been a long time since he'd felt that way and he was enjoying it way too much. His gaze followed her through the crowd. It was obvious she knew most of the guests. She greeted many of them with fond hugs and kisses and her laughter rang out over the noise.

Her deep purple satin gown was so dark it looked almost black and clung to her gentle curves. Her breasts filled the low-cut neckline. The remembered feel of her hand on his arm filled him with another surge of excitement. Knowing his interest was reciprocated aroused him even more. He hadn't been the only one flirting.

A tiny pulse had fluttered in her neck and she'd grown nervous upon his approach. She might have appeared to be offended at his gibe about living out west, but he was sure she hadn't meant it. The thought of spending a few hours with her at the wedding reception filled him with anticipation and all of a sudden, he was impatient for it to begin.

Hunting around for his newly married brother, he pulled him aside and quietly suggested the wedding party move on to their cars. "The photographer's keen to get some photos at the reception center," he murmured, making up the excuse to leave.

"Yeah, no problem, bro. I'll find Samantha and get things moving." Rohan's gaze softened and his voice dropped to a husky drawl. "Thanks for being here for me today, Lachie. It means a lot. Especially without Dad."

Lachlan swallowed the lump in his throat and nodded. Their father, Bill Coleridge, had died from a heart attack six months earlier. Lachlan still thought about him every day.

"I wouldn't have missed it, Rohan and I was as proud as anyone to stand beside you as your best man. Dad's looking down on us; you can be sure about that."

The two brothers hugged briefly. "Thanks, again, Lachie."

Rohan turned away. Lachlan's gaze snagged on a man who stood by a giant oak tree, a frown darkening his face. It was a curious expression for a wedding guest and looked out of place amongst the jovial crowd. The man stared at something in front of him. Lachlan followed the man's line of sight and was surprised to discover Ava was the recipient of the man's scowl.

"Hey, Rohan," he called out softly. "Who's the guy over there looking like his world has come to an end?"

Rohan turned and stared in the direction Lachlan indicated and then shrugged. "He looks a bit like the guy Ava used to be with. I don't know what he's doing here. Are you ready to go?"

Lachlan filed the information away and nodded. "Yeah. Give me a minute and I'll go and round up the drivers. I'll see you there."

"No problem. Can Sam's mother and sisters ride with you?"

Lachlan tamped down the surge of excitement at his brother's suggestion and nodded again. "Sure. I'll go and give them the good news."

Ava spied Lachlan striding toward her and did her best to keep her nerves at bay. Ever since he'd introduced himself, her heart had been beating double time. And then she'd been forced to share a car with him, pressed up against him on the back seat. Okay, her twin had also been seated beside them and her mother was up in front, but still...

Though she looked around for a means of escape, she couldn't deny she was eager for more of his company. The speeches had been made and the cake had been cut. The wedding feast was winding down. The three-piece band played a slow song in the background and she swayed a little to the beat.

"Would you like to dance?" Lachlan's warm, minty breath tickled her ear and she shivered from the impact. A thousand butterflies swarmed in her stomach. She licked her suddenly dry lips. Knowing she shouldn't, but helpless against the magnetic pull in his eyes, she nodded.

"Thank you. I'd love to."

He took her hand and pulled her in close, leading her across the dance floor with an air of possessive confidence. He danced well and as she listened to the music she found herself relaxing in his arms.

"Have you had a good night?" he murmured and then swung her around.

She gasped and tightened her hold on his arm, and again took note of the tautness of his muscles. "Yes, thank you. And you?"

His hooded gaze raked over her and then finally landed on her mouth. "The best."

The nerves in her belly intensified and she licked her lips again. "You're a good dancer," she blurted out, unable to think of anything else to say.

"Thank you. My mom insisted on all of us taking ballroom dancing lessons in high school. We whined about it at the time, but right now, I'm glad I did. By the way," he added in the same low, conversational tone, "who's that guy boring a hole into my back? I noticed him outside the church. He's been staring at you all night."

Ava made a show of looking around, but she knew exactly who Lachlan referred to. Her ex-boyfriend had been trying his hardest all night to convince her they were worth another shot. She was trying just as hard to dissuade him.

"That's Ian Rutherford. My ex," she added.

"Ex-husband?"

"No, ex-boyfriend."

Lachlan nodded and glanced in Ian's direction. The man continued to frown at them as they moved around the dance floor.

"He doesn't seem to be handling the ex-thing very well," Lachlan said. "I take it you were the one who broke things off."

"Yes."

"How long ago?"

"Two weeks."

Lachlan winced. "*Ouch*. The wounds are still raw."

Ava shrugged. "I did what I had to do. It's not my fault he's proving a little hard to convince."

"And yet you invited him to your sister's wedding..."

Ava grimaced. "Yes, well I didn't exactly have any choice. The invitations had already been posted and the RSVPs received. The place holders had been printed and the seating arrangements finalized. Samantha nearly had a fit when I suggested we remove Ian from the list."

Lachlan chuckled and the movement crinkled up his eyes, making him even more attractive. Ava guessed his age to be somewhere around her own, maybe even a little younger.

"So, you got stuck with the ex at the wedding and now you're dancing with me. Is this a targeted ploy to force him to accept you've moved on, and so should he?"

"Hey, you asked *me* to dance, remember?"

Lachlan's hold tightened and he drew her even closer, until their bodies pressed together. "So I did," he murmured against her ear.

The feel of his lips so close to her skin sent a tingle of awareness rushing through her. Even through his suit and shirt, she felt his heat. Her heart skipped a beat and then began to pound. She struggled to stay focused on their conversation.

"How long were you together?" Lachlan asked a few moments later.

"A little over a year."

He stopped and pulled back slightly. "It took you that long to work out he wasn't the right one?"

Ava's defenses slid into place and she lifted her chin. "I like to take my time, see where things lead. I like to give people a chance to prove themselves. Real life's not like it is in silly romance novels. I have yet to meet a man who, with just one look, can sweep me off my feet."

Even as she said the words, she couldn't help but think of Lachlan and her explosive reaction to him. Her heart had been doing double time since the moment she spied him in the church and her stomach was still taut with nerves. As if sensing the lie in her words, he threw her a knowing look.

"Is that right? All I can say is you have way too much patience. Life's too short to waste." He shook his head. "Twelve months. Way too long."

She glared at him, stung. "Really? And how long does it take you to work out whether a girl is worth taking home?"

"Ah, now, that's where you're going wrong. Choosing a girl to take home has nothing to do with knowing if she's the *one*. It's like store-bought chocolate and baked, triple-chocolate cheesecake. One is consumed for instant gratification. The other needs a little time to reach the point where it's edible and can be savored at leisure, piece by decadent piece."

The pad of his thumb brushed across the soft fullness of her lower lip. She sucked in a breath and it was all she could do not to poke out her tongue and taste him. Need throbbed hot and heavy between her legs and she wondered what it would be like to be consumed by him like a rich and expensive piece of chocolate.

His voice had lowered to a husky drawl. Her gaze was snared by his. She stared at him, mesmerized as much by his voice as by the sensual look in his eyes. His head lowered and she had only the tiniest sliver of time to realize he was going to kiss her. And then his lips were on hers and every other thought evaporated.

His lips were warm and supple and moved sensuously over hers. Heat trailed in their wake. He nibbled at the corners of her mouth and then moved back to press his tongue against her lips. She opened her mouth in silent acquiescence. His tongue swept inside and neither of them could hold back a groan.

He tasted of mint and alcohol. He smelled of expensive cologne. Her arms crept up around his neck. Her fingers caressed his skin. He was taut and hard and breathing fast. Her breath came just as quick. A moment later, he pulled away and rested his forehead on hers.

"This is madness," he rasped.

She nodded, unable to manage anything else.

"Your ex is watching us with murderous intent," he murmured. "Here, come with me."

Taking her hand, he tugged her off the dance floor and headed toward the cloakroom. Aware of his intention, she wanted to pull away from him, but was helpless to resist. He opened the door and closed it behind them. A second later, his body pinned her against the wooden panel.

His erection felt huge and hard against the softness of her stomach. He ground his hips against hers. She gasped. A shaft of heat surged through her and centered in her core. She moved restlessly against him.

"Can you feel how much I want you?" he groaned against her lips.

She nodded and then shocked herself by whispering, "I want you, too."

Her words sent him into a frenzy and it was like he couldn't get enough. His kisses were filled with pent-up passion. His body held her in place. With his hands on either side of her head, there was no escaping him.

Not that she wanted to. Escape was the furthest thing from her mind. She burned with a need so great, she didn't think it could ever be assuaged. As if reading her thoughts, his hand reached down and gathered up a bundle of her skirts. Sliding his hand up her leg, he skimmed over her stockings and garter belt, then pushed her lace panties out of the way. His fingers found her warm, moist heat and slid between her slick folds. Plunging them inside her, they both groaned aloud their relief.

"Fuck, you feel so good. So wet. So ready."

Despite her shock at his vulgarity, Ava was excited by his words. She'd never been with a man so coarse and raw and...needy. Yes, *needy*. She could see it in his eyes. He needed her. He wanted her. As much as she wanted him.

While his fingers moved inside her, she reached for the leather belt around his waist. She managed to slide it free and then unbuttoned his pants. The slide of his zipper was barely audible over their harsh breathing. Grinding her hips upon his hand, she reached for his erection.

Her hand closed over the hard, silky length and she marveled at the size. He was huge and hot and throbbing and all of a sudden, she was impatient to feel him inside her. Staring down at her, Lachlan seemed to sense her need and with a muffled oath, removed his hand. He tore down his pants and underwear and fumbled for a condom. Fully sheathed, he lifted her higher against the door.

She gasped and tightened her legs around his naked hips. His hand pulled aside her lace panties with a force that excited her. She heard the tear of the fabric, but was beyond caring. His cock found her wet entrance. Without pause, he plunged all the way in.

"Oh, my!" she gasped again, as he stretched her and filled her way deep inside.

"Christ, you're so tight." He groaned and pumped his hips again.

She clung to him, with her head thrown back against the door. Hot, heavy need built up inside her. Her fingernails dug into his shoulders and still she couldn't get enough. His cock slid in and out in a frantic rhythm until she reached her peak.

With a cry, she fell over the other side and gasped and panted as she climaxed over and over again. Her inner walls flexed and tightened around his cock. He groaned.

"I'm gonna come, babe. Fuck, I'm gonna come."

He thrust into her faster and harder and his breath came harsh in her ear. A moment later, he tensed and groaned and finally collapsed against her. Her legs went slack and he loosened his hold. Stepping back, his cock sprang free and he slid her carefully down until her feet reached the floor, still clad in her stilettoes.

In silence, she adjusted her clothing and he did the same. Her mind raced. She ought to feel embarrassed, ashamed of what she'd done. She'd never acted so wantonly in her life. He was almost a total stranger and she'd just had sex with him in a closet. At her sister's wedding. Her mother would be appalled. Enid Wolfe had raised her children better than that. Ava had let her libido get away with her. She'd totally lost control. *What would he think of her?*

"Don't overthink it, Ava and for Christ's sake don't go laying blame. We're two consenting adults who just enjoyed some wild, uninhibited, mind-blowing sex. We both wanted it. Let's just leave it at that."

She nodded and wished she could match his cavalier attitude. She couldn't help but wonder how often he engaged in fast and furious sex with almost strangers. As if reading her mind, he moved closer and cupped a hand around her cheek.

"That was amazing. *You* were amazing."

"So were you. I... I take it you've had quite a bit of practice at this kind of thing?"

"If you mean do I make it a habit of sweeping beautiful women I barely know off their feet to fuck them mindless in a closet, the answer is, no. In fact, you're the first woman I've ever fucked in a closet. I don't know what came over me. It was like I just had to have you."

His eyes had deepened to emerald green and his voice had lowered to a husky rasp. He stared at her, as if trying to see inside her, to work out what hold she had over him. And then he dropped his hand and half turned away and the moment was gone.

Ava drew in a shaky breath and bent down to retrieve her ruined underwear from the floor.

"Sorry about your panties," he murmured with an unrepentant grin. "They were kind of in the way."

"Yeah, I noticed," she replied with an answering

smile. "I... I guess we'd better go and re-join the party. Do you think we were missed?" Though it was a little late now to wonder, she couldn't help but hope nobody had noticed their absence.

He gave her a lopsided grin and pressed a quick kiss against her lips. "By your ex, probably. As for anyone else, I'm not sure, but you'll have more of a chance of getting away with it if you return via the restrooms. Your hair is a little...mussed."

Heat spread across her cheeks and she hastily dropped her gaze. Patting her hair down with her hand, she looked around for her purse. Too late, she remembered they'd been dancing right before... Her purse was where she'd left it, under the table. She'd have to retire to the powder room and repair what damage she could without the aid of her hairbrush or lip gloss.

"Are you all right?" Lachlan's voice was soft and low.

"Yes, I... I was hoping I had my purse with me. I need it to help repair the damage."

"I'm happy to fetch it for you."

"No, thank you. That's fine. Go back to the party. I'll be out in a little while."

He stared at her. "Are you sure?"

She nodded, all of a sudden anxious to be left alone. "Yes."

After a long inscrutable look, he turned away and opened the door. A moment later, he disappeared through the opening.

And, with that, he was gone.

CHAPTER 3

One month later

In stark contrast to the balmy night air, heavy with the scent of flowers, Detective Constable Lachlan Coleridge stood still and silent, filled with nervous anticipation. A trickle of sweat ran down the side of his face and slid inside his headgear. His heart thumped a steady staccato against his chest. The moments before a police raid were always tense and this time was no different.

He took comfort from the knowledge that the police intelligence was sound. Two officers had been conducting covert operations for the past fortnight. According to their information, behind the walls of the nondescript, California-style bungalow, situated off a quiet street in the small rural town of Moree, lay a drug lab the likes of which neither of them had ever seen.

The meth lab was supposed to be as sophisticated as they came. With state-of-the-art equipment and a seemingly endless supply of chemicals and other drug paraphernalia, the lab was producing enough crystal meth—or ice, as it was known on the streets—to supply most of New South Wales. As head of the taskforce, it was Lachlan's job to ensure that the lab was shut down and anyone associated with its illegal activities hauled away in cuffs. He was on the cusp of having that goal realized.

A slight noise from inside the house snagged his attention and halted his breath. He glanced at his partner of five years. Detective Constable Martin Griffin looked back at him, his expression solemn behind the night vision goggles that obscured one half of his face.

"What was that?" Martin whispered.

"I'm not sure," Lachlan replied, matching Martin's tone. "It sounds like someone walking around."

"Perhaps they got up for a glass of water, or maybe they need to take a piss."

Lachlan considered Martin's suggestions and compressed his lips. "We can't take the risk they might have spotted us. We're going to have to go in. Tell the others."

Lachlan watched while Martin moved off. The thick, overgrown grass silenced his partner's booted feet as he moved from one officer to another, motioning to alert them to the fact the time had come for them to enter the property.

Lachlan sent a silent text to his men gathered at the rear of the house. Any moment now they'd storm the building and pandemonium would break loose. A shiver of apprehension danced along his spine, like it always did just before a bust. He drew in a deep breath and stepped out of the shadows.

"Go! Go! Go! Police! Open up!" he screamed amidst the din of pounding on wood. The door gave way beneath the onslaught and Lachlan and his men poured in.

The front room was dark and musty. A couch with most of its stuffing missing stood in one corner of the room. Three dirty mattresses covered the floor. The officers were greeted with shouts of alarm and confusion as four men, dazed from sleep, faced a torrent of heavily armed policemen.

"Hands up!"

"On the floor!"

"Don't even think about it!" Lachlan yelled, pointing his gun at one of the occupants who appeared to be looking around for an avenue of escape.

Ensuring that the four prisoners were properly secured, Lachlan left them in the company of some of his men and motioned with his head for Martin to follow him further down the hall. With guns drawn and ready, they proceeded forward, kicking open each closed door.

One room held nothing but chemicals, another held a table piled high with packets of ice. A thousand pounds of crystal meth, at least. They continued on down the darkened hallway. It appeared the rest of the house was empty of people. Lachlan's tension subsided.

"What's that smell?" Martin murmured.

Lachlan frowned and then it hit him. "Smoke."

It was coming from beneath the closed door that stood at the end of the corridor. Lachlan had barely enough time to register its presence when there was an almighty roar. The force of the blast lifted him off his feet and threw him against the wall. He heard the snap of bone and winced at the pain in his shoulder. Fire licked at the wooden paneling and quickly spread into the hall. There had been some kind of explosion. They had to get out before it happened again.

With his eyes stinging from the smoke, he peered around for Martin and found him lying on the floor a few feet away. Scrambling toward him, Lachlan reached for him and gently turned him over. Blood poured from a gash on Martin's head. He looked dazed, but otherwise unharmed. Lachlan shook him hard. He moaned and Lachlan shook him again.

"Martin, we have to get out of here. There's a fire and it's building steam. This whole shit box could blow any minute. Can you walk?"

Martin blinked and then struggled to sit. Wheezing and coughing, Lachlan helped him to his feet. "Are you all right?" he asked.

Martin nodded slowly and then winced, reaching up to touch the wound on his head. "Yeah, I think so. I must have hit my head. I can't see for shit."

"It's the smoke." Lachlan hurried to reassure him, hoping to hell he was right.

Putting his uninjured arm around Martin's shoulders, together they stumbled back the way they'd come. The flames, no longer confined, now licked at the corridor walls. The heat from the fire scorched Lachlan's lungs, but still he stumbled forward.

Gasping and coughing, with his eyes streaming tears, Lachlan dragged his partner out of the house and collapsed with him on the front lawn. The sound of the half-panicked voices of Lachlan's men around him reassured him they'd safely exited the building. Leaving Martin resting on the grass, he winced at the pain in his shoulder and awkwardly pushed himself to his feet.

"Is everyone out?" he rasped at the first officer he saw.

"Yes, Detective," Constable David Jacobs replied. "Everyone has been accounted for."

"Where are the prisoners?" Lachlan asked, his voice raw.

"They're secured in the back of the police vans," David answered.

Lachlan nodded, relieved that at least part of their operation had gone smoothly.

"Are you all right, Detective? Your arm looks weird."

Lachlan frowned at David's comment and then glanced at his injured left shoulder. It hung at an odd angle. All of a sudden, the pain intensified and he swore aloud.

"I think I've broken my collarbone. I was thrown hard against the wall in that explosion and I heard something snap." Lachlan looked back at the burning building. "Has anyone called the fire brigade?"

"I'll do it now," David offered and tugged out his phone. "And I'll get them to send an ambulance, too."

"Good idea. Martin might need to be checked out." Lachlan had barely completed the sentence when another explosion rocked the house. Everyone dove for cover.

"Jesus!" David whispered.

"The whole fucking place is going to blow," Lachlan muttered. Keeping his head down and doing his best to protect his injured shoulder, he half-ran, half-crawled to where Martin lay, now still and silent on the ground.

The man's eyes were closed and even in the dimness, Lachlan could see his partner was now deathly pale. With increasing panic, he shook him, then slapped him hard on the cheek.

"Martin! Wake up, mate! Shit, open your eyes! Talk to me!"

Martin remained unresponsive and a fresh wave of panic washed over him. With no time to waste, he bent and awkwardly heaved his partner's bulky form against his chest, half-dragging him across the lawn and away from the inferno.

"David! Get that ambulance!" he screamed, oblivious to the agony in his shoulder. "I need a fucking ambulance! We have a man down!"

David appeared before him and Lachlan blinked to clear his vision.

"The ambulance is on its way, Detective. I—"

David's words were drowned out by the sound of another almighty explosion. This time flames shot high into the night sky, bathing all of them in a hot, red glow. Screams could be heard coming from inside the house and the sound of them brought Lachlan up cold. Setting Martin down gently on the opposite side of the road, he spun on his heel and eyeballed the constable.

"I thought you told me the prisoners were safe."

"They are, Detective. They're in the back of the van."

"Then why the fuck can I hear people screaming? There shouldn't be anyone else in that house."

David frowned. The sounds of the screams were fainter, but still audible. His face lost all color. "Jesus... We must have missed someone. I thought we'd cleared all the rooms, but it all happened so fast. We..."

Ignoring the pain in his shoulder, Lachlan tore back toward the house. Flames leaped high around him and scorched his face as he readied himself to enter.

"Detective! Are you crazy! You can't go back in there!" David reached for him and pulled him up short.

Lachlan struggled against his hold and cursed. "For fuck's sake, David, let me go! There are people in there! We have to get them out!"

David stared at him, his face now flushed an angry red. "Look at the place, Detective! It's consumed by the fire! It's gone way beyond anything we can deal with. There's nothing we can do. If you go inside, you're asking for trouble. You'll only go and get yourself killed and what good will that do? Think about your wife and kids and don't be so fucking stupid. Besides, you're injured." David's stare remained hard. "Leave it to the fire brigade. They're the only ones who have any chance of helping them now."

Lachlan continued to struggle against his colleague's hold, biting down hard on the pain and staring with desperation into the billowing flames. Though it cut him into pieces to acknowledge the truth of David's words, slowly his struggles ceased.

The sound of sirens in the distance brought with it a feeling of relief. The fire brigade would take over and do everything they could. He only hoped it would be enough.

Hours later, the mid-morning sun shone down on the white sling, applied to immobilize Lachlan's shoulder, as he and his men picked their way carefully through what remained of the makeshift meth lab. The acrid smell of smoke and burned flesh scorched his nose. The rooms of the house they'd so recently stormed were barely recognizable.

"Jesus," Martin whispered, slowly shaking his head.

Lachlan shot him a grim look of understanding, relieved his friend had recovered sufficiently from his head injury to accompany them into the ruins.

"It looks like a bomb went off," David murmured. Lachlan silently agreed.

The house was a mess of charred wood and ashes. Remnants of smoke still rose from the floorboards. Lachlan picked his way over fallen debris and came to what used to be the room at the back of the house. Dread weighed heavy in his gut.

"I don't know where the hell that screaming came from. The place looks deserted." The words were no sooner out of David's mouth when Lachlan spied them.

Two small charred bodies lay entwined, as if seeking comfort from one another. What was left of their faces were frozen into masks of terror and pain. Lachie kneeled down beside them and his stomach somersaulted from the sight. The smell of burning flesh sickened him.

"Oh, Jesus!" Martin breathed in horror. "They're fucking children!"

Lachlan stared down at the bodies and nodded grimly. "Yeah, they are."

"What the fuck were they doing here?" David exploded behind him.

Lachlan shrugged, though his mind rebelled against the knowledge that the children had been burned to death. "This is the remains of the cookhouse. They must have been working here, cooking meth. There's no other explanation."

"Fuck!" Martin cursed and then promptly turned and vomited a few feet away.

Lachlan was also struggling to keep his breakfast down. He forced himself closer to the bodies and went through what was left of their clothing, looking for some ID. He found nothing.

Standing, he cursed softly under his breath. "We'll have to interview the assholes we took into custody early this morning. Someone must know who these kids are."

Martin nodded. David looked grim. Together, they turned and left the room.

———

Ava packed the last of her things into her final suitcase and managed to tug the zipper closed.

"Are you sure you have everything, dear?" Mrs Christie enquired.

Though her tone was polite, Ava was almost certain she detected a gleam of wicked humor in her elderly neighbor's gaze.

"Yes, thank you, Mrs Christie," she replied, refusing to rise to the bait. Her neighbour wasn't the first person to comment on the volume of her luggage when she traveled and no doubt, she wouldn't be the last. Ava liked to be prepared for all occasions. That's all it was.

"Thank you again for offering to keep an eye on my condominium," she added, hefting her bulging toiletry bag off the bed.

"That's no trouble at all, dear. How long did you say you'll be away?"

"A month, Mrs Christie. I'll be back by the end of April."

"And where did you say you were going? Somewhere in the country?"

"Yes, Mrs Christie. I'm going to Moree. It's a

small rural town in north-west New South Wales, not far from the Queensland border. About a seven-hour drive from Sydney."

The old woman shuddered, a look of horror on her face. "Seven *hours*! That's forever away! It sounds positively dreadful! Why would you ever want to spend a month in a place so far away from home?"

Ava smiled. "First of all, Mrs Christie, I'm flying, which shouldn't take too long at all. And secondly, I'm doing a favor for a friend of mine. She moved to Moree a few years ago from Grafton and has set up a private psychiatry practice. There's been a family emergency—her younger sister isn't well—and she's had to return home. She's asked me to cover for her. I've agreed to do a four-week locum. Don't worry, I'll be back. I'm not cut out for a permanent life in the country. My blood sings with the sounds of the city."

Mrs Christie continued to study her doubtfully. "She must be an awfully good friend if you're willing to spend so long away from here. I couldn't imagine being away from the hustle and bustle for that long. How do you know this Moree place even has decent coffee?"

Ava laughed. "Oh, Mrs Christie, you're so funny! We're living in the twenty-first century. Everyone knows how to make decent coffee." Ava hoped silently that it was true.

The elderly woman's mouth tightened in disdain and she lifted her head. "You might scoff at me, young lady, but I've been around a time or two. Some of these backwater towns are plain...backward. You mark my words! You'll see!"

Ava chuckled and shook her head, refusing to believe Phoebe would settle in such a place. Prior to moving to Grafton and then more recently, Moree, her friend had spent years living in Sydney. Ava couldn't imagine Phoebe settling down in the kind of place Mrs Christie described, but instead of arguing with her neighbour, she simply smiled again and murmured, "You're right. I guess I will."

Hours later, as the small passenger plane touched down in Moree, Ava couldn't quell the sudden rush of nerves. She hadn't told anyone the real reason behind her eagerness to accept Phoebe's invitation. The mention of Moree had instantly brought back memories of her fleeting moments with Lachlan Coleridge and their interlude in the cloakroom.

Ever since the wedding, she hadn't been able to get him off her mind. Samantha and Rohan had left immediately afterwards for a month-long honeymoon overseas, and not being able to hound her sister for more details about the man who made her pulse beat faster, had driven her to distraction.

She hadn't breathed a word to anyone about what had happened at the wedding, not even to her twin. She didn't know if it was a brief moment in history that would never be repeated or if there could ever be something more between them. He was a cop in the outback. She was a city girl. Any kind of relationship between them would be next to impossible, wouldn't it?

She didn't have any answers, but the fact was,

the city girl had just arrived in the bush. A surge of excitement and nervousness flooded through her at the thought of seeing him again. Moree was a town of less than ten thousand people. Surely it wouldn't be too hard to locate a police officer by the name of Lachlan Coleridge. She couldn't wait to find out.

"All right, everyone, listen up." Detective Superintendent Nigel Becker's voice rang out across the squad room. It was changeover and the modest squad room was crowded and noisy from several simultaneous conversations. The officers who'd kept the small rural town of Moree, New South Wales, safe and protected throughout the past twelve hours were coming to the end of their shift. It had been a helluva day.

Lachlan pushed away from his desk and gathered around his boss, along with the rest of the detectives in the room. Becker towered above most men. At least six foot four or five, most people he came into contact with couldn't help but think of a bear. This impression was emphasized by the man's dark coloring and enormous body mass. He weighed over two hundred pounds, with only the slightest hint of a middle-age spread. There was no doubt about it. He was an impressive physical specimen.

"I want to congratulate you all on the success of your mission," Becker announced. "Thanks to your efforts, two of the four prisoners have already confessed."

A loud cheer went up among those gathered. Lachlan allowed himself a brief smile of satisfaction.

"It's a pity about those kids," Becker continued in a casual tone, "but that's what you get for working in a shithole meth lab with a bunch of fucking amateurs." A general murmur of agreement went around the room. Lachlan's gut tightened.

"By the way," Becker continued, "if any of you need to talk about what happened, don't forget the lovely people in the Employee Assistance Program are waiting to take your call."

The smirk that immediately followed Becker's words irritated Lachlan like a burr caught in his sock, but he clenched his jaw to prevent himself from commenting. Becker's contemptuous attitude toward not only the dead children, but the effect of their deaths on his men came as no surprise, and speaking out against it would only hurt Lachlan's chances of promotion.

He didn't need to be reminded that as police officers, they were built tougher than most. It was their job and their duty to take traumatic situations on the chin. The shit they were subjected to day after day, the awful things they saw, weren't meant to affect them like it did the average man. It was just the way it was and it was no secret any officer who sought counseling through the EAP was putting his career prospects on the line.

The counseling was meant to be confidential, but that was a load of shit. Lachlan never could work out how it happened, but the handful of times one or another of his colleagues had reached out for that kind of help, everyone in the station found out about it.

With Becker's speech over, Lachlan wandered back to his desk and collected his keys and then headed toward the locker room. He and Martin had already met with the officers who were taking over for the night.

After hours of interrogation, along with the confessions, one of the prisoners had finally given up the identity of the two boys found in the burned-out house.

Michael Fernando and Trevor Cross were fifteen and sixteen, respectively. Lachlan had run their names through the database and was saddened to see the list of petty juvenile crimes that were listed underneath both names. They were well known to the local police, but still, nobody deserved to be burned alive. Lachlan was grateful the night shift had agreed to break the news to their families.

"Hey, Lachie, wait up," Martin called out and then hurried to catch up to him. "What a day, huh?"

Lachlan grimaced. "Yeah."

"Fancy a drink downtown?"

Lachlan shook his head. "No, mate. I'm bushed. I'm heading straight for the shower and then to bed."

Martin nodded and then changed the subject. "How's Kristy?"

Lachlan shrugged his uninjured shoulder and kept walking, ignoring the stab of guilt. He'd done his best to keep thoughts of his wife pushed to the furthest recesses of his mind and after the past eighteen hours he'd endured, he sure as hell didn't want to talk about her now.

At his brother's wedding, he'd been relieved when he'd been able to satisfy his family's curiosity at Kristy's absence by claiming she wasn't well enough to attend. They'd all expressed their sympathy and their well wishes that she return to good health soon. He'd burned with guilt over his hasty lies, but he hadn't had a choice. He wasn't ready to tell anyone that his wife had walked out on him more than six weeks ago and had taken their kids.

His head had been all over the place, then and now. It was the reason he'd had mind-blowing, amazing sex with a woman he barely knew. A woman who wasn't his wife. More than a month later, he still hadn't been able to bring himself to speak about any of it. He was filled with guilt every time he thought about Ava Wolfe.

It shouldn't have mattered that his wife had walked out on their marriage and that he was no longer thinking straight. He shouldn't have had sex with her. At the very least, he should have told her he was separated.

The truth was, he hadn't been thinking about anything other than an escape from the dark and pain. He was sick of the bullshit that kept going round and round in his head. He'd wanted to forget about everything, even for a few moments, and do nothing but *feel*.

It was selfish and wrong and any number of

other things, but he couldn't bring himself to regret it, even as a part of him hoped Kristy would come back and they could try harder on their marriage—and nobody would be the wiser about how close they had come, least of all his kids. But that was a stupid way of thinking—his kids were four and two. Surely, Charlotte, his eldest child, would have cottoned on that something was up. She hadn't seen her daddy for six weeks. Pain flooded his heart. He wondered what Kristy had told them.

Ignoring his silence, Martin continued. "Pam and I are having a barbeque on Sunday. Some friends of ours are visiting from Sydney. Why don't you and the family come around? It's been ages since we had you over."

Lachlan reached his locker and, with his good arm, threw open the door. With a little difficulty, he peeled off his grimy shirt and tossed it in his bag. The last thing he wanted to do was go to Martin's gathering and spend an afternoon pretending all was normal with his life, but Martin was waiting for his answer, an expectant look on his face.

Lachlan sighed inwardly. After what they'd just been through, the least he could do was give his partner a little show of support.

"Sure, why not?" he forced himself to reply. "But it will be just me, I'm afraid. Kristy and the kids have gone away for a while."

The lie tasted sour on his lips but he still wasn't ready to confess the truth. His wife had left him, accusing him of being cold and selfish and emotionless, unwilling to think of anyone but himself. If she only knew how hard it was for him to keep the darkness at bay. Refusing to discuss his problems was the only thing that kept him sane.

Martin shot him a curious look. "How long will they be gone?"

"A couple of weeks. Maybe more. Kristy's mother had a hip replacement. She's gone to help out for a while."

Once again, the lies fell from his lips. This time, it was easier. Martin nodded in acceptance. "That's all right. You're welcome to come on your own. Pam will have a fit because the numbers won't work out, but don't worry about that." He grinned and Lachlan forced himself to smile.

"Does Kristy know about your injury?" Martin asked, nodding toward the white sling.

Lachlan averted his gaze. "No. It's nothing. A broken collarbone. There's nothing anyone can do. I just need to keep it immobile for a few weeks. I didn't want to worry her about something as trivial as this."

"I guess," Martin replied, looking unconvinced, "but don't say I didn't warn you if she gives you an earful when she finds out. Women get weird over crap like that."

Lachlan winked. "You'll be there to defend me if the shit hits the fan."

"Humph! Don't bet on it," Martin mumbled, but Lachlan saw through his bluff.

He and Martin had known each other ever since Lachlan moved to Moree five years earlier. Over that time, they'd become close friends. Lachlan was filled with guilt at the thought of not confiding in him, but that would mean opening up a can of worms that he just wasn't ready to face.

"Come around at three," Martin added, tugging off his shirt. "We'll have time to watch the game before dinner."

Lachlan managed a nod and escaped into the shower.

CHAPTER 4

Lachlan pulled his white Ford Ranger pickup over to the curb outside Martin's home and killed the engine. His arm ached and he was already sick and tired of the sling, but according to the emergency room doctor, if he wanted the bone to heal properly, he had to put up with it, at least for three or four weeks. Too bad the pain wasn't bad enough that he could use it as an excuse not to attend the barbeque.

Lachlan stared at the neat, two-storey brick home where Martin and Pam Griffin lived with their kids. Two bikes lay abandoned on the front lawn, one sporting a cute white basket covered in bright plastic flowers. A neatly trimmed hedge bordered the house and the garden beds looked freshly mulched. The warm and friendly exterior was amplified on the inside and more often than not, Lachlan couldn't wait to step inside and be part of it, but today the house wasn't offering its usual appeal.

The fact was, he didn't want to go in. He didn't

want to mingle and chat and socialize with friends and colleagues and strangers and pretend there was nothing wrong. He didn't want to have to fight against his mind straying to another woman and a few stolen, magical moments in time. He couldn't even garner enough interest to watch the game.

The memory of the two young charred bodies kept coming back to haunt him. He'd seen a lot of awful shit over the course of his career, but nothing quite as horrific as confronting the boys who'd been trapped inside the burning house. He wished that somehow they'd been killed instantly, when the explosion had first occurred, but from the screams he heard that night and the looks of agony on their faces, it hadn't gone down like that. The knowledge was tearing him apart.

He blew his breath out on a heavy sigh. He didn't want to admit it, but the job was getting to him. It might have already cost him his marriage. The thought of his kids coming from a broken home filled him with anguish and pain—but he didn't know what he could do.

He loved being a cop. It was all he wanted to be. He'd applied for the Goulburn Police Academy straight out of high school and had been accepted right away. But the horrors the job had subjected him to, were beginning to take their toll. Short of making the call to the EAP for counseling—and hoping like hell it would help—he was out of options.

"Hey, are you coming in, or are you just going to sit in your vehicle all afternoon?"

Lachlan blinked and cleared his head of his depressing thoughts and forced a grin in the direction of his friend. Martin stood nearby with a pair of barbeque tongs in one hand and a beer in the other.

"Yeah, of course," Lachlan managed. Using his good arm, he awkwardly released his seat belt and opened the car door. "I was just... Never mind. How are those steaks going?"

Collecting a six pack of beer off the back seat, he walked with Martin in the direction of the house. They'd barely entered the backyard before Pam Griffin broke away from a small group of guests and headed toward them.

"Lachie! It's great to see you! Oh, you poor thing! Martin told me you'd broken your collarbone. How are Kristy and the kids?"

Before he could draw breath to answer, Lachlan was engulfed by sweet-smelling perfume and soft woman as Martin's pretty young wife gave him a gentle hug. Pulling away, he smiled at her and forced himself to reply.

"Hi, Pam. They're fine. They're at Kristy's mother's place at the moment. Down on the Central Coast."

"Yes, a hip replacement, right?" Pamela Griffin stared at him and Lachlan flushed under her close perusal. There was no way she could know the truth. Nobody knew.

And then she smiled and shook her head. "Your family have been in the wars, haven't they? Broken collarbone, broken hips. Never mind. Here, let me introduce you around."

Lachlan set his six pack on a table. Pam took him by the hand.

"This is Tom and Lynette. They live on the other side of town. They have George and Elizabeth, the twins. They're in Charlotte and Montana's class, right? And this is Robert and Sue. You've met them before, I think."

Lachlan dutifully nodded greetings and shook hands with the other guests, gritting his teeth at the pain whenever someone got too enthusiastic and pulled on his injured shoulder. Oblivious to his discomfort, Pam tugged him toward the swimming pool where a dark-haired woman stood with her back to him, watching the children splashing in the water.

"And this is Ava. We went to school together in Sydney. She's just arrived off the plane. She's staying in Moree for a while. Ava, come and meet Lachie."

The woman turned slowly and smiled at him. Lachlan felt the impact of her all the way through to his gut. Though she wore large sunglasses that covered almost half her face, there was no doubt in his mind who she was. *Ava Wolfe.* Samantha's sister. The woman he'd...

Bombarded with the memory of erotic sensations, of her tongue down his throat and her legs wrapped around his waist, it took him a moment to respond. Guilt flooded through him. He should have told her earlier about his wife, before anything happened between them. Before things got...complicated.

He hadn't seen her since the wedding, but she

looked as hot now as she had back then. He wondered if his brother or her sister had said anything to her about him, but then dismissed the thought. Her expression was one of surprise and pleasure. He couldn't imagine her looking at him like that if she knew about Kristy. Ignoring the growing sense of dread, he greeted her.

"Ava, wow! What a surprise! What are you doing here? I wasn't expecting to see you!"

She offered him a dry smile. "I can see that."

"It's good to see you again. You look fantastic!"

"What happened to your arm?" she asked, glancing at the sling. "You weren't wearing one of those the last time I saw you."

"Oh, it's nothing. A broken collarbone. I'm fine."

"Don't tell me you two know each other?" Pam asked, bemused.

"Yes," Ava responded, before Lachlan had a chance. "His brother married my sister a month ago. We met at the wedding."

"Oh, that's amazing!" Pam giggled. "Don't you just love it when something like this happens? Six degrees of separation and all that crazy stuff. I can't believe it! Wait until I tell Martin." She turned on her heel and hurried away, leaving the two of them alone. Ava turned back to face the pool.

"Are you on lifeguard duty?" he asked, moving to stand beside her. He was intrigued when she moved a little further away.

"Yes, apparently."

"Which one is yours?"

"None of them. I don't have any kids."

His gaze moved across her face. Tiny crows'

feet lined the corners of her eyes. Rohan had told him Samantha was thirty-four and she was the baby of the family. It was curious her sister hadn't made any moves to have children by now.

"You don't like kids?" he asked, keeping his voice light, unable to believe how much her answer suddenly mattered to him.

She turned to him, her eyes guarded. "Yes, of course I do. I just... I just haven't found the right person to have them with. Some men aren't cut out to be a father."

Lachlan digested the information, recalling the ex-boyfriend. "I take it you're referring to the guy you dumped right before the wedding?"

She blushed and averted her gaze, staring fixedly at the pool. "You remember."

He stared at her. "I remember lots of things." His gaze traveled across the smooth skin that stretched across high cheekbones and skimmed across her mouth. He remembered the taste and feel of her under his lips, the way she'd clung to him, panting, hot and frantic with need.

Blood surged through him and centered in his cock and yet, he brazenly continued to look his fill. The bodice of her light summer dress cupped the soft fullness of her breasts. The floral fabric flared over womanly hips and ended in a flurry above her knees. It was now fall, but her legs were bare and golden with the last vestiges of her summer tan. Toenails, painted in a soft pink, peeked out from the open toes of low-heeled, brown sandals.

He remembered the warm wet feel of her as he'd plunged all the way inside and he stifled a groan. *What the hell was he doing?* As far as his friends knew, he was a happily married man. And she had no idea about his circumstances. Despite what had happened between them and how much he longed for it to happen again, he wasn't prepared to concede his marriage was over.

Remaining at the party now seemed foolhardy. His attraction to Ava was so powerful and strong, it wouldn't take his friends long to become aware of it and where would that leave him? His secret would be laid bare for all to see and he sure as hell wasn't capable of dealing with that kind of fallout at the moment. He didn't know if he'd ever find the courage to admit to his friends and colleagues that his marriage might be over, let alone that he was the reason it had failed.

Those thoughts cooled his ardor and with effort, he reined in his wayward libido and put a little more distance between them. She frowned at him, but remained silent, her gaze still fixed on the children in the pool.

"How do you like living in the country?" she asked, as if the last few moments hadn't happened.

He stared at her and then finally nodded. *Fine, if that's the way she wanted to play it.* Pretending those minutes of madness between them had never happened was probably the best way to go. After all, she was only here for a visit. Soon, she'd return to Sydney and her normal life. A life that couldn't include him.

"I love it," he answered honestly.

"Were you born here?"

"No, my brothers and sisters were all born in Sydney. Mom and Dad lived in Cronulla for all of their married lives. Dad's buried in the cemetery at Sutherland."

Ava nodded, her expression softening. "I remember Samantha telling me your dad died the same night our mom received her kidney transplant. It was a difficult and emotional time for all of us."

"Yes. It was. Mom's still coming to terms with Dad's sudden passing. It was a shock, that's for sure."

"How many brothers and sisters do you have? I seem to recall a fair number of them at the wedding."

Lachlan chuckled, his heart filling with pride. "Four brothers and three sisters."

"There are *eight* of you? Wow! I thought growing up with a brother and two sisters was unusual."

"You're right. Large families don't seem to be in fashion anymore."

She looked at him quizzically. "I'm not sure it has anything to do with fashion. More likely the cost of raising kids. I have friends with kids in daycare and I'm telling you, it costs a bomb."

"Yeah, you have that right. Even out here in the country, childcare doesn't come cheap."

Ava stared at the man who had filled far too

many of her dreams and wondered about his comment. It sounded like he had personal experience dealing with the financial reality of having children in paid care. She suddenly wished she'd made more of an effort to contact Samantha and ask if Lachlan were married. From the sound of it, even if he weren't, he definitely had young kids. Keeping her voice light, she asked him.

"You sound like you're talking from experience."

He flashed her a wary smile, but his tone remained light. "I am."

Tension pooled in her belly. "You have kids?" she managed.

"Yes. A boy and a girl. Harry's two and Charlotte's four."

She swallowed hard and tried to keep the dismay from her voice. After all, it wasn't his fault she hadn't asked these questions before they'd had sex in the cloakroom at her sister's wedding.

"You're... You're married?"

He grimaced and looked away, his expression sad and distant. "Yes. No. Kind of."

Ava shook her head, filled with confusion and a burgeoning anger. She stared at him through narrowed eyes. "You're not making sense. It's an easy question. Surely, you're either married, or you're not."

He heaved a heavy sigh and his shoulders slumped. When he turned back to face her, she almost gasped at the pain in his eyes.

"I wish it was that easy. The truth is, I am

married, but I'm not sure for how much longer. My wife walked out and took our kids a fortnight before Rohan and Samantha's wedding. I haven't seen them since they left. Kristy hasn't even let me talk to Charlotte and Harry. She says it will only upset them. I miss them both so much."

He looked away. Ava was too surprised by his revelations to speak. Lachlan dragged in a ragged breath and continued.

"I... I haven't told anyone. I guess I didn't want to face the truth. We'd been having problems for a long time, but I've been clinging to the hope we might get back together, work things out for the sake of the kids." He scoffed and his voice filled with disgust. "Who am I kidding? She can barely bring herself to talk to me and when she has, it's only been over the phone. As soon as the required twelve months are up, I expect she'll ask for a divorce."

Ava continued to stare at him in surprise. She was still upset he hadn't told her at the wedding, but she could understand why it hadn't come up. She'd been just as impatient as he'd been to lose herself in a stranger's arms. And it wasn't like she'd helped to break up his marriage. Apparently, that damage had already been done.

The tension eased out of her. "What happened?" she asked quietly.

He drew in another breath and his body shuddered as he exhaled. "Life happened, I guess. We got married young. I was barely out of the Academy. Fresh and eager to face the world." His lips twisted on another grimace. "Little did we know life would suck me in and spit me out, until I had nothing left to give. Kristy accused me of shutting her out, refusing to let her in." He turned to stare at Ava, his green eyes dark and tortured. "And she was right."

Ava sucked in a breath at the bitterness in his voice. His suffering was obvious. She recalled him telling her at the wedding he was a detective and couldn't imagine the things he'd seen and done in the course of his job. She wondered if he'd sought any professional help and then voiced her thoughts aloud.

"Police officers, suffering from Post Traumatic Stress Disorder… It happens way more often than you think. PTSD isn't a sign of weakness. It's just a normal reaction to the kind of trauma you and your colleagues see. Have you talked to anyone about it? A psychologist?"

He gave a derisive laugh and shook his head. "You're kidding me, right?"

She kept her gaze on his, her voice serious. "No, I'm not. The police service makes provision for mental health issues. You're entitled to three paid therapy sessions; more if it's required."

He frowned and his gaze narrowed. "How the hell do you know all this? Are you a cop?"

"No, I'm a psychiatrist and at the moment, I'm doing some locum work in the area for Doctor Phoebe Jamison. She's a friend of mine and she asked me to cover her practice for the next month. Many of her clientele comprise high stress professionals, including a number of police officers, so I made it my business to become familiar with the procedures and the requirements to receive benefits, including the police service benefits, in case some of their employees require my services."

His lips compressed and he stared down at his feet. Ava could tell he wasn't impressed by her answer. She wasn't sure if it was because she was advocating therapy for police officers or whether his dismissal of the information was something more personal. When he spoke, his voice was low and thick with emotion.

"You people don't know shit about how it works in the real world."

Ava tensed reflexively and then forced herself to relax. She reminded herself he was lashing out at the system, not her.

"Why do you say that?" she asked, keeping her tone even.

Anger flashed in his eyes. "Do you have any idea what it would do to my career if it got out that I was seeking therapy to deal with the crap in my head? We're machines, Doc, not New Age men. We're supposed to be able to deal with all the daily shit."

"I guess while you keep telling yourself that, you'll believe it," she said quietly, feeling his frustration and pain. She sympathized with his situation, even though she didn't agree with it.

He threw her another hard stare and turned away, muttering under his breath. Without a backward glance, he stalked toward the house, shaking his head.

Her heart ached for him and for others like him.

She wanted to help him, but how could she? No amount of therapy could help someone who wasn't in the right frame of mind to embrace it or admit they needed help.

"Ava! Ava! Look at me!"

The high-pitched squeals of Montana Griffin snagged Ava's attention. Forcing away her dark thoughts, she smiled and clapped her hands in encouragement at Pam and Martin's youngest. Four-year-old Montana climbed out of the pool and once again hurled herself into the deep end, laughing and shouting with glee.

"You're very clever, Montana," Ava chuckled, impressed with the little girl's enthusiasm and total lack of fear. Ava couldn't remember being so brave at that age. It was heartening to see.

"Watch me, Ava! I can dive!"

Ava switched her attention to Patrick. Older by three years, with his dark curly hair and brown eyes, he was the image of his father. She watched while the boy bent his knees and belly flopped into the pool. Sputtering to the surface, the grin on his face stretched his lips wide.

"See! I told you I could dive!"

Ava laughed, unable to help herself. "So you did, Patrick. Did it hurt?"

He nodded, but the grin remained. "A little bit, but I'm gonna try again!"

Ava laughed again and shook her head. The scene before her filled her with satisfaction. Just two regular kids having fun in the pool, building healthy self-esteems. That was the way it was supposed to be. She could only hope they remained as fearless and confident throughout their lives.

Life had a way of knocking people down. She hoped they'd be prepared for that when it happened.

Chapter 5

Dear Diary,

Their laughter is filled with joy and spontaneity and the vibrant innocence of youth. I can hear them from my office, right down the hall. I smile at the sound, but it fails to touch me deep inside and the knowledge cuts me to pieces.

It never used to be like this. I used to take joy in their simple pleasures; in the wonderment of life. The black hole that surrounds me has sucked out every scrap of light until there's nothing left but darkness...and it's eating at my soul.

She watches me with concern and a little anger in her eyes, wanting to help, needing to help—but not knowing how. I've done nothing to assist her; nothing to show her the way. It's not because I don't want to. I'd give anything to be normal, to feel something other than this darkness deep inside, but the truth is, I don't know how.

How can she help me—how can anyone help me—when I can no longer help myself...?

From the corner of his eye, Lachlan spied Martin heading in his direction, coffee cup in hand. It was Monday morning and their shift had barely begun. Lachlan stifled a groan and kept his gaze fixed to the computer screen in front of him. Despite the ache in his shoulder and the difficulty he had typing with one hand, he concentrated hard on the task and did his best to appear engrossed in his work. Undeterred, Martin perched himself on a corner of Lachlan's desk.

"Morning, partner. How are you doing?"

Lachlan glanced at his colleague and gave him a brief nod of acknowledgment before returning his attention to the screen.

"You left the party early. You didn't even stay for the game."

Lachie grimaced. "Yeah, I'm sorry. It had been a rough week. I was tired before I got there. Probably should have stayed at home. I hope I didn't spoil Pam's place settings. Is she mad?"

Martin grinned. "Furious. But she'll get over it. She loves you," he added.

"Hey, tell her I'm sorry. I didn't mean to leave so abruptly. I…" He shrugged helplessly, unable to offer an acceptable explanation.

The truth was, he'd felt so out of sorts after his conversation with Ava, he'd known he wouldn't be good company for anyone. The thought of spending more time with her had been unbearable. She'd touched on a raw nerve when she'd suggested he'd do well to seek professional help and he wasn't prepared to sit politely and listen to any more of it over the dinner table.

"I saw you with Ava Wolfe. You looked pretty friendly. Pam said you knew her from before."

"Her sister's married to one of my brothers. We met at their wedding."

Martin nodded in comprehension. "No wonder you appeared so cozy with each other. For a moment, I thought you were coming on to her. I knew I was being stupid. You'd never do anything to hurt Kristy."

Lachlan listened and the familiar feelings of guilt and dread resurfaced. It grew and solidified in his gut until it felt like he was being pulled down into a quagmire from which there was no escape. He sucked in a breath and did his best to steady his racing heart.

He still couldn't understand why he'd told Ava his marriage was as good as over. He'd managed to keep Kristy's leaving a secret all this time—and then just like that, he not only revealed it, but to a woman who was almost a stranger. He had no idea if he could trust her to keep her mouth shut. It might be only a matter of time before word spread that his wife had left and taken the kids. Permanently. He had to tell Martin. His friend would never forgive him if he heard it from someone else.

"Are you all right, Lachie?"

Lachlan blinked to clear his head of the heavy fog that suddenly made it difficult to think. Martin's concerned features filled his vision. He did his best to offer him a reassuring smile.

"Yeah, of course. I... I... There's something I need to tell you."

A frown now lined Martin's forehead and a hint of wariness crept into his eyes. "Okay," he said uncertainly.

Lachlan cursed softly beneath his breath and then decided to make it quick and clean and then get the hell out of there.

"Kristy and I split up. She packed up her things and left with the kids six weeks ago."

Martin looked stunned at the news. He stood and moved a few steps away, shaking his head. "Shit. You mean, she just...left?"

"She accused me of shutting her out. I think her exact words were that I was emotionally frigid and had been for most of our marriage. We argued. Again. She told me she wanted a divorce. The next day, I came home from work and the house was empty. She left a note on the fridge."

"Hell, Lachie! I can't believe you've been carrying this shit around for six weeks! Why didn't you tell me? We're friends."

Lachlan winced at the hurt in Martin's voice. Wounding his mate was the last thing he'd wanted to do.

"We are. And I'm sorry. The truth is, I'm still trying to get my head around it. Kristy calling it quits on our marriage, taking the kids... I guess I didn't want to tell anyone because then I'd be forced to accept it. I'd have to look at the reasons she gave for ending it and I don't know that I'm strong enough or brave enough to do that, on top of everything else."

The admission was difficult, but as he said the words, Lachlan realized he was telling the truth.

The fact was, he'd been in a downward spiral for a long time. Continued exposure to the worst that people had to offer had damaged him deep down inside. The only way he'd found to cope was to shut down his thoughts and emotions and that included shutting out his wife. He had no one but himself to blame for the loss of his family. Ava had been right. He needed help.

He pushed away from his desk and stood.

"Where are you off to?" Martin asked.

"I'm going to see the boss."

Surprise filled Martin's face. "About Kristy?"

Lachlan stared at his friend. "Among other things."

"Be careful what you say, Lachie," Martin warned, his voice low.

"Yeah."

Martin didn't need to remind Lachlan how damaging it would be to his career if the boss decided he was unstable, but he had no choice. His life had taken a downward turn. He needed help—and soon.

Knocking briefly on Becker's half-open door, Lachlan entered without waiting to be asked. Becker threw him a sour look.

"What is it, Coleridge?"

"I... I'm in a bad way, boss. I think I need some help." The words fell out before he could stop them.

Becker stared at him in surprise. "You mean like...therapy or something?"

"Yes. It's been building up for a while. Kristy and I have...separated. And there's other crap I have to work through. I thought you should know."

A humorless chuckle fell from Becker's lips and he shook his head slowly back and forth. "I'm sorry to hear about you and Kristy, but don't talk to me about therapy. That counseling shit's for pussies. Man up, Detective. Grow a pair of balls. We all do it tough, from time to time. It comes with the job. Go and have a few scotches and forget about it, like the rest of us do."

Lachlan stared at him in disbelief, shocked at Becker's callous attitude. He'd known his boss didn't think highly of therapy, but he didn't expect the man to be so blunt. After all, the police service prided itself on providing at least the appearance of emotional support for its officers.

Already regretting his decision to confide in the man, Lachlan turned his back on his boss and left the room without another word. It was clear that if he was going to get help, he needed to do it on his own. And he would. He had no choice. It was as simple as that.

The phone that stood on Phoebe's desk pealed. Ava picked it up, silencing the noise. "Ava Wolfe."

"Hi, Doctor. It's Janelle. I'm Phoebe's receptionist. We met this morning in the tea room. I have a call for you on line two."

Ava recalled the gray-haired, grandmotherly type she'd met earlier over a cup of coffee and smiled. "Thank you, Janelle."

Earlier, with coffee in hand, Janelle had given her a brief tour of the building. Two other bedrooms had been converted into generous office spaces. A small, but tidy kitchen used by the staff and modest bathroom facilities made up the rest of the house. In addition to Phoebe's office, an accountant occupied one room and a chiropractor the other. Ava had yet to meet either of them.

The phone on the desk beeped impatiently and Ava finally answered the call. She smiled at the familiar voice on the line.

"Phoebe! How are you doing? I didn't expect you to call! You're dealing with a family crisis and everything is fine here! The last thing you should be doing is worrying about work."

"Tell me about it," Phoebe muttered, "but I wanted to call and make sure you were settling in all right."

"Of course I am," Ava assured her. "How's Danielle?"

Phoebe sighed. "My little sister is fighting us at each and every turn. By some miracle, Dad and I managed to pull off an intervention and get her into rehab, but she's not at all happy about it. Why the hell can't she see we're doing this for her own good?"

"I'm sorry," Ava replied. "I wish there was something I could do."

"You're doing enough. Way past enough. After I got that call from Dad, I was running around chasing my tail. My head was in a spin. I wanted to be there for my family, but my patients needed me, too. I'm so grateful you were able to fill in for me on such short notice."

"It's no problem," Ava hurried to reassure her once again. "I'm your friend, and that's what friends are for. Besides, your files are all in order and you've made comprehensive notes. I'm sure I'll work things out."

"Thank goodness! How's Janelle? Have you met her, yet?"

"Yes. Janelle's been very sweet and helpful. She reminds me of my grandmother. Your office is gorgeous, by the way."

Ava thought of her clinical rooms in the Sydney Harbour Hospital, all steel and glass and concrete. They lacked the warmth and comfort of the room where she now sat. "I officially have office envy!" she added with a laugh.

Phoebe chuckled. "Enjoy my humble country abode. I'm sure it's a little different from what you're used to."

"Yes, but in a good way. A *very* good way."

"It sounds like you've had a chance to go through my files," Phoebe added. I hope you have time to familiarize yourself with some of my clients before they arrive, especially the police officers. They need the help, but they don't want to admit it and it creates a constant struggle. I want you to be prepared."

"Who refers them to you?" Ava asked, curious in light of her discussion with Lachlan.

"The Employee Assistance Program. When an officer makes a call to the EAP, he or she will speak with a psychologist. If the officer requests a face-to-face meeting, it's arranged. For police officers, living out in the country, finding a qualified professional is often difficult. Some of them are forced to drive hundreds of miles."

"The police service doesn't go out of its way to make it easy," Ava observed wryly.

"No, they don't."

"I was speaking with a detective yesterday at a barbeque. He told me any officer putting in a request for counseling, or indeed even admitting to any need for help, is seen as weak and will be looked upon unfavorably when it comes time for promotion. Is it really as bad as that?"

When Phoebe replied, she sounded grim. "I'm afraid so. I wish I could say it wasn't true, but I can't. The cops who find the courage to meet with me are terrified their colleagues might find out. It makes for a tense therapy session."

Ava shook her head, bewildered. "Why would the police service jeopardize the recovery of their people? It doesn't make sense."

"It's an inherited attitude from a different time when men didn't cry or show their emotions. They're meant to be tough and unmoving; able to put up with whatever trauma comes their way without thinking anything of it."

"They're flesh and blood people, not machines."

"Ha!" Phoebe replied, her voice dripping with scorn. "Try telling that to the police hierarchy. They'll laugh you out of town."

"It makes me wonder how your clients find the courage to contact you at all."

Phoebe sighed. "Now you see why I've suggested you familiarize yourself with their files. It's bad enough that we're expecting them to open up to a stranger. It will go a long way to making it easier, if they feel like you understand where they're coming from."

"Yes, of course." Ava hurried to reassure her, filled with sudden sadness for the officers and their stories contained in Phoebe's files. With a surge of determination, Ava silently vowed to do all she could to ease the transition between her and the officers' usual therapist and to do her best for them in her friend's absence.

After promising to stay in touch, Ava wished Phoebe all the best with her family and ended the call. She stared at the phone, recalling the anger and desperation in Lachlan's face when they talked about the effects of his job and the need for proper counseling. She now understood his negative attitude toward therapy. She thought of the officers who had come forward and were actively engaged in counseling and shuddered, wondering at their level of desperation.

The phone rang again, rousing her from her dark thoughts. She leaned over and picked up the handpiece. "Ava Wolfe."

"Doctor, it's Janelle. I have another call for you. Line one."

"Thanks, Janelle." Ava pressed the flashing button. "Ava Wolfe."

"Ava, it's Lachlan. Lachlan Coleridge."

Ava's heart skipped a beat. She'd recognized the deep timbre of his voice even before he identified himself. She cleared her throat of sudden nerves.

"Lachlan, it's nice to hear from you. What can I do for you?"

He was silent for so long, she couldn't help but wonder if he would answer. Her mind flew to the possible reason for his call. *Was he going to apologize for his abrupt departure at the barbeque?*

"I... I need to see someone. I... I'd like to make an appointment."

His desperate admission, barely above a whisper, shocked her. After what he'd said the day before... Not wanting to discourage him, she hurried to collect her thoughts.

"Of course. I assume you have approval from the EAP to attend a private physician?"

"No, I... You're the first person I've called."

Ava found the file Phoebe had left out containing the information and the procedure involved in accepting new police clients. She flipped it open and scanned the pages.

"I'm glad you did," she replied softly, relieved when she located the paragraph she was looking for. "But there's a procedure that must be followed. You need to contact someone in the EAP first and request face-to-face visits with a therapist in your area. Your request will be processed and approval for three paid sessions should thereafter be given. Once you receive notice of that approval, you can contact me and arrange an appointment."

"That sounds like a lot of bullshit and I don't

want to go through the EAP. I'd rather pay for the sessions myself. Is that a problem?"

Ava frowned and hurriedly scanned the rest of Phoebe's procedural file. She couldn't find anything that precluded an officer from paying for his own therapy. It just wasn't the way things were normally done. After all, professional therapist services didn't come cheap.

"I-I guess that would be all right, but I need to tell you I charge four hundred dollars an hour and I require payment upfront."

"Fine. When can I see you? I... I really need to talk to someone."

His voice cracked with emotion and once again, Ava's heart hurt at the thought of his level of desperation. The previous afternoon, he'd scoffed at her suggestion of therapy. Now he was almost begging her for help. She clicked on her computer screen and opened up Phoebe's electronic diary.

"I could see you this afternoon at four. Does that suit?"

"No. I don't finish work until six."

"Okay." She moved the mouse to the next page. "What about ten tomorrow morning?"

"No, I'm rostered on the morning shift. We work from six to six."

Ava cleared her throat and tried to swallow her impatience. He wanted to see her as soon as possible, but he wasn't making it easy. "I don't have anything else for another two days after that."

"I can't wait that long." His voice was low and ragged. She bit her lip against his pain.

"I'm not sure what you want me to do," she said.

"What about after work today? I could be there a little after six."

She normally finished at five. Regular office hours. She'd been looking forward to reclaiming a little work and life balance. Her hours in the city were hectic. So many needy patients and only so much time, but Lachlan had found the courage to call her. He needed her.

"All right," she heard herself saying. "I'll see you then."

CHAPTER 6

Dear Diary,

The darkness is encroaching, keeping me from sleep. Ha! Sleep! It's been so long since I felt rested, I can't remember how it feels. I stare at the walls in the darkness. They are closing in on me; squeezing, choking; suffocating the life out of me. Why hasn't anyone noticed? Why doesn't anyone see? I can't go on like this...

Lachlan replaced the handset in the cradle and sighed. It was done. For better or worse, he was going to receive professional help. Just like Ava had suggested. Ava. His gut clenched. Could he bare his soul for someone he found so attractive, no matter how professional she was? Right now, it wasn't just her he was unsure of...

She'd looked just as sexy at Martin's place as she had a month ago and more recently in his dreams. Her rosy lips, her perky breasts…

"Who were you talking to?" Martin asked, startling him.

Lachlan shrugged, not willing to disclose the reason for his call. "No one. It's nothing."

Martin perched on the corner of Lachlan's desk, his face creased with concern. "You're sure? 'Cause you looked kind of angry and scared. It wasn't Kristy, was it? She's not threatening you, is she?"

Lachlan shook his head. "No, Martin. Nothing like that. We're trying to keep things civil, for the sake of the kids."

Martin nodded in understanding. "How'd it go with the boss? Did he—?"

"Lachlan! Martin!" Becker shouted, tearing out of his office. "There's been a car accident out near the Boolaroo Bridge. A young kid was behind the wheel. He had at least two passengers. You need to get out there."

Lachlan's gut somersaulted at the news and the urgency on his boss' face. It told him a helluva lot more than he needed to know.

"Any fatalities?" he asked, grimacing against the pain in his shoulder as he tugged on his jacket.

Becker's expression narrowed on his. "Are you all right to attend this one?"

Lachlan nodded brusquely. "Yeah, I'm fine."

"The dispatcher was only given sketchy details from someone passing by," Becker replied, "but I believe at least one of the passengers is in pretty bad shape. The paramedics are already on their way."

Lachlan's training kicked into gear. Grabbing his keys, he tossed them to Martin who was also getting himself prepared. "You ready?"

Martin shot him a somber look. "Yep."

"Let's go, then."

Together, they hurried down the short flight of stairs that led out back to the car park. Martin slid behind the wheel of the patrol car. With a squeal of tires, they hit the road.

It seemed to take forever to drive the six miles to the Boolaroo Bridge, but in reality, it was less than five minutes. With lights and siren blazing, Martin brought the 4WD patrol vehicle to a stop. The red and white of the emergency strobe lights came from two ambulances that were pulled off to one side of the road. The bright mid-morning light glinted off the wreckage of an early model Toyota sedan.

Slamming the car door behind him, Lachlan followed Martin to the accident site. Two gurneys stood not far away. The fact that they were unoccupied caused anxiety to settle heavily in Lachlan's gut. He searched for the paramedics and found them. Their movements were unhurried. The dread increased in his veins. There was only one reason why paramedics weren't frantic with urgency at the scene of an accident. That didn't bode well for the occupants of the vehicle.

"Oh, Jesus! Oh, fuck! No! *Nooo!*"

Lachlan's heart thumped at the cries of anguish that were torn from his partner's mouth. Martin had gone ahead of him and now stood beside what was left of the driver's side of the car. The mangled body of a teenage boy was barely recognizable behind the wheel.

The front of the Toyota had come into contact with a huge gum tree and had folded around the thick trunk. From the amount of damage to the vehicle, it was obvious the crash had happened at top speed.

"Jesus! It's Travis! Help him, Lachie! It's Travis! *My brother!*"

Martin's howls were filled with pain and sent shards of ice through Lachlan's heart. He gasped in horror. "Fuck, oh, fuck," he whispered, incapable of anything else.

"We need help over here!" Martin shouted at the paramedics, his agony reflected in his eyes. "For fuck's sake! We need help!"

Lachlan forced himself forward until he came up beside his friend. He didn't need to take a closer look to know that no amount of assistance would save Martin's brother. The console and steering wheel were caught so tightly against the boy's chest, he was almost severed in two.

Blood had poured from a large gash across his forehead and was now congealing in his lap. Broken shards of glass were trapped in his hair and glinted in the sunlight. Smaller cuts and abrasions marked the soft skin of his face and neck. The boy's pale blue eyes were open, staring lifelessly up to the sky.

Lachlan glanced through the rear window and caught sight of two more teenage boys. Their necks were twisted at odd angles. Their eyes were sightless. It was obvious both of them were also dead.

His mind went numb. It was the only way he could deal with it. Although he wasn't related to any of the deceased, he still knew them. Travis Griffin and two of his mates: Barney Howarth and Jayden Leech. Lachlan wondered where Thomas Downton was. The four of them could usually be found hanging out together.

With his good hand, Lachlan tugged on Martin's arm and tried to get him to move away. "Come on, mate. We can't help them anymore. We'll need to wait for the Rural Fire Service. They'll have to cut those boys out of the car. There's no other way to get them free."

Martin's eyes blazed with fury and he pulled away from Lachlan's hold. Ducking his head through the shattered glass of the driver's side window, he grasped his brother's face in his hands. Tears streamed down his cheeks. "I'm not going anywhere! I'm not leaving my brother alone!"

Lachlan swallowed against the tightness in his chest. Martin's pain was palpable, but standing inches away from the battered body of his deceased brother wouldn't help anyone. Lachlan tried again.

"Martin, step away. You need to move away.

This is a crime scene. You need to get out of the way."

"Fuck off and leave me alone!" Martin shouted, sobbing hard.

"Guys, we have another body over here!"

The shout came from one of the paramedics a few yards away. Lachlan glanced at Martin and then made his way over to where the paramedic stood. What was left of Thomas Downton lay bloody and broken on the ground. He'd been thrown out of the front passenger seat on impact. Though his face was unmarked, a stake protruded from his chest. The remnants of an old wooden fence post had brought about his untimely death.

Bile rose in Lachlan's stomach and he turned away and heaved. Warm jets of vomit poured out of his mouth and nose. The acrid taste burned his throat and brought hot tears to his eyes and all he could think about was how his partner would cope with what lay ahead.

———————

Ava glanced at her watch and frowned. Lachlan was late. She'd stayed back especially to meet with him. Her last patient had left more than an hour ago, along with her receptionist, Janelle, and Rob, the accountant. And there was still no sign of the chiropractor.

She hadn't thought to ask Lachlan for his number, so she had no way of contacting him to find out if he was on his way, but there was no reason he couldn't have called her and told her he'd changed his mind. His rudeness irritated her. Making the decision to go home, she pushed away from her desk and went to the small cupboard on the other side of the room where she'd stowed her jacket and handbag.

The sound of the front door banging open and a soft curse halted her progress. As far as she knew, the rest of the staff had gone home. Changing direction, she opened the door to her office and walked down the short corridor that led into the reception area.

Lachlan was in the process of lowering himself awkwardly into one of the pine chairs that lined the waiting room. He spied her in the open doorway and slowly returned to an upright position.

"Ava, I'm sorry. I was called out of town to an accident. I... I'm sorry I didn't phone. I should have."

A reprimand died on her lips. There was something so lost and broken about him, like he'd come to the end of the line. His shoulders slumped and his eyes were dull with pain.

"What happened?" she murmured.

"Can we go in?" he asked, indicating the rooms that came off the corridor behind her.

"Of course." She waited for him to cross the reception area and then turned and headed back the way she'd come. His boots sounded loud on the polished wooden floor. She paused outside the door to her office and waved him in.

"After you," she said.

He entered and stopped just inside the door, as if unsure of what to do. She indicated the chair opposite her desk. He moved toward it and sat down. "This is nice," he murmured, looking around.

The large, airy room that comprised Phoebe Jamison's office was part of what had once been a majestic old house. French doors painted in glossy white opened up onto an enclosed porch where a chair and a comfortable couch were located. A fireplace, containing what looked like original decorative features, was built into one wall. It had been restored with a loving hand, as had the rest of the house.

"You were expecting something more...clinical?" she asked.

He shrugged. "Yeah, I guess. Or something bleak and dreary."

"I wish I could take credit for the styling," she replied, "but I'm afraid my friend Phoebe is singularly responsible for this wonderful space. My office in the city is far less appealing."

"But it probably suits you," he said.

She blinked in surprise. "What's that supposed to mean?"

"Well, you're a city girl, aren't you? You're dabbling in the country air to help out a friend, but I think we both know you're not cut out for the bush."

His observation stung. He hardly knew her. Okay, so he'd touched the most intimate parts of her, but he didn't know *her*. She could get used to living in the country, couldn't she?

"We never know what we're capable of until

we're put to the test," she replied, challenging him with her eyes.

He sighed heavily as if tired of the game. "Yeah, you have that right."

Once again, the quiet desperation in his tone and his tormented expression stopped her. She wondered if the accident he'd attended was responsible for his mood. Seating herself across from him she drew a fresh legal pad toward her and picked up her pen.

"I'm not sure what I'm doing here," he muttered. "I'm not in the mood to talk about myself."

"Okay," she replied. "Then we'll talk about something else. How's your collarbone?"

He grimaced. "It's all right."

"Tell me about your family," she asked, hoping to get him to open up. "I met them all briefly at the wedding, but I'd really like to know more. How's your mom coping without your dad?"

Lachlan's lips compressed, but he nodded slowly. "She's getting there. They were married for nearly forty years. That's a lot of time together. It's going to take her awhile to get used to being on her own."

"What about the rest of your family? How are they coping? I lost my dad when I was barely three years old, so I have only the vaguest of memories of him, but I know when my mom passes on, I'll be devastated. For years, before the kidney transplant, we faced that possibility every day. I didn't realize how tense I'd been until the stress of it was taken away."

He nodded somberly. "She was one of the lucky ones. Many people on transplant lists die before a compatible donor's found."

"Yes," she agreed. "We all feel very lucky. We won the lottery the night Mom's donor came along."

"I'm sorry about your brother. It must be tough, knowing he's—"

"In jail? Yes." She appraised him with frank curiosity. "Your understanding surprises me. Given your occupation, I'd have thought you'd feel the way Rohan did about the need for Alistair to be punished for his deeds."

He stared back at her. "You don't believe your brother did the wrong thing?"

"Of course he did the wrong thing, but he had the best of intentions."

"Oh, that's right. He stole those organs and tissues out of the goodness of his heart."

Lachlan's sarcasm angered her. Okay, her brother was far from saintly and she conceded that he'd benefited mightily from his arrangement to sell human tissue to an overseas corporation. In fact, the police estimated he'd received close to a million dollars for his services before they discovered his illegal activities.

But despite all that, she couldn't help but point out to most people who would listen that many more donor organs had been made available to desperately ill people that would never have been available otherwise and the number of lives saved as a consequence couldn't be measured.

She glanced at the man who sat across from her, tension evident in the harsh lines that were etched into his face. With an effort, she controlled the instinctive urge to return fire. This wasn't about her. It was obvious his mood was heavy and he was there, in her office, seeking help.

She cleared her throat and forced herself to relax. "I haven't heard anyone mention an accident. Was it nearby?"

He grimaced. "About six miles away, at the Boolaroo Bridge. It's out on the highway heading toward Goondiwindi."

"A car accident?"

"Yes."

"Was anyone hurt?"

He squeezed his eyes tightly shut and then opened them on a heavy sigh. "Yes."

Her heart gave a little start. No wonder he looked down. And then another thought occurred to her. Even in the short time she'd been there, she'd worked out that Moree was a small, close-knit community. It wasn't farfetched to imagine the victim might have been someone he'd known. She voiced the question quietly.

His eyes turned to flint. "Yes. I knew all four of them."

As his words sank in, she was filled with surprise. *Four?* There were four people injured?"

"Not injured, Doc. Killed."

Shock and horror flooded through her. "Four fatalities? I take it there were at least two vehicles involved."

"No."

Another wave of shock shuddered through her. "*No?*"

"No. A single motor vehicle driven by a seventeen-year-old boy. Three of his teenaged mates were passengers. It's my guess the driver was traveling at an excessive speed. He lost control of the car and simply ran out of talent. He collided head-on with a massive gum tree. None of them were wearing seatbelts. I'm led to believe all four died instantly."

His words hammered away in Ava's brain, piling shock upon shock on her stunned senses. She wondered how he could sit there and recite the awful facts so calmly, so unemotionally.

And then she understood.

He was a police officer. People relied on him to remain strong and steadfast during times of unspeakable horror. He wasn't allowed the liberty of losing control, of displaying more human emotion. That would be seen as a sign of weakness and weakness was not to be tolerated by the police service or by the community.

Her heart cried out against the injustice of it, even as she accepted it was true. Society demanded more from the men and women who kept them safe night and day. It wasn't right or fair, but it was the way it was.

"I'm sorry," she said softly.

His lip curled up derisively. "For what, Doc?"

She struggled to vocalize her feelings, instinctively knowing he wouldn't accept her sympathy. "I'm sorry that you had to see that. It must have been awful."

"Not as awful as it was for Martin. The driver was his brother."

Ava gasped and her hand flew to cover her mouth. She stared at Lachlan, horrified, barely able to comprehend. "The-the driver...was...Martin's *brother?*"

Lachlan held her gaze, his expression grim. "That's what I said."

Ava looked away and fidgeted with the files on her desk. She couldn't stop thinking about what Lachlan had said. While he remained cool and collected, she was anything, but. While she didn't know much about Martin's family, she'd been friends with Pam since high school. She couldn't imagine what they must be feeling. And then something else Lachlan said hit her hard, like a sudden blow to the head. She looked up at him. Her voice trembled.

"Did Martin attend the scene of the accident? Was he with you when you found them?"

"Yes, Doc. He was there. He realized before I did, it was Travis. He's...understandably upset."

"Upset?" she shouted. "*Upset?*" A flash of anger blazed through her. "He must be devastated, unable to have a coherent thought! To come across a fatal accident is bad enough, but to discover one of the victims is your *brother*..." Her voice caught on a horrified sob and she couldn't complete the thought. Pushing away from her desk, she turned her back on the man who continued to stare at her with a stoic expression on his face.

"It's not right!" she shouted. "It's not normal to

bury your anger and pain so deep and it sure as hell isn't healthy!"

"You think *this* is bad?"

Lachlan's voice, rough and low with pent up emotion, halted her distraught pacing. Slowly, she looked up at him, fearful of what he might say. She wasn't an automaton. She couldn't turn her heart to ice.

And neither could he. The thought struck her deep inside and suddenly, she knew it was true. He wasn't a machine. He felt horror and pain and anguish like anyone else, but over the years he'd learned how to suppress it because he didn't have a choice.

She made her way back to her desk and lowered herself back in her seat. He stared at her, his eyes dark and stormy with emotion. His hands clenched into fists.

"Talk to me," she whispered, her voice ragged.

"Last week, we raided an illegal meth lab," he stated quietly. "There was an explosion. We got out, along with the men who'd been responsible for it. During the explosion, I thought I heard screaming. I tried to get back into the building, but the fire had already taken hold. We didn't realize until the next morning the criminals had two troubled teens working for them. The charred bodies of those children were barely recognizable as people. We found them in the cookhouse."

Ava pressed a hand tightly to her mouth, holding back her horror. Lachlan continued in the same low voice, devoid of emotion.

"The month before that, we attended a

domestic abuse call out. A woman had dialed the police, screaming for help. Her ice-addict boyfriend was beating the crap out of her. By the time we got there, she was unconscious. Then there was the—"

Ava held up a hand to halt him, hiding her desperation. "Please, I... I've heard enough." She drew in a shaky breath, hating her cowardice, but helpless to do anything about it. While she'd been trained to control her emotions, she couldn't divorce herself from the pain his stories evoked. She wasn't sure if she could listen to more of the horrors he endured on a regular basis in the course of his job.

His hard gaze was filled with cynicism. "Am I offending your tender sensibilities, Doc?"

CHAPTER 7

Ava stared at Lachlan. With surreptitious breaths, she regained control over her turbulent emotions. In a voice that was almost calm, she responded.

"I'm not shocked, Detective, if that was your intention. Your words only sadden me because I know you speak the truth. There is much for us to be ashamed of in our society. I admire you greatly for your bravery and courage and willingness to do what most of the rest of us would be too terrified to do, all in the name of protecting your community and keeping them safe."

She peered over her black-framed glasses to gage his reaction. His expression was blank, but his eyes held a keen light that told her he was listening.

"You've been told, no doubt from the first day you stepped inside the police academy, that you're tougher, stronger, braver than the average man and that you're no longer entitled to feel emotion the way the rest of us do. It's hammered into you day after day that those emotions are damaging and will only get in your way."

"You certainly have a way with words, Doc," he drawled and tossed her a sarcastic smile. "Did they teach you all that nonsense in college? I bet you came top of the class."

Her anger flared low in her belly and spread quickly up her neck, but she forced it down. He was needling her on purpose, trying to get a rise—a defensive tactic to deflect her attention from himself. Unperturbed, she continued.

"They feed you that rubbish in the academy because they have to. They want you to believe you're a robot who can be programed to do a job; to switch on and off whenever it's required. What they don't tell you is that, despite all the bullshit and rhetoric, despite their best efforts to convince you otherwise, underneath you're still a man."

She leaned forward in her seat. "You have a brain and a heart that feels love and hate, pain and anger and frustration, even when you don't want them to," she said, hoping desperately to break through his wall of cynicism.

"Every time you force those feelings further back inside you instead of setting them free, you fill another empty place with damaging emotion. Damaging, not because those emotions are bad, but because they're not dealt with properly. Instead, they're left to fester and rot in some deep dark place inside you and when you can't take the pressure anymore, they'll spew forth in a terrible disaster of incomprehension and pain."

Lachlan still slouched in his seat, but his eyes were focused on her, so she continued.

"You'll be shocked when it happens, but everyone around you will know it was only a matter of time. Coming here is the first step toward mental health. The fact that you kept your appointment, despite the day you've had, tells me you know what I say is true. You've been struggling for a long time. You know you need help; that you can't do it on your own."

Reflexively, she reached across the narrow desk and covered one of his clenched fists. He tried to move his hand, but she only tightened her grip. In a soft voice, she continued. "Feel proud of yourself for finding the courage to take this first, important step. You've done what many others cannot. You've sought out help and I promise you, I'll give it. You won't ever have to feel so helpless and alone again."

She stared at him. His eyes filled with emotion. With an impatient sound, he rubbed a hand across his face.

"Thank you, Doc," he muttered, his voice rough. "I'm sorry for my earlier attitude. I was being a prick. You didn't deserve it."

She offered him a gentle smile. "You have to try harder than that to frighten me away. I'm made of sterner stuff."

His gaze held hers for the longest time. Ava's breaths got short. His green eyes had deepened to a beautiful emerald and her pulse kicked up a gear. Her gaze dropped to his lips and all of a sudden, she was bombarded with images of kissing him and him kissing her—the pair of them clinging to each other in a frenzy of want and need.

He leaned closer across the desk, so close his breath whispered across her skin. A moment later, his lips grazed hers and she was once again transported back in time. Hot breath, frantic heartbeat, the ecstasy of skin against skin. It all came back in a rush and she pulled away on a panicked gasp.

"Lachlan! Stop! We can't do this! It isn't right!"

He stared at her with eyes still dark with desire. "Don't you want me anymore?"

She shook her head at the nonsensical notion. "Of course I want you, but this has nothing to do with that! I'm your therapist! There are rules against this kind of thing! I could lose my license; never be allowed to practice again. Besides, have you forgotten you still have a wife?"

She stood and moved further away from him and then turned back to face him with her hands planted firmly on her hips.

"I'm your therapist, Lachlan. Nothing more. At least, not while you're still seeing me professionally. It's nothing personal. And there's still the thing about your wife. Separated or not, I'm unwilling to get involved with a married man." She gave a little helpless shrug. "I hope you understand."

His shoulders slumped on a heavy sigh. His expression reflected his apologetic tone. "I'm sorry, Doc. Of course, I do. I might not like it, but I understand and as much as I'd like to bury myself inside you again, I need your professional help even more. I'm not going to jeopardize my emotional wellbeing for the sake of a few moments of mindless pleasure."

Ava should have taken umbrage at the fact he implied anything between them would be nothing more than a short and frantic interlude, but she was too focused on the fact that he actively wanted to get himself well.

Clearing her throat, she went back to her desk and sat down. Dragging the keyboard toward her, she opened up the electronic diary and scanned the calendar. "Okay, now that we have that out of the way, when can you see me next? My schedule is fairly full, but I'm probably a little more flexible than you."

"I have a couple of rostered days off coming up the day after tomorrow. I could come in on either of those days, whenever it suits you."

Ava nodded and checked her appointments. "How's twelve o'clock on Wednesday sound?"

"It sounds good."

"Great. I'll put you in."

"Great." He looked down at the thick, pale green carpet and then back up at her again. "I... I want to thank you for seeing me, Ava. I appreciate your help. The truth is, I need it. My wife's refused to let me see my kids until I'm in a better headspace."

"She can't—"

Lachlan held up his hand and halted her protest. "Legally, no. But she's right. I'm not in a good place. My kids don't need to see me like this. It's not fair to them. To anyone."

Ava slowly nodded. "Like I said, you've taken a very important step toward improving your mental state. I'm confident, with time, you'll be back to feeling like your old self. What's more, you'll have the right skills to deal with the emotions you've suppressed for so long. It's a win-win situation. For everyone."

"Yes, although right now, that feels like a lifetime away."

"You're right. It won't happen overnight," she cautioned, "but if you really want to get well and you put in the required effort, it's only a matter of time. I promise."

He smiled softly and the tension and residual pain in his face eased. "I like it when you promise me things. You make me feel like I can believe in you, that you understand me and know what I need better than I do. It's...reassuring."

His words were filled with quiet certainty and she sent a silent prayer heavenwards that she wouldn't let him down. He'd taken the hardest step toward finding inner peace. From now on, she was responsible for seeing that he moved in the right direction.

Chapter 8

"Okay, people. Gather close." Once again, Detective Superintendent Nigel Becker commanded the attention of his staff.

Lachlan saved the work on his computer screen and pushed away from his desk. Martin had taken a week of compassionate leave to deal with the death of his brother, but had now returned to work. From the look of him, Lachlan wasn't sure his partner should have come back so soon.

His complexion was pale, with a grayish tinge evident around his tight mouth. His demeanor had been quiet and subdued since he'd walked back through the door; his eyes were dead. He appeared to move around the station in a daze, barely going through the motions.

Lachlan had suggested quietly to his partner that he take a little more time off, but Martin hadn't taken kindly to his advice. As far as Martin was concerned, he didn't need time off to sit around and think about the tragic loss of his younger brother. He needed to be busy. He needed to be at work.

Lachlan could understand that sentiment. There had been many times during the deterioration of his marriage that he'd turned to work for relief. After two more therapy sessions with Ava, he could now see that kind of solution wasn't really a solution at all. It worked in the short term and helped distract people from what was really bugging them, but in the long run, the problem was still there. It didn't disappear or fade away from neglect. In fact, often it worked the opposite. The longer the issue remained unresolved, the bigger it became and the harder it was to deal with.

He thought of telling Martin about the therapy sessions and suggesting his partner might want to have some, too, but his thoughts were interrupted by Becker, addressing the squad of men.

"We have a situation up on Balo Street. There's a guy holding people hostage in the supermarket. I understand he's the estranged husband of one of the employees, but a few shoppers are also caught up in the drama. We need to get over there and see if we can defuse the situation."

"Is he armed?" Lachlan asked.

"Yes. With a twenty-two rifle, I believe."

"How many hostages are we talking?" Martin asked.

"Somewhere between five and ten. Most of them are employees."

"Who's our informant, boss?" Lachlan asked.

"A woman who was passing by. She heard a

shout and screaming and looked through the plate glass window at the front of the shop. She saw a man with a gun herding people toward the back."

Lachlan processed the information. "Do we have any back up?"

Becker nodded. "I've called the police negotiator's office in Tamworth. They're sending over a team, but it will take them the best part of three hours to get here. We have to do what we can until then."

"Are we going to make contact with the perp?" Martin asked.

"That, we'll play by ear," Becker replied. "I don't want anyone upsetting this guy before we have our elite team on the ground. Naturally, if things deteriorate to the point where the perp's directly threatening any of the hostages, we're going to have to do something. The goal is to keep everyone alive."

Lachlan listened and his gut filled with the usual mix of dread and anticipation. Ava had been teaching him ways to cope with the stress of his job and he called on some of those techniques now. Breathing deeply, he leisurely counted to ten until his pulse was slow and even. The technique helped to calm him and keep him focused.

"Coleridge, how's the shoulder?" Becker asked.

"It's almost as good as new, boss," Lachlan lied.

Becker nodded. "Very well, you go with Martin and see what you can find out. Talk to whoever you can find downtown. We need to know more about our perp. If we know what's driving his behavior, we have a better chance of making him see reason." Becker swung around to face Martin. "Are you all right with that?"

Martin nodded grimly. "Of course."

"Good. The rest of you get down there and secure the area. Make sure no one enters that supermarket. We don't need any more innocents stumbling onto the scene."

Quiet nods and murmurs came from the rest of those gathered around and they began to disperse. Lachlan looked at Martin as he reached for his jacket.

"Are you sure you're all right with this?" he asked.

Martin stared back at him and nodded. "Yeah, I'm fine."

Lachlan held his gaze a moment longer. Satisfied with the sincerity in his friend's eyes, he replied. "All right then. Let's go. We'll talk more in the car."

The downtown streets were busy with mid-afternoon shoppers. School was out and a mix of children and parents and other people lined the pavement. A crowd had gathered outside the supermarket and even a few stupid souls had their faces pressed against the glass shopfront, hoping to see in.

Lachlan brought the squad car to a sudden halt and he and Martin leaped from the vehicle.

Another carload of officers pulled in behind them. They needed to secure the scene and enforce a ten-yard danger zone. Who knew what might happen over the minutes and hours ahead.

"Move on, people," Lachlan ordered, striding toward the bystanders. "This area is out of bounds. You need to move right out of the way."

"What is it? What's happening?" a plump woman asked, tugging at Lachlan's sleeve.

He frowned down at her. "You have to move away from here, ma'am. We have a situation inside the supermarket."

The woman's flushed face turned pale. "What kind of situation?"

"We're not exactly sure, but we're asking everyone to move away. It could be dangerous."

The woman gasped. "But my mother's in there! I dropped her off to buy some bread and milk and a few other necessities while I went to the post office. I've only been gone fifteen minutes. I need to go to her and make sure she's all right. She doesn't hear so well, anymore. I have to—"

Lachlan sympathized with her plight, but now wasn't the time for leniency. "I'm sorry, ma'am, but I can't let you in there. Now, please. Move out of the way."

The woman looked like she was going to argue until Martin stepped closer and pinned her with a dark frown. Her words sputtered and died under his added authority. With a half-sob, she turned and disappeared into the thinning crowd.

With a sigh of relief, Lachlan flashed his partner a look of thanks and with the help of the other officers, managed to cordon off the scene with police tape. With several officers placed around the perimeter of the building keeping watch, Lachlan and Martin moved closer to the plate glass shop front and tried to peer inside.

"Do we have a phone number for the store manager, or anyone else inside?" Martin asked.

"There's a number for home deliveries painted on the door. We could try that."

Martin nodded in agreement and Lachlan pulled out his phone. To his surprise, the call was answered after the third ring.

"It's Detective Lachlan Coleridge from the Moree police. Who am I talking to?"

"It's Jill Sanders. I-I work upstairs in the office."

Lachlan strained to hear her whispered reply. "Jill, are you able to talk?"

"Yes."

"I understand you have a situation in there. Can you tell me what's happening?"

"I-I'm not exactly sure. Barry Irwin stormed in about twenty minutes ago, waving a gun around and demanding to see his wife."

"Who's his wife?"

"Elsie Irwin. She works in the deli. Has worked here for thirteen years."

"Who else is in the store?"

"There are six other staff members, including the two girls on the checkouts and probably half a dozen shoppers. I'm not sure of exact numbers. Some of them might be hiding in one of the other aisles."

"Where is Barry?" Lachlan asked.

"He's down near the deli. He has Elsie and her two co-workers holed up behind the deli counter. He's angry, Detective, and getting angrier by the minute. A moment ago, he threatened to shoot them all."

A sense of urgency raced through Lachlan and his mind kicked into overdrive. The situation was escalating. They couldn't wait for the trained police negotiators to arrive. There simply wasn't time. He turned to Martin.

"We're going to have to try and make contact with him. His wife works in the store. She's one of the hostages. It sounds like some kind of domestic dispute. We might be able to convince him to let everyone else go."

Martin nodded, his expression grim. He touched the weapon holstered on his hip. "I'm ready whenever you are."

Lachlan frowned. "We're going to try and end this peacefully. There isn't any room to be a hero."

"Okay, I get it," Martin replied brusquely. "Let's just get in there and see what's going on."

"The delicatessen's located part-way down the store on the left hand side. We'll go in through the back. So it will be on our right. Our guy probably won't expect anyone to come in the back entrance," Lachlan said.

Martin nodded and together they headed along the side of the building and into the deli through the delivery entrance. Empty pallets and crates were stacked in a haphazard pile against one wall. The rear of the shop was eerily silent. Where staff normally sorted through groceries and fresh produce, ready to be packed onto shelves, there was no one.

Quickly and quietly, they made their way through the storeroom and eased open the double doors that led into the shop. Once again, Lachlan was struck by the silence. Creeping forward, he rounded a shelf stacked high with cat food and came to a halt. A man of average height and build, sporting a receding hairline stalked back and forth in front of the delicatessen counter, waving a rifle.

Lachlan turned back to Martin, who stood a short distance away. Using hand signals, he indicated the whereabouts of their man. Martin nodded in acknowledgement and with a few more hand signals and whispers, they split up with the goal to approach the deli from opposite ends. With a deep breath and a quick and silent prayer, Lachlan stepped out from behind the shelf of cat food and showed himself to Barry Irwin.

"Stop right there! Don't move!" the man shouted, spinning on his heel and pointing the rifle at Lachlan.

Keeping calm, Lachlan halted and raised his hands in a sign of surrender. "It's all right, Barry. I'm Detective Coleridge. What can I do, mate? I'd like to help."

"Help? How can *you* help? Can you turn back time to when my wife still loved me? To the time when she didn't feel the need to sleep with one of my friends?" He shook his head scornfully. "You can't help me. No one can."

"It sounds like it's a problem between you and

your wife, Barry. How about we let these other good people go? They have nothing to do with what's going on and besides, you don't want them to hear your business, do you?"

Lachlan held his breath as Barry appeared to consider his suggestion and then let it out on a rush of relief when the man nodded.

"Yeah, you're right. I don't want anyone else to hear. This is between me and Elsie. She knows exactly why I'm here." He swung back around to face the counter and narrowed his gaze at a middle-aged woman who cowered against the wall. "We're going to sort this out here and now, Elsie. You hear me?"

His shout reverberated off the back wall and the women behind the counter jumped. "You! And you! Get out of here!" Barry ordered, pointing the gun at Elsie's colleagues.

The women didn't need to be told twice. They scrambled to get away. Within moments, it was just Barry and Elsie and Lachlan and Martin—who Lachlan assumed stood somewhere nearby. More footsteps heard from further away disappeared down other aisles. The front doors opened and closed several times before the shop fell silent again. Lachlan turned his attention back to Barry.

"Now that it's just us, we might be able to sort this out—but first, I want you to hand over the rifle."

In a heartbeat, Barry's mood changed. His eyes narrowed with menace. "The hell I will! You're not taking my gun. I came here to put an end to the deceitful, wicked woman I married and that's what I intend to do. Running behind my back with my best friend! That kind of behavior deserves severe punishment. Even God would agree with me on that!"

A dark red flush stained the side of Barry's neck and his eyes were wild with anger. Lachlan forced himself to remain calm and tried to think of another way to pacify the man.

"Are you sure that she's been unfaithful, Barry? Have you tried to talk to Elsie about it? Even if she has done what you say she has, God also preaches forgiveness. I'm not condoning adultery, but maybe she had her reasons."

"You've got it all wrong, Barry!" Elsie cried from behind the deli counter. "I would never cheat on you! Adam and I are friends! That's all! You come home from work and lock yourself away in your den, drinking into the wee hours of the night. You never talk to me about your day, or ask about mine. You never share anything with me. I... I was lonely."

She hiccupped on a sob. "Adam was there for me, Barry, when you weren't. He listened to my trials and tribulations. He celebrated my wins. He cared about me... But, I never betrayed you. I could *never* do something like that! I promised in my marriage vows to be faithful to you, and I have. There's never been anyone for me, but you. I love you, Barry! I'll love you until I die."

Barry stared at her, confused and angry and uncertain. Lachlan could see the war being waged inside him. Barry didn't know whether to believe his wife. And then he came to a decision.

"No! I don't believe you, Elsie! I saw the way you looked at him! And I saw the way he looked at you! Don't tell me there's nothing between you! I won't believe it! I won't!"

Tears of rage and pain poured down Barry's cheeks. Elsie sobbed and held her face in her hands, as if she couldn't bear to watch.

Barry brandished the gun wildly, his eyes crazy and unfocused. Lachlan thought fast.

"Barry, listen to me!" He kept his voice low and urgent. "What good will it do to murder your wife? Believe me, it will be murder. Provocation is no defense. The courts won't care what she has or hasn't done. And what about your family? Your kids?"

Lachlan had no idea if the man had children, but he was betting they probably did. Some of the craziness left Barry's eyes and Lachlan kept going. "Why spend the next fifteen years behind bars, Barry, pacing the walls of a prison cell? If Elsie's done wrong, she must be punished, but not by you going to jail. That achieves nothing."

Watching the man closely, he was relieved to see that Barry appeared to take notice of what had just been said. He lowered the gun slightly and his stance became less belligerent. Lachlan swallowed a sigh of relief. But it wasn't over, yet.

"Give me the gun, Barry. Please, let me have the gun."

The man turned to face Lachlan and he could see the defeat in Barry's eyes. A little more coaxing and he might just get the man to comply with his request.

"Come on, Barry. You know it's for the best. Give me the gun."

Out of the corner of Lachlan's eye, he noticed Elsie inching away. She was almost to the exit door that led to the storerooms in the back when Barry caught sight of her. Spinning on his heel, he brought the rifle around and raised it once again.

The loud report of gunfire ricocheted around the room and nearly deafened Lachlan. With ears ringing, he watched blood blossom on Barry's chest. A look of surprise flooded the man's features a moment before he collapsed at Lachlan's feet.

"Somebody get an ambulance!" Lachlan screamed, still trying to comprehend what had happened. He looked up as Martin came around one of the shelves, his gun hanging loose in his hand.

"What the fuck happened?" he shouted above Elsie's terrified shrieks. "I had him. He was nearly there. Another minute or two and this would have all been over." He shook his head, still in shock and disbelief at how quickly the situation had gone off the rails.

"What the fuck happened?" he yelled at Martin again, eyeballing his partner.

"I... I thought he was going to shoot her. I saw him lift the gun. I got off a shot before he could pull the trigger."

"Jesus!" Lachlan gasped, aghast.

Martin had shot the man dead. Lachie had instinctively called for an ambulance, but he could tell from the way Barry stared fixedly at the ceiling that lifesaving medical attention would no longer be required.

Elsie's hysterical cries of panic and pain echoed throughout the quiet of the store. Dread weighed heavy and viscous in Lachlan's gut. He stared at Martin and all he could do was slowly shake his head.

What had his colleague been thinking? Surely he'd realized Lachlan had the situation under control? And even if he hadn't, they'd never employed the policy of shooting first and asking questions later. That was left to stupid TV shows where the baddies confessed by the end of the program and the guy always got the girl. Real life wasn't like that and Martin sure as hell knew it.

When the media got hold of this... The Moree police would be drawn and quartered. He and Martin would be embroiled in a lengthy internal affairs investigation. That kind of shit always happened over something like this.

As if the pair of them didn't have enough to deal with. Martin had only just buried his little brother. Lachlan was still in the very early stages of coming to terms with his depression and learning how to deal with it. The last thing either of them needed was the stress of an internal investigation.

Lachlan sighed at the thought of the mountain of questions and paperwork that lay ahead. There was nothing to be done about it now. All they could do was keep a low profile, give them what they wanted and get on with it.

He looked across at Martin who was now pale and trembling, suffering from delayed shock.

Moving closer, Lachlan rested a hand on his friend's shoulder. "Are you all right?" he murmured.

"Yeah, I'm... I'm fine." Shrugging off Lachlan's hand, Martin turned his back on the body that lay still and bloody on the floor and went to lean on the deli counter. A moment later, Lachlan heard a sob, followed by a howl of pain. Martin's shoulders shook from the force of his distress.

A commotion of noise and shouting sounded from the direction of the front door. A moment later, Lachlan was surrounded by paramedics and uniformed police officers. Becker strode into view, his face contorted with shock and anger.

"What the fuck happened, Coleridge? You were meant to wait for the Tamworth boys."

"Yeah." It was all Lachlan could manage.

His brief answer only served to incite his boss' anger. Becker's cheeks went crimson with fury. His breath came fast and his eyes blazed. Lachlan hoped they wouldn't have another dead body to deal with.

"What happened?" Becker demanded again through gritted teeth. His tone brooked no argument.

"The victim raised his gun in the direction of his wife. He'd threatened to shoot her. Martin shot first."

Becker's gaze lifted to where Martin stood, his shoulders still shaking with sobs. "For fuck's sake!" Becker growled in disgust and turned away. Without another word, he stalked back the way he'd come.

Lachlan sighed heavily. He looked around at the other officers who now filled the store, but none of their eyes met his. Paramedics arrived with a stretcher and halted beside Barry's body. The paramedics tossed Lachlan curious stares, but refrained from asking questions. It wouldn't take long for them to find their tongues.

By nightfall, the whole town would be talking about it. His and Martin's actions would be examined and discussed and analyzed from every angle. Truth would give way to a better story. By the time the townsfolk of Moree had finished, what they believed happened in their supermarket would barely resemble the truth. Lachlan accepted that for what it was and braced himself for the impact.

CHAPTER 9

Dear Diary,

The pain just keeps going round and round, ever tighter around my heart. I'm drowning, gasping for air; desperate to stay alive. And nobody notices. Nobody sees my pain.

I thought I was getting better; would have sworn that it was true. But I'm back where I started, surrounded by blackness, hurtling full speed into the abyss...

———————

Ava took a sip of coffee and flipped open the *Moree Champion*. She liked to immerse herself in the happenings of the community where she worked and Moree was no different. The newspaper usually held various stories that affected the surrounding farming community and often included the dire predictions for poor crop yields if the current dry weather held.

The café on Balo Street where she'd taken to eating breakfast was housed in an original art deco building and much to her relief, the owner knew how to serve decent coffee. She'd have to remember to tell Mrs Christie when she returned to the city.

The interior of the shop had recently undergone a major renovation and now resembled something like one of the cafés she might frequent in the eastern suburbs of Sydney. The stainless steel seating complemented the dark wood tables, and the glossy marble floor tiles reflected the modern lighting. Rural landscapes by local artists lined the walls. The clatter of plates and cutlery from the direction of the kitchen and the murmur of other patrons had become a familiar, soothing sound.

Focusing on the newspaper, Ava read the headline on the front page and gasped. The day before, there had been a shooting at the local supermarket. It was the same store she frequented, only a hundred yards away from where she sat, but on the opposite side of the street. The article was short on detail, but she was concerned to discover Lachlan Coleridge and Martin Griffin had been involved in a fatal shooting at the store.

She hadn't seen Lachlan since his appointment on Friday of the week before. They'd agreed to keep their relationship platonic, at least while he was her patient. In three weeks' time when Phoebe returned and took over her practice once again, well... Who knew what might happen? But for now, they were strictly friends.

She frowned at the thought of Lachlan and Martin being at the scene of another fatality. Lachlan had been making good progress and Ava had been pleased with his improvement. He'd been opening up more and more and had even spoken to her about his wife. As much as hearing about his family made her uncomfortable, that aspect was an integral part of him and dealing with that was another important part of his healing.

He'd told her one of his main goals of getting better was to gain access to his kids. Ava couldn't help but wonder if a reunion with his estranged wife might also be on the table. She wanted to protest the unwelcome thought, but the truth was, she had no hold on him.

She'd met him at a low point in his life and had provided a welcome distraction and relief. By his own admission, the wedding had come at a time when he'd recently split up with his wife. The fact that their brief moment of passion in the cloakroom had impacted upon Ava's heart was no one's fault but her own. She'd not long turned thirty-six. She knew sex didn't equate to love, no matter how much she wanted it to.

And it wasn't like she was in love with him. That was utter nonsense. She barely knew him. But the more he opened up to her, the more she got to see the real Lachlan Coleridge and the more she wanted to know about him. Memories of just how he could make her body sing didn't help her addiction. If it weren't for the fact he was her patient, she might just throw caution to the wind and see where it led...

Ava shook her head, annoyed with the direction of her thoughts. He wasn't available. Separation wasn't the same as divorce and there was always the possibility he'd reconcile with his wife. No, the sensible thing to do was to put all thoughts of romance with Lachlan Coleridge out of her mind.

Her phone tinkled, indicating an incoming call. Taking another sip of her coffee, she glanced at the screen and smiled. It was her baby sister.

"Sammie! How are you? How was the honeymoon? How's married life treating you?"

"It's amazing, Ava. You and Jessie should try it sometime. You don't know what you're missing."

Images of green eyes that had seen too much suddenly flooded Ava's mind and it was all she could do to concentrate on what her sister was saying.

"The sightseeing was great, but it's good to be back home. How's life in the thriving metropolis of Moree?" Samantha continued.

"It's going well. Phoebe has a busy practice. I'm at work for a good solid eight or nine hours a day, sometimes longer. There are so few professional services out in the bush. We city dwellers don't know how good we have it."

"And how's Lachlan? Rohan told me the two of you had hooked up."

Ava blushed, despite the fact no one knew of her illicit encounter with Lachlan at the wedding. Ava must have been referring to the barbeque they'd both attended a little over a week earlier at the Griffins.

"He's...fine. We've chatted here and there. He's...nice."

"*Nice!* He's more than that! He's hot, like all of Rohan's brothers. Too bad this one's married. Hasn't he got the cutest little kids?"

Ava's blush got hotter. She squirmed on her seat. "Um... I guess. I haven't met his wife or children. I think they're visiting with her mom."

"Oh, well, anyway, I just hope Rohan and I breed kids that cute. On that note... I have some news."

"*Oooh!*" Ava squealed. "Don't tell me you're pregnant!"

"Four weeks along. We're not past the danger period, yet, so we're only telling family."

"Does Lachlan know?"

"I guess so. Rohan said he'd call him."

"Congratulations, Sammie. I'm thrilled to bits. Mom must be beside herself. It's so long since she held a grandbaby."

"Yes, Mom's over the moon. Her only complaint is that she still has so long to wait."

Ava chuckled, and was filled with a surge of yearning. Her little sister was married and about to have a baby. It was the way things were meant to be. Ava had dreamed of her prince charming since she was a young girl, like all young girls did. She longed to have someone to share her life with, to love her, to hold her, to father her kids...

Still, there was no point moping about it. If it didn't happen, it didn't happen. She could still feel happy for her sister. And she did.

After wishing Sam all the best with her

pregnancy, Ava promised to speak again soon and then ended the call. She thought about Lachlan and his children and vowed to do everything she could to bring him back to a place of wellness where his family could once again enjoy his company. It was the right thing to do. It was the way it had to be.

Her phone beeped, indicating a new text message. She picked it up and checked the screen. Her heart skipped a beat. It was Lachlan.

I really need to c u. R u free?

He wasn't scheduled for another appointment until later in the week, but there was something desperate about his brief text. Her first patient wasn't until ten o'clock. It was only a little after eight. She'd intended on enjoying a lazy breakfast and catching up on the local news, but Lachlan needed her and that was reason enough to bring her relaxing morning to an end.

Give me 20 minutes. Can u get here by then?

No problem. C u soon.

Ava tamped down on the surge of excitement and anticipation that rushed through her at the thought of seeing him again. He was still married. He was still battling to get himself well. He was still her patient. It was her job to get him there. End of story.

———————

"What are you up to?"

Lachlan glanced up from his desk and spied

Martin heading toward him. "I was just texting Ava Wolfe," he replied.

Until now, he'd kept the fact he was seeing Ava professionally from everyone, including his partner, but after their earlier discussion with Becker and seeing the fear lying just below the surface of Martin's eyes, Lachlan decided his friend would be better served knowing help was available.

"I made an appointment to talk to her," Lachlan added.

Surprise filled Martin's face. He walked closer and lowered his voice. "You mean, you've been getting therapy?"

Lachlan held his colleague's gaze and hoped he wasn't making a mistake. The reasons he'd wanted to keep his visits to Ava quiet were still valid. "Yes."

Martin's eyes flared wide. "Really?"

"Yes, really. And I'm glad I found the guts to give it a go. I think it's helping."

"With what?"

Lachlan shook his head, irritated by Martin's show of ignorance. "With dealing with the shit we face every day. And now we have IA on our ass. I need to get on top of things. Kristy won't let me see the kids until I get my shit together. Apart from anything else, I owe it to my family to get well."

He'd said the words before, to Ava, but she was his therapist. Hearing them now, he realized how much he meant them and how committed he was to returning to a healthier emotional state.

"You ought to give it a go," he added and wasn't surprised when Martin vigorously shook his head.

"No way! It might make you feel better and I'm happy for you, mate, I really am. But that kind of shit's not for me. I'll have a few beers and put yesterday's troubles behind me. It's how I always deal with it. Besides, I've put in for that promotion. They're supposed to make a decision about it in a week. I can't take the risk that they'll discover I'm in therapy.

"Patrick just started at a private school. In a few years, it will be Montana's turn. Then I'll be paying for two of them. Those school fees cost a packet. I need that promotion. Besides..." He shook his head slowly back and forth. "Have you forgotten about Gerry? The only reason he missed out on that job was because he'd been seeing some shrink in Tamworth."

Lachlan swallowed a sigh, unable to argue against Martin's reasoning. "What about the IA investigation Becker mentioned this morning? They'll be here to interview us tomorrow. Have you given any thought to how you want to proceed?"

Martin's face flushed with anger. "It's bullshit, that's what it is! Fucking IA! You were there! We did nothing wrong!" His eyes took on a frantic light. "You're gonna tell them that, right?"

Lachlan stared at him, disquiet knotting his gut. "Yeah, of course."

Pushing away from his desk, Lachlan stood and collected his wallet and keys. "I'm heading out. I'll see you later."

He left Martin staring morosely at the empty coffee cup that sat on Lachlan's desk.

CHAPTER 10

Dear Diary,

Despite my best efforts, the darkness descends upon me once more and I dream about my children. My little boy and girl. They're caught in the house and it's on fire and there's nothing I can do. Flames lick their hair. My heart snags on their screams. They cry for help in fear and terror, in agony, begging me to help them, save them.

"Please, Daddy! Please!"

My feet are filled with lead. I cannot take a step. They're going to die, be burned alive and there's nothing I can do...

———

Lachlan came awake with a start. The sheets were twisted around his body. His pillow was damp with sweat. He'd been having a dream. More like a nightmare. It was about his kids. They were calling for him in the darkness and he couldn't find them.

The constant ache of sadness that had resided in his gut ever since Kristy walked out renewed itself with a vengeance. The pain of separation from his children hadn't lessened. His sessions with Ava were helping, but he still had a long way to go.

The IA investigators were interviewing him and Martin that morning. His gut filled with dread at the thought. Though his conscience was clear and he was confident they'd find he did nothing wrong, the process would still be a test of endurance, made even more difficult by the necessity of having to speak about his friend's role in what had gone down.

Lachlan sighed heavily. If only Martin hadn't pulled the trigger... If only he'd waited just that little bit longer. Lachlan didn't believe Barry intended to kill his wife. He'd been in policing long enough to recognize bluff and bluster. If he'd been given just a few more minutes with the guy, he was sure he could have gotten Barry to hand over the weapon.

But they hadn't been given those few extra moments and now Barry was dead, Elsie was widowed and Lachlan and Martin were caught in the middle of an IA investigation. Not the best way to start the day and definitely not something any officer wanted in their personnel file. Still, there was nothing to be done about it now.

He'd attended a therapy session with Ava the day before and had talked about the shooting. She'd already read scant details of it in the paper.

She'd been saddened by the outcome of the negotiations with the victim and had told him she understood how difficult it was for both of them and in particular, for Martin, who'd been the one to fire the fatal shot.

It was comforting to have her support. It had been a long time since he'd felt like he had someone in his corner, someone who understood. She had a way of cutting through the bullshit and prodding the darkness that filled his soul.

Inch by inch, hour by hour, she seemed to be turning the blackness into gray. He felt lighter than he had for a long time. It was only in the dead of night, during dreams which were out of his control, that he fell backwards into the abyss and woke exhausted and out of breath.

He wondered if she had any idea what power she held in her hands. He'd been attracted to her from the first instant he'd set eyes on her, as she made her way down the aisle. The taste of her full lips, the softness of her curves, had driven him wild with need. He'd been overwhelmed by the loneliness that had been a constant companion since Kristy left and had lost all thought of anything other than losing himself in the arms of the beautiful stranger.

He should have known it wouldn't solve anything. His moment of uninhibited passion with Ava had been exhilarating, but afterward, reality had crashed back into him and the darkness had once again triumphed.

But that was then, more than a month ago. He was in a different place, a better place now, and he truly had Ava to thank for that. Now, when he thought of Kristy, his heart didn't twist in anger and hurt. He understood her need to get away from him and protect their children from his pain. Though he ached every day to see his kids, it made him want to strive harder to reach a better mind space. A place where he could be a good father, a good man, a good friend. Including a better friend to Martin.

Knowing he couldn't put it off any longer, Lachlan threw back the covers and strode, naked, to the shower. Turning the water on as far as the lever would go, he stood under the hot spray and let it beat down on his head. Feeling invigorated, he dressed in a clean shirt, suit and tie and spent a few minutes polishing his black boots. He'd face the IA investigators with his head held high. After all, he had nothing to hide. And neither did Martin.

———————————

Lachlan stared at the IA officer who'd identified himself as Senior Sergeant Walter Miles and tried to hold on to his temper. The man who sat across from him wore round, black-rimmed wire glasses and a satisfied smirk. It was almost as if he'd already made up his mind about what happened and was letting Lachlan know that nothing he said would change his mind.

"So, Detective Coleridge, despite the fact a team of experienced negotiators were only a few hours away, you and your maverick buddy decided to go in and interfere with an extremely delicate situation, right?"

Lachlan gritted his teeth and forced himself to remain calm. As much as he wanted to drive his fist into the slimy-faced bastard, it wouldn't be the wisest move. The man held Lachlan's career in the palm of his hand, and Lachlan needed to remember that.

And not only Lachlan's career. Martin's career was also at stake. His colleague had yet to put in an appearance at the station. Lachlan had seen his partner's pickup parked outside the local watering hole on his way home the night before. He could only hope Martin hadn't used booze to ease his current problems. He needed a clear head to face the IA bastards. Lachlan crossed his fingers that his friend and partner arrived in the squad room in good shape.

"The victim was holding three civilians at gunpoint," Lachlan finally answered through his tightly clenched jaw. "There were several other people in the store. Three hours is a long time to wait when lives hang in the balance."

Miles scoffed. "You make it sound so melodramatic, Detective. The man was having an argument with his wife. Lives were hardly hanging in the balance."

Lachlan held on to his temper by his fingernails. "I'm calling the situation as I read it. At the time, the victim made vocal threats. He was armed and his actions were aggressive. He told me he was going to kill his wife."

"He used those words?" the other IA investigator asked.

Lachlan concentrated his attention on the younger officer who had introduced himself as George Kitchener.

"I'm not sure that he used those exact words. I think it was more along the lines that he was going to do away with her, but coupled with the fact he had a .22 rifle in his hands, his intentions were clear."

"How far away was Detective Griffin?" Kitchener asked.

"I'm not sure," Lachlan replied slowly. "We'd agreed to split up, so we could approach the situation from different angles."

"Could you see Detective Griffin from your vantage point?" Miles asked.

"No, but I knew he was somewhere nearby."

Miles narrowed his gaze. "How did you know, Detective Coleridge?"

Lachlan returned the asshole's stare. "Because that was the course of action we'd agreed upon."

"And Detective Griffin always follows orders, right?" Miles murmured, an insinuating gleam in his eyes. "That's not what your superior told me when I met with him earlier. In fact, wasn't there a situation only a week ago when Detective Griffin expressly disobeyed an order?"

Anger once again surged through Lachlan and he held it in check by sheer force of will. The supermarket scene had nothing to do with the car accident. It didn't involve Martin's brother, for one thing. It wasn't fair to compare the two situations.

It just wasn't. *Fucking Becker.* When Lachlan replied, his voice was full of steel.

"Detective Griffin and I have worked together for the past five years. We know each other well. I was confident Detective Griffin was where I'd asked him to be."

Miles merely smiled. "Your loyalty's commendable, Detective Coleridge. Perhaps a little misplaced, but commendable just the same."

Lachlan's hands tightened around the edges of the Formica table. He leaned forward, wanting to smash his fist into the guy's face. A tiny voice in his head once again whispered caution and with an effort, he forced himself back in his seat.

"Think what you like," he growled. "Your opinion means nothing to me."

Miles chuckled. "Brave words from an officer in the midst of an ugly IA investigation. "They sure breed them tough in the country, don't they, George?" Miles smiled at his colleague. Kitchener merely offered a shrug. At least they both weren't pricks. Lachlan had to be grateful for that.

"You say the victim made threats against his wife," Kitchener asked in a mild tone.

Lachlan nodded cautiously. "That's right."

"Was Detective Griffin close enough to hear?"

"I believe so."

"Tell us about the moment before Detective Griffin shot the victim dead," Miles demanded.

Lachlan drew in a deep breath and eased it out. "By that time, I'd managed to get the victim to let the two other hostages, and others who were hiding in the aisles, go free. It was only the victim's wife, Elsie Irwin, behind the counter, and her husband. I was maintaining communication with the armed man, urging him to hand over his gun. She was heading toward the exit while I tried to talk him down. I assume he caught her movement, because without warning, he raised the gun in Elsie's direction. That's when Detective Griffin discharged his weapon."

"Did Mr Irwin say anything at the point where he raised his rifle?" Kitchener asked.

"No, I don't think so. It happened very quickly. One moment I was talking to the gunman, the next he swung around and aimed."

"Could you see Detective Griffin at this point?" Kitchener asked.

"No, my attention was focused on Barry Irwin, but I knew Martin was nearby."

Kitchener nodded and made a note on the pad in front of him. Miles simply threw Lachlan a hard stare.

"Thank you for your time, Detective," Kitchener murmured.

"We'll be in touch," Miles growled.

"That's it?" Lachlan asked.

"For now," Miles added. "Don't go leaving town."

Lachlan spied Martin at his desk looking none the worse for wear and was filled with relief. Martin looked up at his approach, his eyes full of fear.

"How did it go?"

"As well as could be expected. Miles is a prick and Kitchener is only marginally better." Lachlan shrugged. "They're from IA. It's the way they're made."

"What did you say? Did you cover for me?"

Lachlan frowned at the desperation in Martin's voice. "I didn't need to cover for you, Martin. All I did was tell them the truth."

Lachlan's reassurance didn't appear to have an effect on Martin's state of mind. The tension in his face remained and his lips were taut with fear. A surge of sympathy went through Lachlan at the thought of what his partner was about to endure. If Lachlan could ease Martin's burden, he'd have done so. Unfortunately, there was nothing he could do.

"You'll be fine, buddy. Answer their questions honestly and they'll have nothing to hang on you. You were right to fire that bullet. Irwin turned without warning and aimed. You thought he was going to shoot his wife. Who knows, if you hadn't, we might have been burying *her*. Then he'd be in a jail cell and we'd probably still be fronting IA, explaining why we let it happen." Lachlan shrugged. "Sometimes you can't win, mate. All you can do is get through each day as best you can and hope you live to see another."

Martin's lips twisted upwards in a parody of a grin. "It's a wonderful life we lead, isn't it? Who'd want to be a cop?"

"Beats me," Lachlan quipped.

Martin flashed him the whisper of a smile and

Lachlan sighed quietly in relief. As his partner pushed away from his desk and stood, Lachlan gave him a friendly slap on the back. "You'll be fine, mate. Just get in there and tell the truth. It will be over before you know it."

It was nearly three hours later when Lachlan looked up and spied Martin exiting the interview room. His face was pale. Even his lips were bloodless. At the desolate expression in Martin's eyes, dread filled Lachlan's gut. Martin turned and headed straight for the door. Lachlan got to his feet and moved to intercept him.

"Martin! Wait up! What is it? What happened?" he asked, trying to keep the urgency from his voice.

Martin stopped and slowly turned. "They think I shot him on purpose."

Lachlan gasped in shock. "You have to be fucking kidding!"

"No."

"How the hell could they arrive at that conclusion?"

Martin laughed without humor. "I don't know, but that's exactly what Miles implied."

"What did he say?"

"I can't remember the exact words, but his meaning was darn well clear."

"That's bullshit!" Lachlan exploded. "They can't pin that on you! You made a split-second decision to save a woman's life. That's exactly what happened."

Lachlan stared at his friend. Tears glinted in Martin's eyes.

"They've stood me down, Lachie."

Shock held Lachlan momentarily speechless. "Fuck," he eventually murmured.

"Without pay," Martin added, his voice hoarse. "What am I going to do, Lachie? What the fuck am I going to do?"

"Don't worry about the money," Lachlan hastened to reassure him. "We'll work something out."

"You have no idea. The mortgage has us stretched tight and then we have the private school fees. This shit could go on for months. How the hell am I going to manage?"

"Go and see Becker. Take all of your leave. You must have some owing."

Martin closed his eyes and his shoulders slumped in defeat. "Yeah, three or four weeks. I guess it's better than nothing."

"You'll be all right, Martin. We'll get through this. The IA bastards will speak with Elsie Irwin and she'll corroborate our story. We thought her husband was going to shoot her and I'm sure she did, too. You saved her life, buddy. It's as simple as that."

"Let's hope she sees it that way," Martin muttered and slowly turned back toward the exit. Feeling helpless and with an impending sense of doom, Lachlan watched his partner stumble away.

CHAPTER 11

Ava glanced at her watch and her heart skipped a beat. Lachlan was due for his appointment any minute. Except for that first time, when he'd been nearly thirty minutes late, he'd been very punctual. She liked that about him. She liked lots of things about him. She wondered what would have happened if he hadn't made that first call; if he hadn't become her patient.

Would they be lovers now, enjoying a torrid, but fleeting, affair? Although she wasn't one for meaningless flings, for Lachlan Coleridge, she might have made an exception. It wasn't every day that a sexy, sensitive, thoughtful man came waltzing into her life. The fact that he was related to her brother-in-law hadn't been a deterrent at the wedding, but his marriage certainly was now.

She'd assumed he was single at the wedding and hadn't given much thought to asking pertinent questions. Now that she knew he had a wife and children, things were different.

"Tell me more about Kristy," she said not long after he'd settled himself on the couch.

They'd taken to having their therapy sessions out on the enclosed porch. Ava sat in the leather recliner with a notepad and pen on her lap, while Lachlan stretched his long body out on the settee. With his boots kicked off, his feet crossed at the ankles and his head nestled against a tapestry covered cushion, he looked comfortable and relaxed until she posed her question.

Almost immediately, his body tensed and he turned toward her with a frown. "Why would you want to hear more about my wife?"

Ava shrugged. "She's the mother of your children. She's an important part of your life. At some stage, she was important enough for you to marry. I'd like to hear more about her and what happened to cause your marriage to fall apart."

His lips twisted derisively. "That's easy, Doc. I already told you. *I'm* what happened. I treated her like shit."

"In what way?" Ava asked carefully.

Lachlan made an impatient sound in the back of his throat. "I didn't hit her, if that's what you're thinking. I'd never do anything like that, but I didn't treat her very well, either. When I wasn't at work, I was often propping up the bar, swapping shoptalk with my mates. When I did make it home, the kids were usually in bed and Kristy was hopping mad. She'd accuse me of shirking my responsibilities, of never being there for her and the kids." He flicked her a glance and then stared at his feet. "She was right."

"Was it always like that?" Ava asked quietly.

"No." He drew in a deep breath and blew it out on a heavy sigh.

"We got married straight after I graduated from the academy. We had the world at our feet. We were high school sweethearts, in love with life and each other. We didn't imagine anything bad could come our way. He laughed without humor. "Hell, I can't believe how innocent we were! We didn't have a clue!"

Ava started in surprise. She remembered him telling her at Martin and Pam's barbeque that his children were four and two. She guessed him to somewhere near thirty. If he'd entered the police academy right after high school graduation, it took quite a few years for the children to come along. She was curious to know why.

"You didn't have children right away."

"No, I wanted to wait until I established myself, became more settled. In the early days of a police career, you tend to get moved around a bit, especially if you want to climb the ladder. We moved three times around the state before I was transferred to Moree as a detective. Of course, Kristy wasn't particularly pleased with the waiting. If she'd had her way, we'd have had kids the first year we'd married."

"It was a source of tension," Ava guessed.

Lachlan grimaced. "Yes."

"Did Kristy work during your marriage?"

"Yes, a probationary police officer doesn't get paid anything fancy. She'd trained as a secretary, out of high school. She was lucky to pick up work in most places we lived. We were far from rich, but we did okay. It got a little tighter when the kids arrived, but by then I'd made junior detective and the pay was better."

Ava digested the information. So far, he described the typical early years of a young couple. Once again, she wondered where it had all gone wrong.

"Something changed along the way, didn't it?" she asked softly.

His body tensed, like it had the first time she'd mentioned his wife. When he was silent for so long, she wondered if he would answer. Though he'd attended several therapy sessions and was making progress, they hadn't discussed anything as intimate as the precise reasons behind the breakdown of his marriage. But if he was sincere in wanting to heal and find himself in a better place—and Ava believed he was—it was imperative that they deal with the difficult issues that were closest to his heart, starting with what caused his wife to leave.

"It was my fault," he finally murmured, his voice low and filled with regret. "Kristy was the same cheerful, kind-hearted girl I married. *I* was the one who changed. The kind of stuff I saw at work every day... Even now, the thought of it fills me with dread. You can't imagine how awful it gets. No one teaches you how to deal with that kind of stuff—you're just supposed to suck it up and get on with it. Being subjected to that kind of trauma over a long and extensive period of time gets to you after awhile, no matter how hard you try to forget."

He turned to look at her with eyes that were dark with remembered horror and pain. "How am I supposed to forget about the baby I found, strapped into his car seat and drowned when his mom, high on drugs and full of alcohol, took a corner too fast? Or the man who beat his eight-year-old step-daughter to death and then cut her up and stuffed her in a suitcase?"

His voice grew hoarse. He dragged in a ragged breath. "I could go on and on and on, Doc. I've been a cop for more than ten years. The things I've seen... It does your head in. If there was somewhere we could go at the end of every shift and de-program all the shit we've seen, perhaps we'd be in a better headspace and there'd be fewer of us depressed as hell and feeling isolated and alone, with no one to talk to but the bartender."

He stared at her. "I don't know what the stats are, but broken relationships are high amongst police officers. It's probably a direct result of what we're forced to endure on any given day without any outlet or way to talk through it, to understand it, to deal with it when it happens.

"We learn early on that our spouses and girlfriends aren't good sounding boards. The average person has no idea what we see and do and they don't *want* to know. It doesn't mean they don't care, but most people on the outside simply can't bear the thought. They're horrified and disgusted by our stories. It doesn't take a cop long to work out the war stories are best left at the office, or shared with colleagues."

"That must put a strain on personal relationships," she said.

"You've got that right, Doc. Now you're getting the picture. I'm not trying to find excuses for why I fucked up my marriage, but most people come home from work and talk about their day. They trade stories back and forth, maybe share a laugh at something funny or commiserate over something that turned out wrong. A cop doesn't have that kind of easy back and forth. We come home from dealing with something unspeakable, and we don't say a word. Not because we don't want to talk about it, but because we know it's better for our spouses if we keep quiet. We learn, you see, that it's better to say nothing than risk distressing the ones we love."

The rawness in Lachlan's voice tore at Ava's heart. She wanted to go to him and hold him close and tell him she'd never be like that. She'd listen to whatever he wanted to tell her, even the worst of the worst, and she'd be grateful that he shared it with her, despite the ugliness of it.

Marriage was supposed to be a partnership, taking the good with the bad. Okay, so most people didn't deal with the bad quite like police officers did, but the principle was still the same. Unfortunately, a lot of people took the easy way out.

Lachlan stared at her. "I can see from your expression you're blaming Kristy for not wanting me to open up, but the truth is, I didn't want to shock her or disgust her or frighten her with details from my job. She was young and good and innocent. I didn't want to tarnish that."

Ava challenged him with her stare. "And yet, if you had, if you'd shared more with her and given her the chance to understand, she might not have left."

Lachlan nodded sadly. "I get that and it tears me up, but it is what it is. We do the best we can at the time... Kristy accused me of shutting her out, of never opening up, but the truth is, she didn't want to know. She didn't want to know about all the shitty things I go through almost every day. She wanted to ask about my day and be told that everything was fine. She'd never admit it, but that's true."

"How do you feel about her now?" The question fell out of Ava's mouth and she waited, on edge, for his answer. All of a sudden, she very much wanted to know.

Lachlan sighed heavily. "Kristy and I fell out of love a long time ago. As far as I know, there's no one else involved. I guess we just drifted apart. She had her life, raising the kids, attending pre-school functions, having lunch with her friends—and I had mine. I went to work, paid the bills, kept a roof over our heads. Sometimes, I met a colleague for a drink and swapped some shop talk. It was the only outlet I had.

"Unfortunately, Kristy didn't see it that way. She accused me of having time to spend with my friends, but no time for her and the kids. The more tense things became at home, the more times I'd find myself in a bar." He shrugged sadly. "It was only a matter of time before things deteriorated to a point where something had to happen."

"So she punished you by packing up and leaving with your children," Ava finished.

"Yes, but I don't blame her. Like I said, it was my fault. I should have talked to her, tried to make her understand. I should have tried harder to share my work life with her. After all, it's the largest part of my day. While I was never cross or angry with my kids, I wasn't there for them, either. Not like I should have been."

His voice hitched with emotion and Ava's heart clenched tight.

"My dad meant the world to me," he continued in a husky voice. "I thought he'd hung the moon and the stars. My earliest memories are of my dad with me and Rohan sitting on his knee. He'd tell us stories of the old days, back when he was young. We'd sit for hours on his lap, engrossed in every word. And now he's gone and there won't be any more memories. Charlotte only met him twice and Harry—Harry won't ever remember him."

He turned to look at Ava and his gaze was tortured. "I don't want my kids to grow up without memories of me. I'm their *dad!* I deserve to be part of their lives. I get that I wasn't ever going to win Father of the Year, but I never abused my kids. I loved them with everything I had! I still do."

Tears glinted in his eyes and Ava could no longer remain aloof. Setting the notepad and pen aside, she stood and went to him. It was against every ethical rule in the book, but right at that moment, she didn't give a damn. He was hurting and he needed her help and she was darn well going to give it to him.

Taking a seat beside him, she pulled him into her arms. With his head in her lap, he cried quietly. She stroked his hair with her fingers and urged him to release the pain. He'd bottled it up for way too long. It was time he let it go.

Awhile later, he raised his head, looking embarrassed. "I'm sorry. I shouldn't have blubbered all over you like a child." He sat up and moved away. She immediately felt bereft and then was filled with irritation. This wasn't about her. It had never been about her. It was about the man she cared for way too much and his struggle back to health.

"I didn't tell you about what happened today at the station," Lachlan said to Ava a little while later, still embarrassed about his outburst. The night was fast closing in, but he hadn't been able to move from her comfortable couch.

What had he been thinking, falling apart like that? He hadn't cried since his father's funeral and that was different than losing it with his therapist over the shitty hand he'd been dealt. So, he'd been doing it tough; he'd lost his wife and kids. That didn't give him permission to break down like a girl.

All his life, he'd been raised to believe boys

were tougher, stronger; able to withstand higher degrees of pain. It was the men who women turned to for strength and endurance, for support when things went wrong. It had been that way for his parents and it had been that way between him and Kristy—at least in the early years. It was only recently, when he discovered he wasn't as invincible as he thought, that the foundations had begun to crumble.

"I wondered what brought you here for the second time in as many days," Ava replied and threw him an encouraging smile.

Lachlan cleared his throat and told her about the IA interview and how they'd stood Martin Griffin down.

"Oh, no! He must be devastated!" she replied, bringing her hand up to her mouth. "After everything he's been through lately with his brother, and now this. How's he coping?"

Lachlan remained silent. He'd been wondering the same thing. "I suggested he come and see you—for therapy—but he dismissed the idea out of hand. He... He's going for a promotion. He's worried any hint that he might not be coping will affect his chances. Of course, the IA thing is going to blow everything out of the water for him, anyway. The investigation's supposed to be confidential until a decision is reached, but there's no doubt the people on the job interview panel will know."

Ava shook her head, looking sad and concerned. "Poor, Martin! I must call Pam and see if there's anything I can do. Perhaps I could babysit the children one night so they can have some time alone. She must be feeling as bad as he is."

Lachlan looked at her and saw the sincerity in her eyes. She was a good woman with a kind heart. To reach out to a friend in need was admirable. He wondered if there was something *he* could do.

The thought had no sooner formed when he remembered that the fair was coming to town. His kids loved going to the annual festival and they'd often gone with Martin and his family. Though his own children weren't around for this one, he could see if the Griffins wanted to come and take their minds off things for a while.

His gaze slid to Ava. She was writing in her notes. He wondered if she'd be interested in coming along. His heart skipped a beat at the thought of issuing the invitation. Holding on to his courage, he dragged in a deep breath and forged ahead.

"Listen, the fair's coming to town tomorrow night. Out here in the country, it's kind of a big deal. People come from all over the district to get together and have a good time. There are displays of farm machinery, livestock; arts and crafts. Cooking and flower displays, crazy rides and at least four different colors of cotton candy. It's fun. I could ask Martin and Pam if they want to come and they could bring their kids. It could be good for all of them; something to distract them from their troubles." He risked a glance in Ava's direction. "What do you think?"

Her smile was soft, her eyes luminous. She pulled off her glasses and nodded. "I think it's a lovely idea."

He blushed under her close regard and all of a sudden was at a loss for words. "Would you... Would you like to come with us?"

Her expression grew solemn. "I'm your therapist. I'm not sure that would be appropriate."

"But you're also Pam's friend. You just said you wanted to do something for them and it's not like a date, or anything." Another wave of heat crept up his neck and he looked away, praying she wouldn't notice.

She stared at him thoughtfully. "Just friends, right?"

He nodded emphatically. "Right. Just a group of friends enjoying each other's company."

"Right. Because I haven't forgotten you're married," she murmured.

"On paper, perhaps. I think Kristy and I both know it's been over for quite a while."

Ava's eyes flared with some indefinable emotion and he couldn't help but wonder if his announcement meant something to her. He couldn't believe how much he wanted it to. Things had started out between them as a passionate fling between two disconnected strangers. They were both seeking something that night and he sure as hell had found it. For those few mindless moments of ecstasy, he'd forgotten the turmoil of his life and had lived only for the pleasure he found with her in his arms.

But now, he'd gotten to know her on a much

more personal level. She wasn't just a sexy-as-hell wedding guest, satisfying a mutual need. She was a real person, warm and kind and giving. She was smart and funny and beautiful. She was everything he wanted.

He wondered if the knowledge would frighten her and then was suddenly impatient to find out. Friends, be damned. He'd never been one for playing games. Besides, he was too old for that kind of shit. He drew in a breath and spoke again.

"I really like you, Ava," he said, laying it all out bare.

Her expression grew troubled. She slipped on her glasses. "I like you, too, Lachlan," she admitted quietly and his breath rushed out.

"But," she held up a hand as if to silence his yelp of elation, "I'm still your therapist and you're still married. As long as those situations remain as they are, we can never be more than friends."

He held her gaze, desperate to make her see. "Before I started coming here, I was convinced I was the reason my marriage had failed. I even told you as much. But thanks to you and the help you've given me, I'm now seeing things more clearly. My gradual emotional withdrawal from Kristy was only the catalyst for bringing our marriage to an end. I believe now, it was inevitable. My job didn't help, but the truth is, we married far too young and we drifted apart. I don't love her anymore. When the time comes and she serves me with divorce papers, I'll sign them without a fight."

To his surprise, Ava's eyes blazed with emotion.

Heightened color reddened her cheeks. She leaned forward in her chair. "*Why?* Why are you giving up on your marriage? You promised to love her until you parted in death! Didn't those words *mean* anything? I've come to know you quite well over these past couple of weeks and I never pegged you as a quitter, or a coward."

Anger stirred low in his gut. "Did you just call me a coward?"

She held his gaze without flinching. "You're giving up on your marriage. What would you call it?"

His heart thumped and blood rushed through his ears. He couldn't believe what she was saying. "Didn't you hear what I said? I don't love my wife anymore. I haven't for a very long time. My father once told me the very best thing I could do for my kids was to love their mother with all my heart. And I don't! I *don't!* The way I see it, the best thing for everyone is to call it quits."

She glared at him. "And what about your children? How will they cope with being raised in a broken home?"

He shook his head, bewildered. "I don't get it. I thought you just said you liked me, that you wanted to spend time with me."

"I do."

"Then why the hell are you pushing me back into Kristy's arms? Why the hell do you want me to stay married?"

She threw up her hands in frustration. "I'm not saying that. I don't want you to stay married, but I want you to end it for the right reasons! I want you to be very sure this is what you want. You've been through a terrible time emotionally; you still have terrible times to come. I don't want you to think you can solve your problems by running away from them. Running away never solves anything. Haven't you learned that much?"

By the time she was finished, her chest was heaving from the force of her emotions. Lachlan stared at her and then with a muttered oath pushed away from the couch.

What the hell? She wanted him to reconcile, to try again?

He strode into the adjoining room and retrieved his coat from the closet. The nights had turned chilly. Winter was on its way. Awkwardly, he did his best to shrug it on. A sharp pain surged down his arm and he grimaced. He'd gotten rid of the sling and was putting on a brave face at work, but every now and then he was reminded the bone was far from healed.

Ava's mixed messages confused the hell out of him, but deep down, she was right. He needed to reconnect with Kristy, to give his marriage one last chance. He needed to know that if they went their separate ways, he'd given it all he had. He might not be in love with her now, but he had been, in the past. For his kids' sake, was there a chance he could learn to love her again...?

He turned slowly and faced Ava. She stood just inside the doorway to her office, pale and still.

"You're right," he said, "about everything. I'll call Kristy and see if she'll meet me somewhere. I need to do what I can to save my marriage."

With that, he turned back toward the door and let himself out.

Ava watched him disappear from sight. A sob escaped her tightly compressed lips and she jammed her fist against her mouth in an effort to hold her sorrow in. She'd fallen for him, hard and fast, and yet, she'd all but pushed him away, back to Kristy—back to his wife.

What the hell was wrong with her? Why couldn't she be happy with the knowledge he liked her, really liked her, and wanted out of his marriage? The fact was, he wasn't in any position emotionally to be making such life-changing decisions and she didn't want to be anyone's rebound relationship.

If she was going to give her heart and soul to him, she needed to know he'd be there for her, for all time: the good times and the bad, the easy and the hard. She needed to be sure he had what it took to commit to a woman for a lifetime.

Okay, so maybe he was right and he and Kristy had married too young, before they even knew who they were. There was a lot of difference between two young people in high school and those same people a decade or so down the track. People changed, grew apart. She knew, better than most, the reasons people gave for filing for divorce, but she wanted to believe the man she gave her heart to would fight for her to the death.

If pushing Lachlan back into the arms of his wife was what had to happen to prove he had the courage and tenacity she needed, then so be it. It sounded like a warped way of dealing with the situation, but it was all she had, despite the fact the very thought of him resurrecting his marriage devastated her.

The first sob was followed by another and then another until she was heaving from the strength of her tears. Stumbling back toward the couch he'd so recently vacated, she collapsed onto it and poured out her heartache and grief. Another old adage came to mind: If you love something, let it go. If it comes back, it's yours. If it doesn't, it never was.

The wise words pounded gently into her heart. Slowly, softly, they eased her pain and with that, came the faintest flare of hope.

CHAPTER 12

The day of the fair bloomed bright and sunny and boded well for a pleasant evening. Ava hadn't heard from Lachlan since their last therapy session and wasn't even sure whether the "non-date" was still happening. Given the way he'd left, she doubted it. That thought filled her with disappointment, but she'd resolved, during the long hours she'd spent tossing and turning in bed before the arrival of the dawn, to stand by what she'd said.

With a sigh, she made a note in the patient file on her desk and then flipped over the page. Her phone beeped with an incoming text and she dug her cell out of her handbag and checked the screen. It was a message from Pam.

The kids r so excited about going 2 the fair 2 night. Lachlan told Martin the 2 of u will meet us there at 6. Can't wait 2 catch up! Talk soon!

Ava stared at the words and frowned. It took her a moment to comprehend their meaning. Lachlan hadn't been in contact with her, but it was obvious he'd been in touch with the Griffins. She wondered what it meant that Lachlan still wanted to spend time with her, despite the fact he'd vowed to reconnect with his wife. For once, Ava didn't have any answers. She'd just have to wait and see.

She glanced at her watch and suppressed a sigh. It was barely midday. She had a whole six hours before the appointed meeting time. At the thought of seeing Lachlan again, a flurry of nerves moved around in her stomach. She frowned. Over the course of their therapy sessions, they'd spent several hours alone. She had no reason to feel jittery.

But this was different. This was a social outing to the fair with friends, under the cover of a blanket of stars. Even when she was a little girl, a trip to the fair had been a time of anticipation and great excitement. She and Alistair and her sisters would talk about the rides they'd go on and the color of the cotton candy they'd eat. They'd dream about toffee apples and soda pop and the anticipation was almost as exciting as the real thing.

Even when she was a teenager, the fair held a special appeal. She could remember being allowed to go one year with her then high school boyfriend, Bernie Atkins, who escorted her there and back. They went on fast rides and she shrieked and screamed as the wind rushed through her hair. Bernie had even stolen a kiss while they'd sat in their carriage, swinging at the very top of the Ferris wheel.

The thought of Lachlan kissing her while they

were snuggled on the seats of one of the rides sent another wave of nervous excitement rushing through her. She still meant what she'd said to him the night before, but that didn't mean she couldn't hope and dream for more. Then she remembered that if he worked things out with Kristy, she might never feel his arms around her again.

Did she have the courage to give herself another night with him and then let him return to his wife? The thought was quickly followed by a shaft of pain. Was it better to know love, even for a short time, than not to know it at all? She was sure there was an old Stevie Nicks song about something along those lines.

She sighed. The song was right. She'd give herself the gift of one more magical night with Lachlan and then let him go. If he never came back to her, she'd have her memories. If he did, there would be plenty more memories to make.

The phone on her desk trilled, interrupting her thoughts. She reached over and picked up the receiver. "Ava Wolfe."

"Doctor Wolfe, its Janelle. Your next appointment has arrived."

"Thank you, Janelle. I'll be out in a minute."

Hanging up the phone, Ava let out another little sigh and then determined to get on with her day.

Butterflies swirled around in Lachlan's gut as he tucked his long-sleeved, tailored shirt into his jeans. His hair was washed and his teeth were clean and his jaw was freshly shaved. He splashed on some cologne and wondered if Ava liked the way it smelled and then immediately dismissed the thought. She'd made it plain they were only friends and this wasn't a proper date.

The thought of collecting her from her apartment and taking her to the fair sent another rush of nerves surging through him. He'd never been to her place before. He'd texted her a few hours earlier to confirm arrangements, not at all sure until she'd responded that she was still agreeable to coming along.

He wouldn't have blamed her if she'd turned him down. He'd declared he was going to try and fix things between him and Kristy. *What kind of woman accepted a date with a man who was determined to get back with his wife?*

He'd even gone so far as to contact Kristy and set up a time and place to meet. She'd sounded cautious on the phone, but had agreed. It was all he could hope for. He wanted to give it his best shot. What Ava had said was true. He owed it to his kids to exhaust all options before he made them another statistic.

But that didn't mean his heart didn't yearn quietly for the woman who was helping him heal. It was a conundrum for which he had no answers. Right now, all he wanted to do was enjoy a night out with Ava—date or no date. He didn't care what she called it. If he could also make Martin and Pam and their kids happy, even for a few hours, then it was a win for everyone.

With that thought in mind, he pulled on his polished black boots and finger combed his short hair. With a final look in the mirror, he grabbed his wallet and keys and a jacket and headed out into the night.

He pulled up outside a small apartment block and checked the address details on his phone. Climbing out of the car, he headed in the direction of Ava's apartment. She lived in an upscale complex that was close to the shops and other amenities. He figured since she was only there for a month, that she'd taken a short term lease. Still, the paintwork was fresh and the gardens were tidy. She hadn't scrimped on her needs. He was pleased to see she took care of herself, even temporarily.

He wondered if she was punctual. He glanced at his watch and noted he was right on time. Arriving at her doorstep on the ground floor, he pressed the doorbell and swallowed against a fresh wave of nerves. He didn't have long to wait.

The door opened just as he was smoothing his damp palms on his jeans. Blushing, he glanced away and then looked quickly back at her again. Like him, she was dressed simply in jeans and a shirt. Her top's pale pink color brought out the rosiness of her cheeks. Her black hair hung soft and loose with only a scrap of a pink fabric headband to hold it in check. She smiled, looking far younger than her thirty-six years.

He'd discovered her age from his brother.

When Rohan called with the news Sam was pregnant and enquired after Kristy and their kids, Lachlan had broken down and told him they were separated. A few conversations later, Rohan had been more than curious about Lachlan's reasons for enquiring about Ava Wolfe's age.

The fact that she was six years older didn't faze him one little bit. He'd married his high school sweetheart, but that didn't mean he only found women his age attractive. Ava was fit and healthy and looked no older than him and even if she did, it wouldn't have mattered. He'd fallen for *her*—her wit, her charm, her brains—the way she looked was only part of what made up the woman who was Ava Wolfe.

"Hi," she greeted him with a soft smile.

He stared back at her. Like at the wedding, she wasn't wearing glasses. He could only assume they were for close-up work. She always had them on in her office. Or perhaps she wore contacts on social outings? He didn't know and he didn't care. She was gorgeous, either way.

Her dark brown eyes shone brightly and her teeth glowed white in the porch light. A faint scent of cinnamon and vanilla, and warm, soft skin reached his nose. All of a sudden, he couldn't wait to spend the next few hours with her by his side.

"You look beautiful," he said and then leaned in and kissed her cheek. He couldn't help it. He needed to touch her.

She tensed a little, as if taken by surprise and then reached out for his hand. Giving it a gentle squeeze, she murmured, "Thank you. So do you."

"Shall we?" he asked, indicating his white Ford Ranger parked in the drive.

She smiled again and nodded. "Sure. Lead the way."

Ava followed Lachlan to his car and her heart beat double time. It had been that way ever since he'd kissed her. Okay, so it hadn't been a real kiss, full of passion and fire, but her cheek felt warm where his lips had brushed her skin and the smell of his expensive cologne still lingered in the air. She drew in a surreptitious breath in an effort to get her pulse rate back under control and caught the teasing look he tossed her way.

"Are you all right?" he asked softly.

"Yes, just a little...nervous."

He breathed out a sigh of relief and laughed. "Good. So am I."

Ava raised her eyebrows in surprise. "Really? You look so calm, cool and collected."

He laughed again. "That just goes to show how good an actor I am. I was sweating buckets a moment before you opened the door."

She smiled in relief. Their eyes connected and an arc of awareness ran between them. They reached the car and, as if in a daze, Lachlan stepped forward to open her door. Halting mid-stride, as if changing his mind, a moment later, he pressed her back against the cold panel and threaded his hands through her hair. She gasped at the need in his eyes.

"Lach—"

His mouth came down on hers and ignited a blaze of heady desire. Warm and full, his lips moved across hers, urgent, but somehow gentle.

"You taste so good. As good as I remember," he murmured against her lips.

Ava could do nothing but moan in agreement. Her arms crept around his neck. She leaned into him, needing to get close. His body pressed hard and urgent against hers. His erection strained against her stomach. There was no question he wanted her as much as she wanted him.

But they were supposed to be meeting their friends for an evening of fun at the country fair. It was ludicrous to think for even a moment that they could call the night off and spend it in each other's arms. As much as the idea appealed, common sense prevailed. Loosening her hold on him, she gently pushed him away.

"We're double dating with the Griffins, remember?"

He smiled, slow and sexy and her heart did a somersault. "Ah, so it *is* a date."

She ducked her head, but then gave him a grin. "Would you rather have it any other way?"

The townsfolk of Moree and the surrounding district had come out in full force to enjoy the spirit of the annual fair. The balmy fall evening was filled with the sounds of cheerful screaming as people terrified themselves on the rides. Music pounded out from each stall, doing its best to entice customers. The bellowing of cattle penned up in anticipation of the rodeo added to the cacophony of sound.

Lachlan sauntered along beside Martin, while Ava and Pam walked a little ahead. The two Griffin kids, Montana and Patrick, ran to and fro, taking in the sights and sounds, smiles of delight on their faces. It warmed Lachlan's heart to see the innocent pleasure in their expressions and the stress-free look on the face of their dad. It was the most relaxed Lachlan had seen Martin in a long time and he was filled with contentment.

His gaze drifted to the rounded curve of Ava's bottom, hugged lovingly by her jeans. He remembered the feel of her pressed against him and forced down a surge of need. He intended to keep his promise to do what he could to save his marriage, but he couldn't deny his feelings for his therapist would make the task more difficult.

Martin looked at him sideways and then looked back at Ava and Pam. "She's a good-looking chick," he murmured.

"Yes, you're a lucky man," Lachlan replied, deliberately misunderstanding him.

"Don't be a cock, Coleridge. You know I was referring to Ava. Are you sure there isn't more between you than the fact that she's your therapist? You've barely been able to drag your eyes away from her all night. What gives?"

"Nothing," Lachlan replied, averting his gaze. "We're friends. That's all. In fact, I'm meeting up with Kristy in a couple of days."

The distraction worked as he'd hoped. Martin's eyes widened in surprise. "Wow, that's great. From the way you spoke before about it, I sort of figured your marriage was over. Like, for good."

"Yeah, well, things didn't end well, that's for sure, but I'm now in a better place. I want to see if she's willing to give me another chance."

"I see." Martin's tone was non-committal. Lachlan narrowed his gaze.

"What the hell's that supposed to mean?" he demanded.

"Nothing. It's just that, it was obvious you two weren't exactly getting on, even before. In fact, the more I think about it, the more I recall you two would argue just as soon as look at each other right from the moment you and I met. Pam and I figured you were just one of those couples who liked to fight a lot. Some people get off on it, you know. They fight so they can enjoy the make-up sex. If you ask me, it sounds like a whole lot of trouble for not a lot of return, but each to his own."

Lachlan shook his head, unable to believe what his friend was saying. "We weren't like that! You're exaggerating! I don't think Kristy and I ever had make-up sex. We fought and didn't talk to each other, sometimes for days on end. Then, eventually one of us would get over whatever it was we were fighting about and things would return to normal."

"Until the next time," Martin quipped.

Lachlan stared at his friend as the grim memories came flooding back. "Yeah," he said slowly, "until the next time."

"Hurry up, you two! You're falling way behind!" Unaware of the somber tone of the conversation taking place behind her, Ava smiled laughingly back at him and his heart clenched.

She was so sweet and kind and beautiful. She wanted him as much as he wanted her. He was sure of it, and yet, she'd urged him to try and reconcile with his wife, to do what he could to fight for his marriage.

And for what? She had nothing to gain by him returning to Kristy's side. No, she'd made the suggestion because she believed in everything marriage stood for and the commitment he'd made to his wife.

No doubt as a psychiatrist, she also knew firsthand the effect divorce had on the kids. It was a sad reality and one he didn't take lightly. As much as he wanted to ignore her suggestion, he knew he'd follow through on his promise. He'd meet with Kristy and gage the strength of their relationship and whether they had what it took to take it the distance. He owed it to Ava. He owed it to his kids.

"Daddy! Take me on the merry-go-round!" Montana tugged on her father's hand. Martin smiled softly down at his little daughter and then bent down until he was at eye level. With a gentle hand, he brushed the hair out of her eyes and gave her a wink.

"Of course I'll take you on the merry-go-round, Miss Montana. Now, which carriage would you like to ride in?"

"The blue one, Daddy! The blue one!"

"All right, the blue one it is."

Martin stood upright and then picked up Montana in his arms. She squealed in delight when he tossed her high and then safely caught her.

"Higher, Daddy! Higher! As high as the merry-go-round!" she shouted, laughing.

"Wow, that's pretty high, Miss Montana. I'm not sure I can toss you as high as that."

"Of course you can! Nobody's as strong and tall as you! Throw me higher, Daddy!"

Lachlan watched the two of them together and swallowed a lump in his throat. Montana was the same age as his daughter and he couldn't help but think about how much time he'd lost with Charlotte. It had been two months since Kristy had taken his children. Two months since he'd seen his kids. Kissed them. Hugged them. Tossed them in the air. His heart ached with loss.

It was time he lay it all bare for Kristy and convince her that he'd changed. He felt almost like he used to, before he became a cop. Like he'd told Martin, he was in a much better place now. He deserved to be a father and to take an active role with his kids.

As for him and Kristy, they'd have to wait and see. He was less sure of his footing where she was concerned and even less certain he wanted to try all over again.

CHAPTER 13

From the neon lights of the fairground rides, Ava watched the shadows chase themselves across Lachlan's face and wondered at their cause. Earlier, she'd seen him look with longing at Martin and Montana and could only imagine he was missing his own kids. It had been a couple of months since he'd seen them. It had to be tough.

Amid sticky trails of pink cotton candy and soft, sleepy good-byes, she and Lachlan said farewell to the Griffin family and continued to wander around the fair. Lachlan wowed her with his target shooting by winning a huge panda bear. He handed it to her with a wide smile and a flourish and she could hardly believe the carefree man with the sexy grin was the same tortured officer who'd first appeared in her office.

He'd worked hard on his therapy and deserved the mental health benefits that were obvious for all to see. Apart from the frown that now creased his brow, he appeared to be at peace.

"What's the matter?" she asked quietly, reaching for his hand.

He entwined his fingers with hers and applied gentle pressure. She loved the feeling of his hand, warm and strong and secure. *Safe.* That's exactly how he made her feel.

"I'm meeting with Kristy the day after tomorrow," he replied without inflection. "I wanted to let you know."

Her heart tightened with dread, but she nodded bravely in encouragement. "Good. I'm glad."

He stopped and turned to face her, shaking his head back and forth. His expression flooded with confusion.

"I don't get it. Why do you keep pushing me away? I know you feel the same connection that I do and it goes way beyond the sex. And yet, it's like you're prepared to sacrifice the way we feel, sacrifice a chance at true love. For what? I just don't get it."

She stared up at him and her heart thumped. "I don't get it, either. In the light of day, it seems the right thing to do. I'm not going to be responsible for breaking up your marriage. But... Right now, with the warm evening breeze ruffling your hair and your cologne overwhelming my senses, my reasons seem...less than compelling."

She heard his sharp intake of breath and desire glittered in his eyes. In silence, he drew her unresisting form further into the shadows. His warm lips found hers and she groaned a heartfelt sigh of relief. For this night only, she belonged in his arms.

The kiss deepened. Ava opened her mouth and his tongue stole inside. He tasted of cold beer and corndog and spicy ketchup. He tasted delicious. She pressed herself against him and threaded her fingers in his hair. Holding his head in place, she kissed him until she was breathless.

They pulled apart simultaneously, both of them panting hard. "Let's go back to my place," he murmured against her ear, his voice husky with need.

She managed to nod and together they walked hand in hand back to his truck. She didn't know where he lived, but she hoped it wasn't far.

―――――

Lachlan stepped on the gas and arrived at his modest, four-bedroom, brick-and-tile house in record time. He unlocked the front door and ushered Ava inside. She looked around at the homey furnishings and the family photos that hung on the wall. Too late, he realized the last thing she probably needed was a reminder of his marriage.

"You have a nice place," she said quietly and pulled off her jacket. Hanging it over the back of the couch, she continued down the hall.

He followed her slowly, a little uncertain about how to put her at ease. She came to a halt in the doorway of his bedroom. Like the living room, it contained photos and other evidence of his wife.

"Let's go outside," he suggested hurriedly and reached for her hand. Leading her back the way they'd come, he strode through the open-concept kitchen and dining room and then opened the door that led to the deck.

Though it was late, the night was mild and the sky was filled with stars. He led her across the back porch and down the stairs. Halfway across the yard, he came to a halt. The outline of a trampoline glinted in the moonlight. In silence, he turned to her and with one hand, lifted her up in the air.

She gasped and clung to his shoulders. "Your sore arm! Put me down! I'm way too heavy!"

"It's fine," he murmured and set her gently down on the pad.

She bounced lightly up and down and giggled. "I haven't been on a trampoline since I was a kid."

He smiled. "Well, tonight you're in for a treat. Lie back and enjoy the ride."

Giggling again, she lay back on the pad and stared up at the sky. Lachlan joined her.

"It's beautiful, isn't it?" she whispered. "I never get to see the stars like this in the city. Too many tall buildings. Too much light. It's so dark here, it's like the sky is cloaked in sequin-covered, black velvet."

He reached for her hand and pressed it against his lips. In silence, they absorbed the grandeur of the night around them. Crickets chirped in the grass. An owl hooted in the distance. The air was filled with the scent of orange blossom from the Murraya hedge that bordered the back fence.

Lachlan traced the soft skin of Ava's hand with his finger, learning its unique shape and feel. He heard her soft intake of breath and was pleased. Though they'd both done their best to ignore it, there was something special between them; a connection he couldn't explain. And it wasn't just in a physical sense. It was like they really understood each other; saw beneath the tough exteriors, the faces they showed to the world, to the real Lachlan Coleridge and Ava Wolfe, beneath.

He'd never felt like this with any woman, certainly not with Kristy. They'd fallen madly in love in high school and things had been great for a while, but as they grew older and more mature, they'd seemed to have less and less in common. The stresses and strains of his job didn't help. His emotional withdrawal had been the final blow.

Still, he meant it when he said he'd meet with his estranged wife and be completely honest with her—and see if there was anything worth fighting for.

But for now, he'd enjoy his time with the woman in his arms. Knowing it might be the last time he held her filled him with a sad melancholy that was bittersweet, but he wouldn't change anything about it; wouldn't deny himself this precious time. The future would bring its own set of problems. For now, he'd surround himself with the wonders of the present.

Turning on his uninjured side, he drew her close against him. The gentle slope of the trampoline aided his cause. She rolled into him and her hands splayed across his chest.

"I can feel your heart beat," she whispered.

He stared at her with all the longing in his heart.

Moving slowly, his head inched toward her mouth. He grazed her lips with the lightest of pressure, loving their taste and feel. Needing more, he returned to her mouth and kissed her once again. This time, he didn't hold back.

She opened her mouth and he deepened the kiss. Her tongue tangled eagerly with his. He pulled her in tightly against him, relishing the feel of her breasts. Even with their clothes between them, their soft fullness imprinted themselves on his chest. He longed to feel her naked, his skin to hers.

As if reading his mind, she eased his shirt from his jeans. Her hands slid under the cotton fabric and her fingers caressed the muscles of his chest. He sucked in a breath at the wonder of it, his heart pounding.

Her fingers continued their exploration, dipping into his navel and then sliding upwards to skim across his pectorals. They tangled in his chest hair and then grazed his nipples.

Sensation rocketed through his veins and pooled heavily in his balls. His cock throbbed. He ached for her to touch him. Once again, she seemed in tune with his needs. Reaching under the waistband of his jeans, her hand encircled his erection and squeezed.

"Ah, sweet Jesus! That feels so good."

Her hand moved up and down his shaft in an agonizing rhythm of pleasure and pain. He wanted to flip her over onto her back and spread her thighs. Instead, he submitted to her heated attentions for as long as he could endure and then tenderly removed her hand.

"My turn," he murmured, his voice husky with need.

She smiled and lay back against the trampoline pad, swaying gently with the movement. He started on the buttons of her shirt. His still-healing collarbone made it a little more difficult, but he managed to slide each button out of its hole. He took his time, relishing the sight and feel of her soft, smooth skin, as he revealed more, inch by inch. At last, her shirt lay open and with the aid of the moon, he stared at her beautiful breasts.

During their first encounter in the cloakroom, he'd been in such a hurry, he hadn't had time to fully appreciate their magnificence. Her white lacy bra was filled to overflowing. He traced the swell of one breast with his finger and then moved to the other. She watched him, her eyes half closed and responded to his touch. He bent his head and through the lace, flicked his tongue over each of her rosy nipples. They puckered and hardened and all of a sudden, he couldn't stand even the thin barrier of lace. Reaching around behind her with his good arm, he found the clasp and released it.

They both sighed simultaneously—he with wonder, she with relief. He smiled and she smiled back at him and then groaned when he filled his hands with her unbound breasts. They were round and soft and silky to the touch and overflowed his palms. He kneaded them gently over and over and then once again bent his head.

This time, he took her nipple into his mouth and suckled the nub between his lips. His tongue flicked over the sensitive peak, tasting her sweetness as he breathed in her light perfume. She moved restlessly beneath him and then reached up and tangled her hands in his hair. Holding his head in place, she sighed again.

"Your mouth feels like magic," she murmured. "So darn good."

"You taste and smell delicious," he replied and moved his attentions to her other breast.

Once again, she moaned her contentment and drew his head down close. The rasp of his stubble scratched against her soft skin, but she didn't protest. Her heart pounded beneath his cheek.

With his mouth still loving her breast, his hand stole lower and inched across the smoothness of her belly. Lower still, he slipped beneath the waistband of her jeans and tangled in her curls. His finger slid along slick folds, moist and warm with need. She arched against his hand and he responded by increasing the pressure.

She gasped and her hands tightened around his head. His cock jerked with need. He had to have her. He had to bury himself in her wetness before he disgraced himself. Easing away from her and ignoring her soft cry of disappointment, he awkwardly tugged off his boots and jeans, almost toppling over on the unsteady platform. His shirt and underwear quickly followed. His cock sprang free, hard and proud, glistening with desire. Fire raged through his veins. He'd never wanted anyone so much.

Kneeling a little awkwardly on the trampoline, he tugged off her sandals and undid the button on her jeans. He slid them down her hips. A matching pair of white lace panties were revealed to his heated gaze.

"You're so beautiful," he whispered and leaned forward to kiss her. His lips found hers and they kissed each other with frantic need. The heat between them reached fever pitch. He felt it in every movement of her limbs. Her arms clung to him around his neck, her legs entwined with his. His cock pressed against her soft belly and it was agony and ecstasy, all at once.

"Make love to me, Lachlan."

Ava stared up at Lachlan in the moonlight and relished the feel of his weight against her. Naked at last, she clung to him, skin to skin. The trampoline swayed gently beneath them. Taking his weight on his uninjured arm, he rose above her, all bronzed male magnificence, and sheathed his cock. She wondered briefly about where he'd found the condom, but then he nudged her legs apart and settled between her hips and she could focus on nothing but the feel of his erection pressing against her.

Unlike the first time they came together, this time, he moved at a more leisurely pace. His cock slid inside her one tantalizing inch at a time. Twisting her hips, she moved against him, wordlessly urging him on. She was eager to feel the full, hard length of him inside her.

"Easy, honey. There's no rush," he murmured huskily against her ear. "I want to remember this moment forever."

The words sent equal parts of joy and pain searing through her heart. He was right to savor it. This might be the last time they were together. With that thought in mind, she relaxed against him and immersed herself in the feel of him slowly easing inside her.

When he could go no further, he stilled. His forehead rested against hers and his breath came fast and harsh. The tension in his body told her he was fighting hard to remain immobile. And then, as if he couldn't stand it a moment longer, he groaned deeply, pulled out and then thrust hard all the way inside.

His breath was harsh against her ear, but she loved the feel of him stretching her wide. Bracing himself awkwardly on one arm, his movements became faster, more urgent, aided by the sway of the trampoline. She wondered briefly about his injured shoulder, but then pushed the thought aside and lifted her hips and met each thrust. He appeared to be coping with the exuberant activity just fine. Panting, she clung to his arms and seared the memory of him, of them, in her brain.

"Oh, sweet Jesus. Ava, you're so wet. I'm gonna come, babe. Fuck, I'm gonna come."

He groaned and pumped faster, his body hard against hers. The pressure inside her grew stronger. She was close, so close. Her nails dug into his shoulders and her teeth left marks on his skin. He yelped and shuddered above her and the action did her in.

Her orgasm gripped her and wrung her out, tipping her over the other side. Waves of pleasure and relief coursed through her. She gasped and cried out and held on to him, riding out the storm.

It was a long while later when Lachlan stirred and lifted his weight off her. Sliding out of her, he rolled onto his side and quickly disposed of the condom. She frowned, remembering he'd also been prepared the last time they'd been together. There was something about it that was a little strange. It niggled at her. And then it hit her.

"What's a married man doing carrying around a bunch of condoms?"

His brow creased in confusion. "What are you talking about?"

"The condoms. You had one at the wedding. Now you've produced one here. I was just wondering why you'd have condoms at all. I assume you and your wife don't have any need of them."

He sat up slowly, the action made more awkward by the trampoline pad. "What are you trying to say, Ava?"

His voice was low and held a hint of warning. She wanted to forget the whole conversation and go back to feeling great, but somehow, she couldn't let it go.

"I'm just curious why a man who's still married—in fact, who was still living with his wife up until a couple of months ago, has a steady supply of condoms. Do you make a habit of picking up women for sex?"

The words fell out of her mouth and there was no way she could take them back. His body tensed and his eyes flashed with anger.

"What the hell are you implying? That my vows mean so little to me, that now my wife's out of the picture, I spend my time having sex with as many women as I can?" He shook his head in disgust. "Is that how little you think of me?"

She shook her head. The words had come out all wrong. She was curious about why he appeared to have a condom on hand whenever one was needed. That's all. No big deal.

"For your information," he bit out, "Kristy's allergic to 'the Pill.' We tried other methods of contraception, but condoms seem to be the easiest one. So, yes, I do have a steady supply of them. I never know when my wife will be in the mood for sex. Lately, that hasn't been working out so well. I guess it's lucky you came along."

She gasped at the hurtful words and tears sprang to her eyes. She'd never meant for her question to be taken like this. He was angry and she was deeply hurt. He'd cut her to the quick, with his throwaway line and right at that moment, she didn't know if she could ever forgive him. In frantic haste, she climbed off the trampoline and then searched feverishly for her clothes.

"Ava, I'm sorry. I didn't mean it. Jesus, please don't go. I'm sorry." He looked as devastated as she felt, but she wasn't in the mood to placate him. The cool professionalism she worked so hard to maintain with her patients had disappeared.

"It's fine. I understand," she managed. "Go and make up with your wife." And with that, she left.

Chapter 14

Dear Diary,

Just when I thought the blackness would consume me, I find myself peering into the light. Little by little, I'm gaining ground, winning the war against the faceless beast. My wife does the best she can. My kids love me, no matter what. They don't even know they're my rock. I cling to them and fight off the darkness...

I feel better than I have for a long time and I have my friends and family to thank. I only hope it continues. The beast is strong. The beast is powerful. The beast is more cunning than I think. I must stay on my guard, be alert or else risk falling back into the abyss...

Ava paid the cab driver and stumbled bare foot into her apartment building. In her haste to dress and leave, she'd forgotten her shoes. She was still smarting from Lachlan's comments and was desperately sad that they'd ruined such a magical night. Despite her brave words, the thought of him renewing his relationship with his wife was more than she could bear.

Flinging open the door to her apartment, she slammed it shut and ran down the hall to her room. Throwing herself across her bed, she let the hot tears fall. She cried for the lost opportunity, the loss of what felt—for her at least—like her opportunity to experience true love. She cried for Lachlan and his family. He was torn between his feelings for her and his loyalty to his wife and kids. It wasn't fair that any of them should be forced to make such a choice.

Why the hell couldn't she have fallen for some other stranger? Someone single and completely unattached? It would have made things so much easier. She could be celebrating her newfound feelings and looking forward to a future filled with love. Instead, her heart was breaking and there was no happy ending anywhere in sight.

She should have known there was a reasonable explanation for the condoms. She'd hurt him with her accusations and he'd lashed out and hurt her in response. The therapist inside her knew exactly what he was doing and why, but it hadn't made it any easier to accept or listen to, at the time.

He'd told her he was meeting Kristy and though Ava only wanted to see him happy, a part of her despaired at the thought that he'd reconnect with his wife and return to his family.

She believed wholeheartedly in marriage and everything it stood for. It was right and good that he did everything he could to make it work, but the possibility tore her heart in two. She'd fallen in love with him and she was almost certain he felt strongly about her, too.

Perhaps she should have tried harder to stay away from him? Give the reinvigoration of his marriage the best start it could? It was her own stupid fault she'd lost her heart to him and risked having it broken.

What a hopeless situation; somebody was bound to lose. If not her, then for his wife and more importantly, his kids. He didn't want his children to come from a broken home and she didn't want that for them, either. But she also wanted *him*. The two needs seemed irrevocably opposed. There was no way each of them could win.

She had to let him go. It was the only thing she could do. With a fresh wave of tears streaming from her eyes, she sobbed like her heart was breaking and prayed desperately for the strength to endure whatever was to be.

———————

Lachlan checked his watch a second time and cursed softly under his breath. Kristy was late. The midday sun beat down on his head, even where he sat on the park bench beneath the shade of a huge gum tree. He'd taken his lunch hour to meet with her—and not for the first time wondered where she was.

Not that she was known for her punctuality. Keeping to a set time had always eluded his wife. It drove him nuts that they'd agree to arrive or leave at a specified time and when that moment came around, she wouldn't be ready. It wasn't unusual for the Coleridge family to be running fifteen or twenty minutes late. It had become so commonplace that among their friends, it was often the source of a joke.

He'd forgotten that irritating habit of Kristy's when he'd made the appointment time. He'd been lulled into a false sense of security. Ava was always punctual. He winced, remembering the last time they'd been together. It was wonderful, magical, soul-destroying perfection...until it wasn't.

He still ached over the hurt and disappointment both of them had caused each other. He could understand her curiosity over the condoms, but still, did she really think he was just sleeping around? She was the only woman he'd had sex with since his wife had walked out. And it wasn't just because he was horny and Ava was willing to help him out.

He'd fallen in love with her and the knowledge was tearing him up inside. He wanted to do the right thing by his wife and kids, but he wasn't sure he had the strength or courage to see it through. If Kristy welcomed him back with open arms, would he turn his back on Ava and all they'd found? He wanted to shout out a furious denial, but the truth was, he didn't know.

His kids deserved a full-time father and a

mother living in the same house. Could he sacrifice his own happiness for theirs? With a tortured cry, he hung his head in his hands, wishing he knew the answer and even more terrified that he already did.

"Lachlan? Are you all right?"

He lifted his head and stared at his wife. She looked the same as she always had. Short and petite with bleached blond hair and blue eyes that now studied him seriously.

"Kristy. Hi, I...didn't see you arrive."

"Yes, I noticed," she replied dryly.

"I... It's not what you think. I was thinking about something that happened...at work."

"That's the problem, Lachlan. There's always something awful happening at work." With a little sigh, she moved closer and perched beside him on the bench. Her tone softened. "How have you been?"

She sounded like she cared about his answer. He swallowed a lump in his throat. For all her faults, she'd once been the love of his life and she'd always be the mother of his kids. For that, she deserved his honesty.

"I've been okay. For a while after you left, I went a little crazy. I was shocked and angry that you'd gone. But lately, I've been able to look at things more clearly and I can see where I went wrong. You did the right thing by taking the kids and leaving. I probably never would have changed my ways if you hadn't forced me to open my eyes."

Her eyebrows rose in surprise. "Wow, I... I didn't

expect you to be so understanding. What happened to make you see?"

Lachlan stared at his hands. "I started getting therapy. I've been seeing a psychiatrist. She's been...helping me through my...problems."

"She?"

Lachlan looked his wife in the eye. "Yes. Her name's Ava."

"Well, I'm just glad you decided to get professional help. It's made a difference. You seem so much more at peace. Calmer, happier." She turned to him and frowned. "*Are* you happier?"

He thought about it and nodded. After all the recent ups and downs, he hadn't stopped to think about how he was feeling. Yes, he was happier: happier about feeling whole; happier about not feeling like he was drowning in misery and depression; happier about finding Ava.

"I'm sorry, Kristy, for all the stuff I put you through. It wasn't fair. I shut you out and wallowed in my own self-pity. I gave up on us and our marriage. You married a man who was strong and resilient, who was fun to be around. I stopped being that man such a long time ago, it's no wonder you left."

Kristy nodded slowly and tears filled her eyes. "Yes, you did. And I was angry at you for becoming such a cold and angry stranger, but... It wasn't the only reason I left."

Lachlan frowned. "No?"

She shook her head. "No. The truth is, I... I fell in love with someone else."

Lachlan gaped in shock. Kristy's admission hit him like a ton of bricks. The tears now streamed down her face, but all he could do was stare at her.

"Lachlan! Please, say something! I'm sorry! I never meant for it to happen. But you were always out, either working or propping up some bar. I was lonely. I needed company. Mike gave that to me."

Lachlan reeled back like she'd slapped him. "*Mike?* Mike Barnes from the hardware store?"

"Yes. I went in there one day looking for something to unblock the drain in the kitchen sink. I'd mentioned it to you a couple of times and you'd promised to fix it, but you never did. I finally decided to darn well do the job myself. We got to talking in the store and Mike offered to come over and help. Afterwards, we had a cup of coffee and...things led to where they are."

"Did you sleep with him in our bed?" The words came out harsher than he intended, but he needed to know.

"Yes."

"How many times?"

"Oh, for goodness sake, Lachlan! Why does it matter? The fact is, things hadn't been good between us for a long time, even before this stuff with you at work. Once, I loved you like crazy, but I haven't felt like that since before Harry was born."

Lachlan shook his head, dazed. "Before Harry? *That* long ago?"

"I'm sorry, Lachlan."

He pushed away from the bench, needing to

put some space between them. If he were honest, he was more shocked than upset by her revelations. He understood her need for attention and for seeking out comfort and love. God knew, he hadn't provided those to her for a very long time.

"Please, don't be angry, Lachlan. I never meant to hurt you. Things with me and Mike just kind of happened. We never planned it."

"Do the kids know?" he asked quietly.

"Charlotte knows more than Harry. Mike's been staying with us."

Lachlan shook his head in surprise. "At your mother's?"

Kristy averted her gaze. A guilty flush stained her cheeks. "No, I... I was only at my mother's for the first week. After that, we found a little place by the beach. Mike has been coming over from Moree on the weekends."

"I see. It sounds awfully cozy. A proper little family." He couldn't keep the sarcasm from his voice.

"Please don't be like that, Lachlan. I want to try and keep things civil. If not for our sake, then for the kids."

He wanted to bite back with another sharp retort, but clenched his jaw and let the moment slide. With an effort, he got his anger under control and realized his pride was hurt more than his heart.

He wanted to see Kristy and his children happy. If that meant sharing them with another man, then so be it. As much as he wanted to keep his family together for the sake of his kids, it wouldn't do them any good to live with two parents who no longer wanted to be together. As sad as that was, it was true.

"Thank you for being honest with me," he said softly.

Kristy looked at him in surprise. He guessed that she anticipated she'd be in for a tougher fight.

"I wanted you to know the truth," she replied simply.

Lachlan drew in a deep breath and blew it out on a heavy sigh. "As long as we're being honest, I should tell you I'm also seeing someone."

"The therapist?"

"Yes. How did you know?"

"Your voice softened when you mentioned her name and a smile came into your eyes. She's very special to you, isn't she?"

His chest went tight with emotion. "Yes," he managed.

Kristy moved closer on the bench and put her arms around him and held him tight. "I'm glad. Good luck, Lachlan. I wish you all the best."

He hugged her back. "You, too."

Standing again, she stepped away and collected her handbag. "I'll be in touch," she said, turning to leave. "We'll work out something with the kids. I can probably bring them over next weekend for a visit. Would that suit?"

Joy and relief surged through him and he offered her a shaky smile. "Yes, that would be great. Thank you."

"Anytime." And with that, she strode off.

Lachlan watched until Kristy disappeared. He sat back down on the park bench, scrubbed a hand through his hair and sighed. It was over. His marriage of nearly ten years was over. The knowledge saddened him, but at the same time, he was relieved he and Kristy had managed to end it amicably. It would make things so much easier when it came to the kids. He was confident next time he spoke to his wife, she'd agree to something more permanent as far as his contact with his children went.

He thought about Mike Barnes and though it was upsetting to know another man was now going to be a big part of his kids' lives, he was glad it was somebody decent and hardworking, like Mike.

His thoughts turned to Ava and his heart skipped a beat. He wanted to go to her right away and tell her about his meeting with Kristy. And then he remembered the way the two of them had parted and his excitement dimmed. He hadn't spoken to her since she'd left.

He assumed she'd caught a cab home. She'd left her car at her apartment. He lived on the opposite side of town. It was way too far to walk. He'd called her office the next morning on the pretext of making an appointment. All he really wanted was to check if she was in. The receptionist, Janelle, assured him she was and he hung up when the woman put him on hold. He was relieved to know that Ava had arrived home, safe and sound.

Perhaps he could call her again and test the

waters? Apologize for his outburst? Beg her forgiveness? His fingers hovered over the keypad of his phone. The instrument rang in his hand. Starting in surprise, he looked at the screen and swallowed his disappointment. It was his partner.

"Hi, Martin. How are you doing? I'm sorry, I'm running a little late, but I'm finished up here, now. I'll be back at the station soon."

"Lachie... Lachie..."

Concern immediately seized Lachlan's chest. "Hell, what is it, Martin? What's the matter?"

"It's...It's about the Irwin matter. I just had a call from IA. They're charging me with manslaughter."

"What?" Lachlan gasped, shocked to his core.

"Yeah. They just got off the plane. They gave me the courtesy of calling ahead, so I could prepare myself." Martin's voice was ragged with fear. "What am I going to do, Lachie? What the fuck am I going to do?"

Lachlan's thoughts turned frantic. Nothing was making sense. "Where the hell do they get off charging you with manslaughter? What happened with Irwin's wife?"

Martin's voice turned desperate. He sounded like he was on the verge of breaking down. "That's the thing. She didn't back up our story. She told IA there was no way in the world Irwin would have shot her. She said he was about to hand over the gun. That's why he raised it. At least, that's what she said."

"Fuck. He raised it because she was trying to get away." Lachlan shook his head back and forth, stunned.

"I need help, Lachie. I need you. I need you to be here when they arrive."

"I'm on my way, Martin. Don't worry about it. We'll get to the bottom of this bullshit. Stay there. I'll see you soon."

CHAPTER 15

Lachlan's thoughts were in a whirlwind as he raced to his vehicle and threw himself behind the wheel. With a screech of the tires, he reversed out of the parking lot, wincing at the pain in his shoulder as he turned toward the station. He couldn't believe Elsie Irwin hadn't backed up their version of events. Lachlan had been in that supermarket. He'd seen Irwin raise the gun when Elsie tried to leave, and so had she. Her story simply didn't make sense.

Unless Martin had misunderstood the phone call? Was it possible in his fear and confusion that the IA investigators hadn't implied that at all? Lachlan gritted his teeth in frustration, not knowing the answer, but critically aware his friend was in a bad way and needed him there.

His thoughts landed briefly on Ava and once again, he was filled with disappointment that he couldn't go to her and do what he could to make amends. As much as he yearned to do so, right at that moment, Martin needed him more. With reluctance, he pushed all thoughts of a reconciliation with Ava behind him and focused on what lay ahead.

Pulling his vehicle into a vacant parking space behind the police station, he half-jogged up the few steps and punched in a security code that allowed him access through the rear of the building. Nodding greetings to several officers and administrative staff, he continued without pause to the first floor where the detectives were housed. He spied Becker coming toward him, his expression grim.

"Martin called me in a panic," Lachlan stated without preamble. "What the hell is going on?"

Becker's expression remained somber. "IA called. Apparently your eye witness, Elsie Irwin, contradicts your statements. She says her husband had no intention of shooting her. That he was ready to hand over his gun. She said Martin overreacted and now her husband is dead. She's threatening to sue."

Lachlan shook his head in disbelief. "Fuck! How the hell could she *say* something like that! He caught her trying to sneak out! I was there. I saw the whole thing. I was the one negotiating with the stupid prick!"

Becker stared hard at Lachlan, his body tense. "And was he listening?"

Lachlan sucked in a breath and blew it out on a heavy sigh. "Yes, he was listening, but even I thought he was going to blow his wife's head off when he lifted that rifle."

Unable to stand still, he moved away and

began to pace, shaking his head back and forth. He still couldn't believe how quickly things had gotten out of control, now or then. Spinning on his heel, he stalked back to Becker.

"This is bullshit, boss. The guy was obviously unstable. He turned up in a supermarket, held people hostage and threatened his wife with a gun. I did my best to calm him down, talk him out of doing anything stupid, but we both know how situations like that can escalate in an instant."

Becker stared at him. "Except your eyewitness disagrees."

Lachlan made a sound of frustration deep in his throat and tugged at his hair. With narrowed eyes, he held Becker's gaze.

"Martin Griffin saw the man raise his gun and point it straight at his wife. Martin called the situation as he saw it. Any one of us would have reacted the same way. It was our duty to protect her. She was an innocent victim. He posed a significant threat. He had to be dealt with."

"I've read the training manuals, Coleridge. You don't need to remind me how it goes."

Lachlan's breath came hard and fast. The tension inside him was tightly coiled. He wanted to scream out his frustration, hit something, hard; force Becker to understand. But it wasn't his boss he had to convince.

"When are those IA assholes expected to arrive? I want to speak with them again," he growled.

"They'll be here any minute. "They called from the airport."

Anger surged through Lachlan's veins and he narrowed his eyes again. "They sure as hell didn't give us much warning."

"No. And I'm not sure how much good it will do you talking to them again. It seems to me like they've already made up their mind."

"That's bullshit!" Lachlan exploded. "What about the other witnesses? The other people in the store? There were two other staff members with Elsie Irwin. What do they have to say?"

Becker tossed him a look that bordered on sympathetic. "Unfortunately, they're not saying much. They agreed Barry Irwin came in with a gun, angry at his wife, but they say they left the supermarket before the situation turned fatal. They didn't see him raise the gun. They didn't see the shooting. They have nothing to add."

Lachlan cursed again. "So, it's me and Martin against Elsie Irwin. The two big bad cops against one defenseless woman. Jesus! We were trying to save her *life!* Doesn't she get that? Doesn't she care Martin will see that poor bastard in his dreams forever more, with a bullet in his heart? Doesn't she realize the decision to shoot was made because he thought he had no *choice?*"

"I get where you're coming from, Coleridge," Becker said, "and I hate this whole shit show as much as you, but there's nothing I can do. It's out of my jurisdiction."

Lachlan's anger boiled over. "We try and do our job, keep the community safe. Something like this happens and we get crucified for it. Where's the fairness in that?"

"I agree. It isn't fair. It isn't right, but unfortunately, we don't get the say. Goons from IA come in here, trying to keep the peace. Their job is to pacify the community, keep the media from our door, and this is what they come up with. They sacrifice one of their own for the greater good."

"That's bullshit, boss, and you know it! Where do they draw the line? How many of us will they sacrifice in order to maintain the peace? It's bullshit! Absolute bullshit!"

Becker stared at him, his expression calm. "Like I said, there's nothing we can do about it, Coleridge. IA's made up its mind. They'll go through the motions of charging Griffin and no doubt there'll be a trial. We can only hope he gets a decent lawyer and a sympathetic jury who sees sense."

Fury and disbelief battled inside Lachlan. He stared back at his boss. "And if he *doesn't?* What then? His career will be over, to say nothing of the time he'll most likely spend in jail! I can't believe you're just standing there, doing nothing to help him! He's our colleague, our friend. He needs our backing and support. He needs to know we're on his side, that we don't think he did anything wrong."

"And I'm sure you'll be prepared to tell him that, Coleridge."

Lachlan shook his head again and bit down on his anger. He couldn't believe his boss was going to walk away from one of the members on his team and hang him out to dry.

"He needs to hear it from *you*, Becker," he shouted. "He needs to know it comes from the top. It's the only way he'll have the courage and spirit to fight this. I know Martin. He... He's been doing it tough. His brother's barely cold in the ground and now...now *this*."

Becker stared at him, unmoved. "I get what you're saying, Detective. I really do. Do you think I don't care about the way IA's treated this whole thing? They've come in and made you and Griffin out to be the baddies, like you're the ones who were doing the wrong thing. It shits me! It shits me every time! But I can't do anything about it. I don't have the power to fix the system. It's just the way it is."

Lachlan clenched his jaw tight, holding back another torrent of words. It was no good venting his anger on Becker. His boss was right when he said he didn't make the rules.

"I'm taking this bullshit to the media," Lachlan said, staring hard at his boss.

"No, Coleridge, you're not. We deal with this internally. We don't want any outside interference."

"And what if that doesn't work?" Lachlan exploded. "What if the media twist it all Elsie Irwin's way? The poor woman who's now been made a widow because of some trigger-happy cop. If they don't know the truth, they'll go with rumors and you can bet your last dollar those won't support Martin."

"You know the protocols, Coleridge," Becker hissed, "and I refuse to antagonize the police commissioner. I forbid you to have any contact with the media. We deal with this in the usual way."

Lachlan opened his mouth again to protest, but Becker shot him a look that brooked no argument. "I said *no*, Detective. That's a direct order. Breach it and I'll report you for insubordination. Be careful, or you might be facing an IA investigation of your own."

Lachlan tensed at the overt threat. He couldn't believe Becker would sell him out that way, and more importantly, Martin. He shot his boss a cold look filled with disgust.

"You spineless prick." Spinning on his heel, he strode away, so angry he could barely think.

"*Coleridge!* You get back here!"

Lachlan ignored Becker's angry shout and continued walking toward the locker room, looking for his partner. He found him huddled on a bench. It looked like Martin had been crying.

"Hey," Lachlan murmured and took a seat beside his friend.

Martin turned slowly to face him and when Lachlan saw the devastation in the other man's eyes he felt like he'd taken a punch to the gut.

"It's all over, Lachie. They're going to hang me out to dry."

Lachlan was overcome with panic. "No, Martin, you're wrong. We're all behind you in this. I just spoke to Becker—"

"Becker's a worthless piece of shit. He cares more for his next promotion than the men under his command. He'll do whatever it takes to protect his own ass. We both know that."

The sad resignation in Martin's voice both frightened and angered Lachlan. It was true what his partner said about their boss, but it scared him to hear the defeat in Martin's tone. He needed to go in there swinging, refusing to accept IA's claims. He needed to be strong and courageous in the face of adversity, not accept it calmly, as if the outcome were a foregone conclusion.

"This is bullshit, mate. We have to fight them," he said a little desperately.

Martin stared at him. Fresh tears welled up in his eyes. "You're a good friend, Lachie, but you and I both know, there is no *us*. It's *me* they have in their sights. *I'm* the one they want. I'm the one who pulled the fucking trigger."

He wanted to shout out in protest, to argue that Martin was wrong, but he couldn't. His partner spoke the truth. The IA pricks were out for blood and they were fixed on Martin's scent. It wouldn't be over until they had their trophy and could feed an acceptable storyline to the media.

Lachlan could only hope the circus would end before there was a trial. That someone higher up in the police command would bring an end to this travesty of justice before it went that far. If Becker wasn't going to do it, by God, *he* would.

As the thought took hold, a tiny frisson of hope blossomed deep inside his gut. Becker and his gag order could go to hell. Lachlan was going to do everything he could to help a friend in need, including paying for the best lawyer he could find.

But first, he had to talk to Ava. He needed the quiet strength and encouragement only she could give.

————————————

The late afternoon sun shone wanly through the window of Ava's office as she tried to concentrate on the monologue coming from the man who sat in the chair opposite her desk. She was grateful he was her last patient of the day and soon, she'd be free to close up and go home. The man was a regular patient of Phoebe's and although he'd been a little disconcerted to discover Phoebe had gone away for a brief while, it hadn't taken him long to feel comfortable with her locum.

A cross-dresser since he was a child, it appeared to Ava that her patient sought therapy more as a way of conversing with someone about his predilection, rather than a need for help. He seemed to vacillate from hating the fact he enjoyed dressing in women's clothing, to wondering why all men didn't partake. Ava had come to the conclusion that he didn't really want or need her advice. He might not have been entirely happy with the way he was, but he didn't appear to want to make an effort to change things.

She didn't usually see patients on the weekend, but the man had phoned in a panic and insisted he needed to see her. He'd arrived at her office looking a little more ruffled than usual. His color was high and his graying hair looked a little bedraggled. He'd then proceeded to regale her with the dramas of his home life.

Despite her best efforts to concentrate, her thoughts wandered to Lachlan. She wondered how his meeting with Kristy had gone and whether, even now, he was busy moving her back in. A shaft of pain went through Ava at the thought, but she had to brace herself against the possibility that the scenario could very well be real.

She made an unconscious sound of distress in the back of her throat and hastily covered her mouth in an effort to force it back in. Her patient stopped mid-sentence and stared at her curiously.

"Are you okay, Doctor Wolfe? You've gone a little pale."

She nodded and forced a smile on her face. "I'm fine, Mr—"

"Nigel, please," he insisted with a smile. "Call me Nigel. I think we know each other well enough for first names, now."

"Yes, well, all right, Nigel. Please, continue. I'd really like to hear how it makes you feel when your wife is angry at you for wearing her clothes."

The man's eyes widened and then his shoulders slumped on a sigh. "Yes, well, now that you mention it, she *does* get really mad, but not because I'm wearing *her* clothes. Her dresses are way too small for me. It's the fact I'm wearing clothes that she feels belong on a woman that gets her riled."

"Does it make her mean and nasty, or is she sad and confused? You told me the last time we met she didn't know you were a cross-dresser in the early days of your marriage. It must have been very difficult for her when she discovered your secret."

"Yes, I guess so, but in the first few years after finding it out, she seemed to understand. At least, that's what she told me. As long as I was discreet, didn't tell another soul and didn't go out in public dressed like that, she'd let it slide. And I followed all her rules. It was only after the kids were born that her attitude toward me and my...habit...changed."

"In what way?" Ava asked, doing her best to appear interested and not at all convinced this warranted an urgent weekend appointment.

"Like you said, she started to get mean and nasty. Only a week ago, she accused me of not being a real man. She... She threatened to divorce me, to take the kids and leave. She told me she'd tell the kids I was dead. That I was better off to them dead than as the joke of a man that I am!"

He stared up at her with tears in his eyes, his large frame shaking with emotion. Her impatience to get the meeting over with dissolved and her heart clenched in sympathy. She wanted so much to help him, but she understood that deep down inside, he wouldn't appreciate suggestions, that he didn't really want to be helped.

"Have you tried not to dress up, like I told you the last time we were together? Have you tried to occupy yourself with other activities? Taking the kids to the park, or a picnic by the river?"

He shook his head helplessly, back and forth, his sobs coming loud and fast. "Yes... Nooo! I tried! I really did! I went three whole days without putting on a single scrap of women's clothing. But it didn't work! I got needier than ever! I couldn't eat, couldn't sleep. My work began to suffer.

"You don't understand, Doctor Wolfe! When I'm Nigella, the world recedes and I don't feel any pain. Nigella doesn't front up to the stress at work, dealing with whatever horror comes her way. Nigella lives for the sunshine. Nigella laughs all the time. I can't give her up, Doctor! I just can't!"

Comprehension and compassion flooded through Ava and all at once, she understood. Nigel used his cross-dressing as a means of escape, like others turned to illicit drugs or alcohol. She hurried to reassure him.

"It's all right, Nigel. Nigella can stay. We'll work something else out."

He breathed a sigh of relief and smiled through his tears. "Thank you, Doctor! You don't know how much comfort your words bring to my battered soul."

Ava nodded sympathetically. Everyone dealt with life's harsh blows differently. Who was she to say whether his outlet was right or wrong? As far as she knew, it wasn't harming anyone.

"How's your wife, now?" she asked. "Has she calmed down? You don't really think she meant those things she said, do you?"

He shrugged. "Who knows? She's been more and more snappy of late. It's like nothing I do pleases her anymore. I wish I knew how to make her happy, but I don't."

"Do you think she'd consider seeing a therapist? It sounds like the two of you are in dire need of couple's counseling."

He shook his head. "No, she's happy for me to go, but she doesn't do this kind of thing."

Ava accepted his comment. There were a lot of people who weren't convinced about the benefits of therapy. It always saddened her to think about all the desperate people who could be supported and helped toward healing if only they'd let someone in.

She was relieved Lachlan had found the courage to seek her out...

Once again, Ava's thoughts switched from her patient and returned to the man who haunted her dreams. She wondered if he'd call her later, after work. Or perhaps she could drive past a couple of the downtown bars and see if his vehicle was parked outside. She could saunter in and order herself a drink. If he noticed her and came over, she could pretend she hadn't realized he was there. She could ask him about his meeting with Kristy and hope he gave her the truth. If he ignored her altogether, she'd have her answer...

Could she do it? Could she play some silly game in order to find out whether the man she'd fallen for had decided to return to his wife? A silent *yes* surged through her. She shook her head slightly in desperation. There was no denying it. She was as sad and hopeless as some of her patients.

Lachlan pulled into the driveway of Ava's apartment block and switched off the ignition. A light shone from at least two of her windows and her car sat in its usual spot. Nerves bounced around in his gut, keeping his tension high. He wanted to go inside and tell her everything, beg her to let him try again... Still, not knowing what kind of reception he would get, held him back.

Coward. The word echoed from somewhere in the back of his head and he grimaced. He'd been a lot of things in his life, but a coward wasn't one of them, despite what Ava had once said.

Even after being warned off by his boss, he was still prepared to contact the media and give them a tell-all exposé on the gutless dealings of IA and to hell with his career. The only thing that held him back was that Martin's arrest hadn't yet been made public and Lachlan refused to add to his partner's burden. It had been bad enough having to stand by while his friend and colleague was led away in cuffs. He couldn't imagine the horror that was going through Martin's head, or the hell that was yet to come. He was only grateful that the IA assholes had given him bail. At least he could be with his family.

The time would come when Lachlan would

stand in front of the cameras and tell the world just how it was. But not tonight. Tonight was his and Ava's. Tonight he'd do everything he could to make amends with the woman he loved.

With that thought uppermost in his mind, he unclipped his seatbelt and climbed out of his car. Locking it behind him, he walked up the concrete path that led to her apartment. The night was quiet, with only the occasional passing vehicle breaking the silence. Even the insects were still. Wiping his dampened palms on his jeans, he drew in a deep breath, squared his shoulders and knocked on her door.

CHAPTER 16

Dear Diary,

The darkness draws me ever nearer, just when I'd begun to find the light. It envelops me in its icy cloak, dank and musty and cold. It whispers to me of days gone by, when I was still a kid. The fun I used to have swimming in the river; playing soccer with my dad.

Those days of innocence are over and I can never go back. Even the love of my family is no longer enough. I'm no good for anything or anyone, but him. He knows me like no other. He knows who I really am... And I love him for it. It's only a matter of time before the world knows our secret.

We all have secrets, but mine is worse than most. I hide my shame like I hide my secret, in the dark. I've tried to seek help. I've even tried counseling, but I don't really want any help or want to change. Even my therapist knows it. I embrace the darkness inside me. I listen for its call. Right now, it's crooning a soft, sweet lullaby... My lover is standing close...

Ava heard the knock on her door over the sound of the six o'clock news on the TV and frowned. She'd had a simple supper of an egg white omelette and greens and was now relaxing after her unscheduled call in to the office. She wasn't expecting visitors.

The knock came again and with a sigh, she set her wine glass on the coffee table and pushed away from the couch. Padding barefoot down the hall, she looked through the peephole and gasped.

Lachlan.

With her heart pounding double time, she glanced down at her old robe. Though it was threadbare at the elbows, she still refused to toss it out. She'd been wearing it since her final year of college and there were a lot of fond memories stored within its woven cloth. Besides, it was comfortable.

With no choice but to open the door and let Lachlan see her in her finest, she undid the security chain and turned the door handle. He looked so sad and despondent, she immediately forgot about her worn attire.

"Lachlan! Are you all right? What are you doing here?"

He stared at her blankly as if trying to comprehend her questions. At last, he blinked and nodded. "Hi. I'm... I'm fine. I needed to see you. I hope you don't mind."

"Of course not," she said, a little warily, wondering what had brought him to her door. She wasn't sure she was ready if he came to tell her he'd reconciled with his wife.

At the possibility, she swallowed a desperate sigh. If that was his reason for being there, she might as well get it over with. Stepping backwards, she opened the door all the way and indicated he could enter. "Come in."

She turned and walked back to the open concept kitchen and living room and muted the TV before turning back to face him. "Can I get you something? A drink?"

"Thanks. A beer would be good, if you have it."

His tone was still quiet and his demeanor remained downcast. She frowned and tossed him another worried look. It was Kristy. It had to be. He was here to tell Ava his wife was moving back.

All of a sudden, Ava's legs turned to concrete and she could barely force herself to move toward the fridge. With her heart heavy with dread, she came to a halt. If the news was bad, she didn't want him staying any longer than he had to. She wanted him to get it over with and then she'd ask him to leave. Like ripping off a Band-Aid. Some things were better done fast and with gritted teeth.

"It's about Kristy, isn't it? You're getting back together, giving your marriage another chance. It's all right. You can tell me. I've been half expecting it. It was my idea, after all." She laughed without humor and tried to fight back the tears. Unable to look at him while he told her that news, she turned her back on him and braced herself.

Instead, she felt his hand upon her shoulder, strong and gentle all at once. She flinched and moved away.

"I'm fine, Lachlan. I am. And...I'm happy for you. For all of you. Your kids—"

"It's not about Kristy, or my family. Well, it is, kind of, but that's not why I'm here. Kristy and I have decided to formally separate. In time, we'll get a divorce. I'm here because I wanted to say I'm sorry for the things I said. I was angry and hurt and..."

He cursed beneath his breath. "What I really want to tell you is that I've fallen in love with you and... I'm wondering how you feel. You told me once you liked me and I can't help hoping there might be a chance the two of us..."

His voice faded off, as if his courage was depleted. She stared at him, so lost and uncertain and joy trickled into her heart. He loved her! He wasn't getting back with his wife. He wanted to know if there could be something between them—if he had a chance.

"Yes! Yes! Yes!" she cried and threw her arms around his neck. In less than a second, she'd gone from despair to wild jubilation.

He grimaced and too late, she remembered his collarbone, but she kissed him anyway, on his lips, his nose, his cheeks. Her glasses made the action more awkward and laughter rumbled through him. He pulled back a little to stare at her, his eyes wide with disbelief.

"Yes? You mean it?"

She nodded and smiled and tugged off her glasses, wiping the moisture from her cheeks. Taking him by the hand, she led him to the couch and sat down beside him. Still holding his hand, she said softly, "Tell me everything."

Over a beer and a glass of wine, Lachlan filled her in on his meeting with his wife. Ava was surprised to hear Kristy had found someone new, but was relieved to know this hadn't factored in Lachlan's decision—or that he wasn't devastated by the news.

"I loved her for a long time," he murmured. "Once, we were good together, but time has a way of playing tricks. We grew up and put our high school days behind us. We could have grown together, matured into our adult life. Unfortunately, the longer we stayed together, the more obvious it became how far we'd grown apart. We had two beautiful kids who I'll love and support until I die, but I can't live my life with their mother, knowing I'm in love with someone else, no matter how hard I try. And I can't ask her to do the same."

Ava stared at him. Lachlan moved closer on the couch, until their thighs were touching. Her short robe had ridden up. His jeans were rough against her naked skin. He shifted his head until his lips were inches from hers.

"You believe in marriage and all it stands for. You cried at your sister's wedding," he murmured, his breath warm on her mouth.

"Y-yes," she said a little uncertainly, unsure where he was heading.

"You're a traditional girl with traditional values. I understand. Believe it or not, I feel that way, too. My marriage to Kristy might not have worked out, but that doesn't mean I'm forever soured against the institution. You want marriage and a lifelong commitment."

He stared into her eyes. He was so close she could see the dark flecks amid the green. Her breath caught at the intensity of emotion in their depths.

"I want to give you that," he whispered against her lips. "If you'll let me. I want to love you until the day I die."

She gasped on a sob of pure joy and happiness and he held her against his chest. His lips found hers and they kissed like they were ravenous. She matched his passion at every turn, loving the feel of him against her. He reached inside her robe and his fingers found her naked breast.

He stroked her nipple back and forth until she was wild with need. She moaned against his lips and lay back on the couch. Careful of his injured arm, she reached up and pulled him down on top of her. He willingly complied with a growl deep in his throat and tugged at the tie around her waist. Spreading her robe wide, he stared down at her nakedness, panting.

"You're so beautiful. I love you, Ava Wolfe."

"I love you, too, Lachlan."

He bent his head and captured her lips and kissed her again and again. She squirmed against his erection, desperate to feel more. Pulling away, he undid the button and zipper and shucked his Levis and boxers down his hips. Returning to his position, he lay naked, fully on top of her and both of them sighed loudly in relief.

"That's better," he growled.

She stared up at him. "You feel so good."

He pressed his cock against her entrance. She was sure he could feel her heat. Slick with wanting, her need coiled tightly inside her.

"Do you want me?" he murmured, his eyes heavy with desire.

Anticipation surged in her belly and tingled through her core. "Yes," she breathed and pulled his head down for another soul-searching kiss.

His cock nudged at her entrance and she suddenly realized he didn't wear protection. "Do you have a condom?" she whispered.

He stilled and drew slightly away from her. "No," he said. "I wasn't sure if you'd even want to see me. I didn't want to appear presumptuous and spoil everything...again."

He stared down at her, his expression solemn. She smiled softly, tenderly and reached up to cup his cheek. "It's all right. That was my fault as much as yours. I'm sorry. I was the one who made assumptions. It was wrong of me."

"Let's just agree to forgive each other and forget. Can we do that?" he asked.

Ava smiled in relief. "I can if you can." Once again, she pulled him down on top of her and kissed him. Passion quickly built up again inside her and she twisted impatiently against him.

"I need you inside me," she murmured.

"What about the condom?"

"I don't care about the condom. I'm free of disease and you look pretty healthy. Besides, I'm taking contraception pills."

With that, Lachlan bent his head and captured one rosy nipple. He suckled and licked until Ava was driven wild with need and then he moved to the other.

"Stop!" she gasped. "Please, I want to feel your cock."

He moved slightly. A moment later, his thickness probed once again at her slick entrance. She lifted her hips and met his thrust and in one smooth movement, he embedded himself to the hilt. He groaned in relief.

Clinging to his shoulders, she urged him on. His thrusts came hard and fast and she kept begging him for more. No man had ever felt the way he did, buried deep inside. She panted with exertion, close to orgasm.

He picked up his pace once again and her hips met every thrust. Her fingernails bit into his shoulders and finally she was on the edge. A breath later she was crying out and toppling over, clinging to him for dear life.

With a triumphant yelp, he thrust into her over and over again. All at once he tensed and then growled low in his throat. His warm seed poured into her and she loved the feeling that they were one. As their breathing returned to normal, he rolled sideways and brought her with him.

"That was..." She shook her head, unable to find the words.

"Amazing, wonderful—out of this world," he supplied.

She smiled tenderly. "Yes to all of that and so much more."

With her head resting against his chest, she wriggled a little, searching for more room.

"This isn't the widest couch in the world," he murmured against her hair, "and my shoulder is kind of sore. Is there somewhere more comfortable we can go?"

She pushed away from him and found her feet. Reaching out, she took his hand, helped him up, and led him down the hall toward her bedroom. She'd left a lamp on earlier, intending to read once she'd finished her wine. The light softly illuminated the room.

"Nice," he said, looking around at the pastel prints on the walls. The pale pinks and blues matched the color of the bedspread. Cushions in contrasting hues decorated a window seat that looked out onto a small courtyard surrounded by garden.

"Don't give me credit for the décor." She winked at him. "The place came fully furnished."

He smiled and tugged her over toward the bed. "Who cares about the décor? The view is so much better from here."

Pulling her down beside him, he snuggled her in his arms. Ava spooned into him and sighed with contentment. Thinking back to how he'd arrived at her door, looking so full of despair, she giggled.

"What's so funny?" he mumbled against her hair.

"I was just thinking how I managed to brighten your mood."

"Yeah," he replied softly.

She turned in his arms and looked at him. "You don't sound altogether convinced."

His expression grew somber. He kissed her

gently on the mouth. "It wasn't just us and our problems that were playing on my mind."

She stared at him and ignored the tiny flash of fear. "Talk to me."

In a heavy voice, Lachlan told her about Martin and the IA investigation and what had happened at the station.

Lachlan's expression hardened. "I hate that Becker doesn't have the guts to go against the party line. This is a friend, a colleague who's being treated like shit. It could happen to any one of us. We need to know the police service and the hierarchy will support us in times like this. Otherwise, what the hell are we doing?" His breath came faster and his eyes flashed. "Tell me, Ava. What the hell are we *doing?*"

The illuminated numbers of the clock on Ava's nightstand read 3:15, but still Lachlan couldn't get to sleep. The woman in his arms had dozed off hours ago, her breathing slow and deep. He wanted nothing more than to join her and escape, even for a little while, from the nightmare of the day. Even so, sleep continued to elude him.

The faint sound of his phone ringing from the other room startled him. Remembering he'd left it in the pocket of his jeans, he carefully eased his arm out from under the sleeping woman and padded down the hall. He glanced at the screen and frowned. *Pam Griffin.*

Why the hell would Pam be calling at this time of night? Dread formed in his gut. He'd attended enough crime scenes to know nothing good ever happened after midnight. His body went cold at the thought, but he answered the call.

"Pam? What is it?" he asked, forcing himself to remain calm.

"Oh, Lachlan! Come quickly! It's Martin! He's been drinking since early evening and now he's turned plain mean. Hurry, Lachlan! Hurry! Oh, God! He's... He's got a gun!"

CHAPTER 17

Lachlan sped through the night, his heart in his throat. The whole time, he murmured a frantic mantra that Martin and his family would be all right. Pam had ended the phone call abruptly and hadn't picked up when he'd called back. He could only hope she'd been able to talk Martin back under control.

Lachlan hadn't even taken the time to wake Ava, or write her a note. She was sound asleep and with a bit of luck, he'd sort things out in the Griffin household and be back in bed before she knew he'd left. At least, he hoped that's how things would pan out.

Taking the corner way too fast, he gritted his teeth as he fought the Ranger's steering wheel, reminding him suddenly that his collarbone was far from healed. With an effort, he managed to bring the vehicle back under control.

The pale, smooth bark of a gum tree flashed by and a thick patch of silky oak. The trees stood silent and ghostly in the moonlight. So far, the streets were free from traffic and he was thankful for it. It meant he could linger less at each intersection and travel even faster in between.

He turned into Martin's street and breathed a sigh of relief. All the houses were dark and quiet, including the one belonging to the Griffins. It was like Pam's panicked phone call had never happened, like somehow it was a dream. He prayed to God that Martin had sobered up and all was once again good with the world.

No, not good. Not with this ongoing IA investigation. Things wouldn't be good for the Griffin family for a long, long time. But he could only hope for tonight at least, everything had righted.

He came to a stop outside the Griffin residence and climbed out of his car. Striding up the driveway, he remembered the last time he'd been there. Had it only been two weeks since he'd spotted Ava by the pool? So much had happened in such a short time. It made his head spin.

Reaching the front door, he knocked on it gently, not wanting to disturb the children. The hour was late. No doubt the two of them were asleep. To his consternation, his knock went unanswered. The house remained quiet and dark. He knocked again, this time a little louder.

"Pam? Martin? It's Lachlan. Are you there?" Once again, there was no reply.

He frowned in concern. It had taken him less than fifteen minutes to drive across town. If Martin was as drunk as Pam had implied, he might have passed out, but surely Pam couldn't have fallen asleep? Perhaps she was upstairs, in the bedroom. Perhaps she hadn't heard him knock.

Tugging out his phone, he dialed her number and listened. He heard a ringing sound coming from inside the house and realized it was Pam's phone. It eventually went through to voicemail and he hung up, feeling even more apprehensive. He tried Martin's number and got the same result.

He turned the doorknob and it moved beneath his fingers. Stepping into the entryway, he felt around for a light. His fingers grazed the switch and he flicked it on. The living room was neat and tidy, like it usually was. As far as he could see, there was nothing out of place. He moved further into the house, calling out a little louder as he went.

"Pam? Martin? Can you hear me?" The house persisted in its stillness—almost eerily so. He shivered with a sudden premonition and then told himself not to be stupid. It was the middle of the night. Of course the house was quiet.

Reaching the bottom of the staircase, he once again felt along the wall and found the light. Switching it on, he blinked against the sudden illumination. The staircase led up to the upper storey, where the bedrooms were. He hadn't been upstairs before. He hadn't needed to. But he had to find the Griffins and reassure himself they were both all right and he wouldn't leave until he'd done so.

With a quick breath, he took the stairs two at a time and reached the landing. The light continued down the hall and after debating in silence for a few moments over which direction to take, he turned left.

The thick carpet muted his footsteps and he called out quietly once again. He didn't want to disturb the children, but he also didn't want to come upon Pam and Martin by surprise. Pam had told him Martin was armed. The last thing he wanted was to be mistaken for an intruder and shot by his partner.

"Pam? Martin? It's Lachlan. Can you hear me?"

The doors to all of the rooms leading off the hall were closed. There were three on the right and two on the left. He pulled up outside the nearest one and eased it open. The faintest glimmer of moonlight peeked through the open blinds. Through the dimness, he made out the shape of a queen-sized bed. On it were the shapes of two adults.

Pam and Martin. It had to be. Using the flashlight on his phone, Lachlan shone it across the bed. A large dark stain pooled beneath Martin's head and dripped onto the floor. With a sickening feeling, Lachlan backpedalled and felt around on the wall for a switch. He found it just inside the door and flipped it on.

"*Nooo!*" The sound tore from his throat, filled with distress and pain. Martin lay dead on the bed, the gun beside him. Inching forward, Lachlan moved around to Pam's side and his breath caught in horror at what he saw.

Martin's wife stared sightlessly at the ceiling, a single bullet wound in her forehead. Blood oozed from the blackened hole and had run down her cheek. Shock ricocheted through Lachlan and he clenched his jaw hard against a surge of bile. It looked like Martin had shot his wife dead and then turned the gun on himself.

"Why, why, *why*?" Lachlan moaned, staring at his friend in disbelief. How could he have missed seeing how close to the edge Martin was? His partner had been doing it tough, but he'd never imagined him capable of something like this.

Knowing there was nothing he could do, he backed out of the room and dialed for the police. Providing scant details only, he gave the dispatcher the address. Pulling the door closed behind him, he went searching for the kids, hoping like hell they hadn't been woken by the shots and gone to investigate.

The next room along the hallway was unoccupied, filled with a double bed and dresser. The bed was neatly made. It was probably the guest room. The doors on the other side of the hall contained a bathroom and separate toilet. Lachlan came to the last door and guessed it had to belong to the kids.

He eased open the door, not wanting to wake them before it was necessary. With any luck, he could get them out before they caught sight of their parents. It was a scene no child should have to see and he was determined to make sure they didn't.

Like the rest of the house, this room was also still and silent. It was also very dark. Lachlan guessed the curtains had been drawn and not even a sliver of moonlight penetrated the blackness. Once again, he used the flashlight on his phone to illuminate his way. He made out two single beds. Both of them were occupied.

Creeping over to the first bed, he peered down at the sleeping face of Montana. She looked so peaceful, like an angel. And then he looked closer. Like her father, a dark stain pooled beneath her head. Filled with a fresh wave of horror, Lachlan reached out and turned the child over.

A bullet had entered above her ear and exited through the back of her head. Though her skin was still warm to the touch, she was lifeless. Lachlan could only guess she'd been murdered by her father.

He forced himself to look at Patrick and his gut flooded with dread. Even with the light from his phone, he could tell that the boy was also dead. White hot fury rushed through him, choking him. He bent over, gasping for breath.

The bastard! The prick! The coward! How *could* he? It was one thing to take his own life, but to take that of his wife and children, too! It was shocking. It was sickening. It was beyond anything Lachlan could ever comprehend.

Lachlan nodded a brief acknowledgement to three of his colleagues who worked to secure the scene. Red and blue and white strobe emergency lights lit up half the street. There were people milling around in the driveway, curious neighbors still in their pajamas, murmuring in shocked voices about the tragedy that had occurred on their block.

Lachlan understood their reaction. He was just as dazed as the bystanders. No matter how hard he tried, he couldn't get the image of the slain Griffin family out of his mind. They'd found evidence that Pam had been shot in the den where two empty whiskey bottles sat on a side table next to the recliner. A third bottle with two fingers remaining in it stood open nearby.

Martin must have shot her not long after she made the emergency call to Lachlan and then carried her upstairs. A bloodied towel was found on the floor beside the bed. From the lack of blood on the staircase, it was surmised Martin had wrapped his wife's head in the towel before taking her upstairs. He'd then laid her down on their bed. It wasn't clear whether he'd attacked the children before or after, but Lachlan guessed it had been after. Pam hadn't said anything about the children being under threat. He was relieved that she'd been spared that much pain, at least.

Still, the level of premeditation required for Martin to murder his wife, carry her to their bed, shoot both of his children and then return to the bedroom and end his life was staggering. The gun's chamber held six bullets. Only four shots had been fired, but the chamber had been empty. Lachlan could only assume Martin had loaded the gun with the minimum bullets required to carry out his deadly mission. The final bullet had been for him.

Lachlan squeezed his eyes closed tightly against another surge of pain. He couldn't conceive what had been going through Martin Griffin's head. Had the man wondered at any time what the hell he was doing as he stood over his wife and kids? It was a devastating, soul-destroying, needless loss of life and Lachlan couldn't help but be angry at his friend.

If things had been that bad, why the hell hadn't Martin sought help? Lachlan had even told him about Ava and suggested therapy. Okay, so Martin was going for a promotion and didn't want to jeopardize his chances, but look what had happened? How could killing his family have been a better option? Did he have any idea he was that close to the edge? Lachlan wanted desperately to believe the answer was an emphatic *no*, but the worse thing was knowing he couldn't be sure.

"Oh, my God! Lachlan! Is it true?"

He looked up and spied Ava running toward him up the drive. She was wearing a ratty old housecoat that had seen much better days. It was vaguely familiar and he suddenly recalled seeing it on her hours earlier. *Had it really only been a matter of hours since he'd felt so blissfully happy and alive?*

He stared at her, dreading the thought of telling her the news, but she was Pam's high school friend. It wasn't fair to keep it from her.

Besides, it was obvious she'd already heard something.

"Yes," he said somberly. "It's true. Martin's murdered his wife and children and then turned the gun on himself."

Ava turned so pale he thought she was about to faint, but instead she cried out in shock and distress and threw herself against him. His arms came around her and held her close. She shuddered and gasped and then began sobbing. Tears pricked the back of his eyes. He stroked her hair and tried to hold himself together.

He needed to be strong for her, for the community and for his men. Once word got around, the whole town would be in shock over the tragic deaths. It would take a long time for them to come to terms with it. No one would ever forget.

Gradually, Ava's sobs quieted and she raised her face to his. Her eyes were red and swollen, filled with confusion and pain.

"W-why?" she stammered. "I-I just don't understand."

It was like all of her training about the human psyche eluded her. She was just as scared and uncertain as the rest of them. He tightened his good arm around her and pulled her back in close against him. "Some things are beyond our understanding."

She remained silent. After a moment, he spoke again.

"How did you know I was here?"

She lifted her head. "I woke and couldn't find

you. Then I realized your truck was gone. I called your phone, but there was no answer, so I decided to go out and look for you. I went to your house, but your truck wasn't there and the house was still and dark. All the bars downtown are closed. So I went to the station. I thought maybe you had gone back there. I... I was worried about you."

Her concern for him warmed his heart, but now wasn't the time to linger over the way she made him feel. "I take it someone at the station told you about the Griffins," he said.

"Yes. The night constable mentioned you were attending an emergency in Helensvale Avenue. As soon as I arrived, I realized it was Pam and Martin's house. I heard some of the neighbors talking about a shooting and that the police had found someone dead."

Shock and disbelief still weighed heavily in her voice. Lachlan understood how she felt. The events of the night had left him shattered. And angry. He was angry at his friend for murdering his family and for not seeking help before things escalated to such a tragic end, but he was also angry at the system and its decided lack of support. Martin had refused to consider therapy because he was afraid it would damage his career prospects. The saddest thing was that he'd been right.

Pressing a kiss to the top of Ava's head, Lachlan set her away from him. "You need to go home. I'll be here for a while, yet."

She stared up at him, her eyes still full of

sadness. "Are you sure? Is there anything I can do?"

"No, but thank you. I appreciate your offer, but this is a crime scene. Besides, you're not exactly dressed for the occasion." His gaze moved lower to her housecoat. "What on earth are you wearing?" He smiled gently, tugging at her robe.

She looked down at herself. Even in the darkness, he saw her blush.

"Oh, my goodness! I forgot all about it! I was in such a hurry to find you, I just pulled on my robe, collected my keys and walked out. I wasn't expecting to..."

Her voice drifted off and she glanced back at the Griffin house, now ablaze with lights. Teams of detectives and forensics officers walked in and out of the building. Lachlan sighed. He needed to get back to work.

Tilting her chin up, he kissed her softly on the mouth. "I love you."

Her arms went around his neck and hugged him tight. "I love you, too."

"Go home and go back to sleep," he urged.

"Yes," she replied, although they both knew she wouldn't. Sleep would be a long time coming for everyone. At that moment, Lachlan couldn't imagine finding restful sleep, ever again.

After watching Ava leave in her car, he turned back toward the crime scene. A few hours earlier, the Griffin house was just like every other house on the tidy street. Now it would be forever known as the house of death. Knowing there was nothing for it but to go back inside and offer to help, he walked up the steps and crossed the front porch. Constable David Jacobs met him at the door.

"Have you seen Becker?" Jacobs asked.

Lachlan shook his head and frowned. "No. Has anyone notified him?"

"I'm not sure. I assumed he'd been called by someone at the station."

"I'll call dispatch and see what I can find out," Lachlan replied and pulled out his phone.

A moment later, the police switchboard operator confirmed that Detective Superintendent Nigel Becker had been contacted thirty minutes earlier and informed of the tragic deaths.

At the news, a fresh wave of anger surged through Lachlan. *Where the hell was he?*

Becker should be here, at the scene of the crime, showing his support for his men. None of them wanted to be here, but they were, because that was their job and it was Becker's job to lead them, to guide them through the darkness, to reassure and support them during the tough times and mourn the tragic loss of their colleague.

But he was nowhere to be found. With an oath, Lachlan scrolled through his contacts and found a number for his boss. When the call was finally picked up, Becker sounded like he'd been roused from sleep.

"Coleridge. What can I do for you?"

"I'm calling about Martin. He's dead and so is his family, but you already knew that. Where the hell are you? We need you here!"

There was a moment of silence and then Becker said, "Yes, it's bloody awful, but there's nothing I can do for Griffin, or his family. As for the rest of you, suck it up and do your job. I'll see you in the morning." And with that, he hung up.

CHAPTER 18

Lachlan's eyes felt gritty and sore and a headache pounded his skull, but his anger remained as white hot and focused as ever. Driving in an easterly direction toward the station, he squinted against the bright, early morning sun. He hoped Becker had found the energy to drag himself out of bed. If he wasn't at the station by the time Lachlan arrived, he'd just as likely make a house call and pull the superintendent out by the hair. After the night Lachlan had endured and all that had happened, he was just in the mood.

He made a right at the intersection and pulled up outside the station with a squeal of brakes. Hours spent at the crime scene had done nothing to improve his mood. He still couldn't believe what Martin had done and he couldn't believe Becker hadn't bothered to attend. For Lachlan, the absence of their boss was the last straw. He was teetering on the edge.

Not even bothering to make an effort to control his anger, he stormed through the front door of the station and continued up the stairs. A younger officer took one look at him and scurried out of the way.

"Is Becker in?" Lachlan growled at him.

"Y-yes, Detective. He's in his office. I-I'm sorry about—"

Lachlan pushed past the officer, not bothering to wait for him to finish. He rounded the corner. The door to Becker's office was closed, but that didn't impede Lachlan for long. Turning the knob, he barged in and planted himself before Becker's untidy desk.

"D-Detective Coleridge! Stop right there! What's the meaning of this?"

Fury like Lachlan had never known boiled up inside his chest. His face burned from the heat of it and his breath rasped in his throat. Though Becker was taller than him and outweighed him by at least fifty pounds, Lachlan rounded the desk and with both hands, grabbed Becker by his shirtfront. Ignoring the pain that shot through his shoulder, he lifted the man off his feet.

"You fucking coward!" he shouted, giving his boss a hard shake. Becker's face went white.

Gasping with anger and pain, Lachlan released the larger man and stumbled back, cursing the fresh wave of agony that burned through his shoulder. "We needed you, you bastard! We needed you there!"

Becker merely shook himself off and found his composure. He regained his seat behind his desk.

"Detective Coleridge, I don't know what you're talking about. You had plenty of men on the scene. A forensics team even came over from Tamworth, or so I was led to believe."

Lachlan stared at Becker and nearly choked on his anger. "You're the *boss*! The team leader! You should have been there for us! We were trying to piece together the meaningless and tragic deaths of one of our own and his entire family and you couldn't even be bothered to get out of bed!"

Lachlan shook his head in disbelief and continued. "No wonder you scoff at counseling. You never get your hands dirty! You never see the shit we do, the kind of crap we're forced to deal with day after day after day. Martin was suffering from depression and post-traumatic stress. You know firsthand the shit he's had to deal with, but did you care? Of course you didn't! You don't give a shit about any of us."

"That's not true, Detective. I—"

"Bullshit!" Lachlan interrupted, unwilling to hear Becker's weak excuses. "If you truly cared you wouldn't have brushed me off when I came to you asking for help. It took a lot of guts for me to approach you. I've been a cop long enough to know how the establishment feels about any sign of weakness, but I was at my lowest ebb. I needed help. In the end, I decided to hell with the job. I needed to get my head right. I had therapy and I'm so much better for it, no thanks to you or to the establishment."

Becker's eyes widened in surprise, but he remained silent. Lachlan was far from finished.

"I could tell Martin was teetering, too," he continued. "I've been there. I know the signs. I suggested he seek counseling, but he was having none of it. He was up for a promotion, you see."

Lachlan let his words sink in. Becker turned an even lighter shade of pale. The bastard knew where this was going. Lachlan's lip curled up in a snarl. He leaned over Becker's desk, in a deliberate effort to intimidate the man. Despite his impressive size, Becker shrank back.

"You see," Lachlan continued in an almost conversational tone, "Martin Griffin knew the system, too. He knew as a law enforcement officer, he was expected to put his life and body on the line in the course of duty. He saw things and did things that no one should ever be forced to see and do and yet he did them regularly and without complaint in an effort to help keep his community safe and provide for his family.

"But when the horror of it all got too much for him, there was nowhere he could turn. Oh, the establishment was there to pay him lip service and provide him with a counselor on the end of the phone. They'd even pay for face-to-face counseling, if he requested. But like you and me and Martin know only too well, any admission of weakness—any sign you aren't coping with the stress on your own—and word gets around.

"Not only are you treated differently by your peers, but you can kiss any hope of a decent promotion good-bye. After all, no one wants a weakling, a pussy on their team. Right, Superintendent?"

Becker's brows came down to meet in the middle. "I don't make the rules, Detective. It sounds very much like you're blaming me for the unfortunate death of Detective Griffin."

The stare Lachlan directed at his boss was deadly. When he spoke, his voice was as cold as the ice that now filled his veins. He leaned even closer to the man before him, until their faces were mere inches apart.

"Make no mistake, Superintendent Becker. Let's be clear on this. *You* killed Martin Griffin and his family, just as surely as if you'd loaded the gun and pulled the trigger. And it's time the world knew it."

Ava made another note in the patient file in front of her and tried to concentrate. Though she'd spent a fair portion of her Sunday at home under the bedcovers, mourning the tragic deaths of the Griffin family, it had been difficult to drag herself out of bed Monday morning and face the day. But, no matter how reluctant she was, she had appointments booked for most of the day and it wasn't fair to her patients to cancel.

Her cell phone vibrated on the desk and she glanced across at the screen. In anticipation of her first appointment, she'd switched the phone to silent mode. The name *Samantha Wolfe* came up on the screen and Ava let out a little sigh. She didn't feel like talking to anyone about what had happened, not even her sister, but there would never be a good time. Sam had known Pam, too, though they'd been in different years. Her sister would be just as devastated as Ava was to hear about her death.

Picking up the phone, she reluctantly answered the call. "Hi, Sam, how are you doing?"

There was a slight pause and then Sam replied. "Ava, are you all right? You sound a little...weird."

"Yes, I'm fine... No, actually, I'm not."

With tears in her eyes, she stumbled through the events that had occurred in the early hours of Sunday morning. Sam was shocked to hear of the terrible deaths.

"I wonder if that's why Lachlan's on the morning news. Rohan just called me and told me to switch on the TV. I'm in the tea room at work. It looks like Lachlan's giving an interview."

Ava frowned. She hadn't spoken to Lachlan since the morning before, outside the Griffin home. She hadn't realized he'd be the one fronting the media. As if he didn't have enough of a burden to carry.

Forcing her anger down, Ava quickly ended the call and searched for the live news stream on her phone. Sure enough, Lachlan had a microphone pinned to his shirt and was talking to the camera. He was dressed in the same clothes he'd worn the night before and looked more than a little tired and disheveled. When Ava turned up the volume she was shocked for a second time.

"This is a travesty!" Lachlan said to the reporter. "The deaths of Martin and Pam Griffin and their young children should never have happened."

"Are you implying this tragedy could have been prevented?" the reporter asked.

Lachlan stared straight down the lens of the camera, his expression fierce. "Yes, that's exactly what I'm saying. Too many police officers take their lives every other day. When are we going to say, enough is enough! When are we going to remove the stigma from depression and post-traumatic stress and get these people the help they need instead of treating them like lepers, as if they're undesirable weak links if they seek help."

"Are you saying the police service is lacking in this area?" the reporter asked.

"Absolutely," Lachlan replied. "But don't take my word for it. Ask any number of police officers. Or better yet, go back and search through some old, and not-so-old records and just take a head count of the number of officers who have committed suicide over the years."

"Many of those have taken their lives after they've left the job," the reporter insisted. "Are you still blaming the police service for their deaths in that instance?"

"Yes," Lachlan replied without flinching. "They've left because they either can't take it anymore or they've been stood down permanently on sick leave. They mightn't be actively on duty when they kill themselves, but make no mistake, it's the job that's brought them to that level of desperation where they see no other way out."

"What do you think should be done about this, Detective Coleridge?" the reporter asked.

"I want to see wholesale changes in the system, starting right at the top. Our police commissioner has a lot to answer for. He and the minister responsible for policing make the rules. It's time those rules were overhauled. It's time attitudes toward mental illness changed and especially the toxic attitude toward it, within the police service. How many more good men and women are we going to let die?" Once again, Lachlan's steady, somber gaze filled the screen.

The interview came to an end and Ava blew out a shaky breath. Her heart was beating double time, but she silently applauded Lachlan's bravery. He'd come a long way from the broken man who couldn't find the courage to seek help. Here he was, fronting the media, speaking in public about the police service's secret shame. She was sure he knew his actions wouldn't be without consequences and that he'd weighed those before stepping forward.

His disloyalty to the thin blue line and wilful breach of the code of silence would have long-term effects on his career and yet, he'd done it anyway. She swiped at the tears of emotion that filled her eyes and smiled. She'd never felt more proud of this man she loved.

"What the hell do you think you're doing?" Becker screamed the minute Lachlan cleared the front entryway of the station.

"What you should have had the guts to do long ago," Lachlan growled without breaking stride.

"Where the hell do you think you're going?" Becker shouted, racing to keep up. "You're not going to go back upstairs and pretend nothing just happened. Not on my watch. Get out! Get out! I don't want you here. We don't need the likes of you."

Lachlan came to a sudden halt and spun on his heel. Two steps higher than his boss on the staircase, Lachlan's face was mere inches from Becker's.

"What?" Lachlan snarled. "You don't need officers with the courage to look people in the eye and say what's right? I told the truth and everyone in the New South Wales Police Service knows it. It's time the rest of the world knew it, too."

"I'll see you dismissed for this, Coleridge," Becker spluttered, pulling back.

Lachlan turned without another word and took the rest of the stairs two at a time. He had no intention of staying. At least, not for the rest of his shift, but he refused to go down without a fight. They'd have to force him to clean out his desk.

Collecting a jacket he'd left in his locker, he shrugged it on, ignoring the fresh pain in his shoulder. No doubt word would have spread. By now, there'd be even more television crews with cameras outside the door. He strode across the squad room and caught the eye of David Jacobs.

"You did good out there, Lachlan," the man said. "Good on you for saying what a lot of us wish like hell we had the guts to say. You have my support."

Lachlan bit down on a sudden surge of emotion and threw the man a grateful nod. What he'd started was only the beginning and it was going to get a lot worse before it got better. He only hoped he'd get to see the day when it *did* get better. That was the reason he'd finally done what he had. It was what he was counting on.

As fast as he'd ascended them, he walked back down the stairs. Becker was still shouting and sputtering in the foyer to anyone who would listen. The man was a disgrace. He spied Lachlan, and launched himself toward him, but Lachlan sidestepped out of the way. He was done with Becker. He had bigger game in his sights.

"I saw you on the news this morning," Ava said as she stroked Lachlan's hair. He'd texted her an hour earlier to ask if he could come over. She'd only just arrived home after a hectic day, but his text sent her fatigue into the ether and she immediately texted him a 'yes'.

She'd met him at the door and without words, he'd taken her in his arms. They'd made sweet, gentle love in silence from the comfort of her bed and now sat on the sofa together. Lachlan's feet dangled over the side and his head was in her lap. He opened his eyes at her comment.

"Really? I thought you were at work?"

"Yes, I was, but Samantha called and told me you were being interviewed."

He smiled softly. "You told your sister about us?"

Ava blushed and shook her head. "No, but she knows that I've met you a few times." She poked him gently in the chest. "Now, don't go trying to change the subject. I'm on to you."

His smile slowly faded. "I had to do it, Ava. I *had* to. Not just for Martin, but for all of us. There are so many officers walking around with undiagnosed mental illnesses. Depression and anxiety, mostly, but a fair number of them have PTSD and the police service hierarchy refuses to acknowledge it."

Favoring his injured shoulder, he sat up, as if unable to remain lying down. He turned to face her.

"Official statistics are only kept on police deaths that occur to serving police officers. No one wants to know about the number of deaths that happen after they retire from the service, or are medically discharged, and in particular, by their own hand. It's not considered acceptable even to mention that kind of thing. No way! We can't go around talking about things like that. If we did, the powers that be might have to acknowledge there is a problem." His voice was thick with sarcasm. "So, we continue to suffer in silence and only those directly affected by it care at all."

Ava's heart broke at the bleakness in Lachlan's voice. His eyes were clouded with pain. This thing went deep and wouldn't be fixed overnight and she wanted to support him every way she could.

"Do you really mean to take this up with the police commissioner?" she asked, recalling what he'd told the reporter.

"Yes, and if I don't get the right answers from him, I'll go even higher. I'll demand a meeting with the state premier before I'm through."

Ava smiled tenderly at the fierce determination in his voice. She knew he'd fight until he had what he wanted and only then would he rest. It had been the same with his marriage. He'd tried to hold it together until it became obvious things were no longer going to work and even then, he'd made the decision not to contest the pending divorce—not for his benefit, but because he believed it was the best thing for his children.

She thought of the way he'd been when he'd first come to see her as a patient and was proud of how far he'd come. She loved that she'd had a tiny part to do with his healing and couldn't wait to spend more time by his side.

"Your locum must be nearly finished," Lachlan murmured in a quieter tone. "I seem to recall you telling me at the Griffin barbeque that you were only taking over from Phoebe Jamison for a month."

"Yes," Ava said and couldn't help the surge of disappointment at the reminder. She wondered what would become of her and Lachlan's new relationship when she had to leave.

Her life was in the city. She had her own private practice at the Sydney Harbour Hospital. He was a country cop. Though he'd been born in the city, as far as she knew he had no intention of moving back. Then her thoughts snagged on something else he'd said and she forgot about their dilemma.

Phoebe Jamison. Her friend and colleague and the daughter of John Jamison: the state premier. She sat forward.

Lachlan lifted his head at her sudden movement and turned to look at her.

"What is it?"

"Phoebe. She's John Jamison's daughter."

"The premier?"

"Yes."

"I didn't know that."

Ava shrugged. "She doesn't advertise it. People have their own opinions about the government, good or bad. She prefers to live her life the way she wants, free from other people's judgements."

"Fair enough."

"But, she *is* the premier's daughter." She stared at him and waited for him to make the obvious connection. It didn't take long.

His eyes lit up in understanding and a smile widened his lips. "She's the premier's daughter," he repeated slowly. "How well do you know her?"

The sudden urgency in his voice made her chuckle. "Well enough. You see where this is going?"

"Oh, I see where this is going all right. If I could get a meeting with the premier, I could bypass the commissioner altogether. I'd rather talk to the butcher, not the block."

Ava chuckled again and shook her head. She was sure the premier and the police commissioner would be appalled by Lachlan's metaphor, but it was apt. Whilst the commissioner was powerful in his own circles, the premier had the power to influence legislation. He could even convince his party to pass new laws to give police officers greater support and more access to real solutions that would make a difference.

It was a good plan. All she needed to do was make the introductions and hope Phoebe had enough influence over her father to convince him to meet with Lachlan.

CHAPTER 19

Lachlan wiped his sweaty palms on his suit pants and tried to quell his nerves. Phoebe Jamison had worked on her father more quickly than he and Ava could have imagined and now he found himself waiting in the grand reception area outside the premier's office in Parliament House, located in the state's capital. It was only a fortnight after his first TV interview.

The speed with which the premier had agreed to see him might also have something to do with the fact that Lachlan had been in high demand by several national current affairs television shows and talkback radio stations. He'd lost count of the number of interviews he'd given since the morning of Martin's death, both in person and over the phone.

He was more tired than he could remember, but if his speaking out meant that people in a position of power listened, then it was worthwhile. He refused to let the death of Martin and his family be in vain or let other officers continue to suffer in silence.

The door to the premier's office opened and a man who introduced himself as one of the premier's advisors ushered Lachlan inside. John Jamison looked a little younger and thinner than he appeared on television, but he was still a portly man. The overhead lights bounced off his shiny balding head, momentarily distracting Lachlan from his purpose. He blinked, averted his gaze and then took the seat that was offered.

The premier nodded in Lachlan's direction from his position behind his large, dark cedar desk. The advisor took up a position in one corner. After exchanging introductions and brief pleasantries, the premier settled his bulk, shifted a few bundles of paper out of the way and clasped his fingers together in front of him.

"Now, Detective Coleridge. I understand you requested to meet with me about the support available to mentally unstable police officers. Is that correct?"

Lachlan held onto his temper. It wouldn't do to antagonize the man who could help him so early into their conversation. He forced a smile.

"I appreciate you taking the time to see me, Premier. And yes, I do have some concerns. But not about mentally unstable police officers. My fears and concerns are for police officers suffering PTS and who are forced all too often to witness unforgettable atrocities. Detective Constable Martin Griffin was a fine officer with a decade of experience. He recently took his life and the lives of his wife and children."

The premier *tut tutted* and shook his head slowly back and forth. "Yes, it was a terrible tragedy. I first heard about it on the news and of course, I was later briefed by the commissioner. I understand the deceased was a colleague of yours. I'm very sad for your loss, but I'm not sure what these deaths have to do with anything."

The premier lasered Lachlan with the piercing Jamison gaze he was renowned for, but Lachlan refused to flinch. Drawing in a deep breath, he returned the premier's forthright stare.

"With all due respect, Premier, the deaths of Martin Griffin and his family have everything to do with my reason for being here. Sadly, Martin's suicide isn't the first—by far. Nobody knows the exact number of officers who have taken their own lives, but I believe the numbers would be staggering. The truly tragic thing is that many of those deaths could have been avoided."

The premier appeared unconvinced. "There's no proof those deaths were job-related. The majority of the suicides you're referring to happened after the officers left the police service. There is evidence quite a number of them had drug and alcohol problems and significant personal issues at the time of their deaths. Isn't that right, Stanley?"

The premier turned toward his advisor, who offered his boss a nod. "That's correct, Premier."

Lachlan's temper rose along with his frustration,

but he forced himself to remain calm. He had to make both of them see.

"That might be so, but what the reports fail to state is that the drug and alcohol and personal problems arose because of an inability by those officers to cope with the extreme psychological demands of their jobs. I accept that none of them came across a fatal car accident and then went home and killed himself because of that one incident, but the causal link is there, just the same—and in an accumulative way. You have to understand, this illness is insidious. It's months and often years of facing that kind of trauma that results in these tragic and preventable deaths."

The premier's expression sharpened. "Preventable? Are you blaming the police service, Detective? Are you saying the support systems in place at the moment are inadequate? Stanley has assured me we provide every police officer with free, direct phone access to the Employee Assistance Program any time they need it. In the case of truly horrific circumstances—attending a fatal car accident, or something of that nature, like you mentioned—I understand it is accepted protocol for team leaders to insist that their officers receive telephone counseling. Are you telling me that's not happening?"

"Yes, Premier. You're correct, but the problem doesn't only lie there, where it's obvious. The problem is systemic, and lies in the ingrained attitude of senior officers who denigrate anyone who puts up his hand for help."

Lachlan shook his head; his frustration was

harder and harder to control. "The thing is," he added, "we've all seen the EAP posters around the tea room and in the corridors—telling us how and where to get help, but the moment anyone admits to needing it or seeking it, they're crucified—by their colleagues and very often, by their boss."

The premier narrowed his eyes and stared at Lachlan. "Have you had personal experience with this, Detective?"

Lachlan held his gaze. "Yes. I have. And so have many others. It's the worst kept secret in the office. The judgement and ridicule isn't necessarily overt, although sometimes it is. About a month ago, I finally found the courage to approach my commanding officer and tell him I was struggling emotionally with the demands of the job; that I needed help."

"And what response did you get?"

"I was told to man up and heal myself with alcohol."

The premier's eyes widened in surprise. "That was certainly direct."

Lachlan grimaced. "Unfortunately, it wasn't an isolated or unpredictable response, Premier. This attitude of casual dismissal of an illness so real and terrible is universal throughout the police service and it's perpetuated from within the highest levels. You don't need to take my word for it. Interview any officer, past or present, and if they have the courage, they'll tell you the same thing."

Jamison leaned his bulk back against his leather chair. It squeaked in protest. Pinning

Lachlan with an assessing gaze, he mused, "Why are you only now bringing this to everyone's attention, Detective? You've been incredibly vocal on the radio and television these last couple of weeks. I get that your friend and colleague recently took his and his family's lives, but you've served as a police officer for at least a decade. You must have seen your fair share of terrible things and other evidence of this so-called dismissive attitude long before now. What's given you the fortitude to come forward at this time?"

Lachlan stared back at him and tried to gather his thoughts. Martin's death had certainly given him impetus, but there was more to it than that. It was getting help through therapy with Ava that had finally given him the courage to break his silence.

"Up until now, Premier, my thoughts have been far from clear and my ability to take action has been impeded by my emotional instability caused by the very kind of thing I mentioned. Fatal accidents, tragic deaths, senseless violence. I've been up and down and all over the place. For a long time, I've been floundering and needed help. I never thought about suicide, but I can understand how officers suffering from mental illnesses get to that scary place. They lose their resiliency and because they're handling additional loads of baggage in the form of PTSD... Well they reach a point where there's just no way to carry more."

He drew in a ragged breath and continued. "These officers have families to support, demands of home and community as well as the inordinate load to serve and protect individuals, businesses, communities and government that they face at work. Any person, experiencing the gauntlet of trauma day in and day out, would experience the same. Only ordinary people can go, unscathed, to counselors or psychiatrists and get the help they need. They move along with their career plans, advance the circumstances of their family...and participate fully in life. For a serving police officer, those things don't come that easy.

"Admitting to my superior that I was struggling was difficult. I was fearful of jeopardizing my career. I've worked hard to get where I am. I've put up with things no normal person should and I did it because I love my job. I love being a cop. But make no mistake, Premier. It comes at a price. It takes its toll in the dark and silent hours before dawn and then, even when the sun's shining, the blackness doesn't completely leave. Families fall apart. Lives blister... It was only after my own recent family breakup, I realized I had a problem and I needed to get help. I was one of the lucky ones who sought help outside work. It's given me the strength and clear mindedness to know speaking out about this is the right thing to do. Martin's death was tragic, and became the catalyst—for pushing for change."

Lachlan's breath came fast. He leaned forward, his heart thumping. "Knowing how many of my colleagues are out there suffering, I can no longer turn a blind eye without doing something to help them. Some have found the courage to seek help, but they're being crucified for it. Others are too afraid of what it will mean for their careers if they admit to any weakness—and *they* are the ones I feel for most because they're the ones most likely to end up another dark statistic."

Anger stirred through him at the thought and he clenched his fists. He glared at the premier. "How many more brave and loyal officers will you let die before you step in and say, enough is enough? Tell me, Premier? I'd really like to know because if one more officer takes his life on your watch through the lack of support of those around him, it will be one life too many and make no mistake—it will be on you."

The premier stared at him with narrowed eyes, but finally heaved a sigh. "You make a good case, Detective. If what you say is true, there are good police officers suffering without support or help and punished when they seek it. The thought that some of our strongest and bravest might even have arrived at the point where they've committed suicide saddens me beyond words."

Lachlan eyeballed him, unmoved by his rhetoric. "You talk pretty words, Premier, but I'm more interested in action. What are you going to do about this? What are you going to do to save the lives of Australia's police officers? They have sworn to serve and protect you and your family and all the families of this fine State, but who is protecting them, Premier? Who is protecting *them*?"

A red flush started up the premier's neck and he squirmed beneath Lachlan's unrelenting glare.

Averting his gaze, Jamison picked up a bundle of papers and moved them to another part of his desk.

"I-I'll look into it, Detective Coleridge. I'll call a meeting with the police minister and the commissioner. I assume one, or both of them, have all of the statistics you're talking about."

Lachlan offered him a bitter smile. "That's the thing, Premier, and that's part of the reason why we have this problem. Like I mentioned before, a lot of the suicides by police officers or former police officers are summarily dismissed by those in charge as being caused by other reasons." He stared pointedly at the man across from him. "Just like you did."

The rekindled knowledge that this went on far too often sent hot anger flooding through Lachlan's veins once again. This time, he let the premier feel the full force of his fury.

"Nobody wants to admit, Premier, that it's the job and the lack of support dealing with the shit that comes our way every single day that's causing good men and women to take their lives. The official stats mean nothing. Go and make further enquires, on your own. I *dare* you!"

Lachlan's breath came harsh and fast, but he refused to back down. Ignoring the concern that filled the face of Jamison's advisor, Lachlan glared at the premier and let him have it again.

"Set up an independent enquiry into the deaths of cops, employed, retired, on medical leave, or who quit, who have attempted or taken their own lives. Remove the rose-tinted glasses and have the guts to see it for what it is. Admit that *you*, as a government, are failing these brave officers and the families that love them. *They* are the ones forced to deal with the devastating consequences."

The premier contemplated him in silence, a frown etching deep grooves into his face. Lachlan struggled to slow down his breathing and get his temper back under control.

"You've made your point, Detective," Jamison said at last, "and I will certainly be taking it under advisement." He glanced at his advisor and then back to Lachlan. "You have my word, I'll meet with the minister and the commissioner and thereafter, I'll formulate a plan."

Lachlan stared at him. "So, you'll set up an enquiry?"

The premier nodded, his expression grave. "If that's what is warranted, I'll make sure it happens. It has to go through the party, of course, but you'll be pleased to know my opinion carries a good deal of weight in these things. Your frequent appearances in the media have done your cause no harm. People are talking about it and wondering. Questions are being asked. Maybe the time is ripe for a change?"

Then the premier shook his head slowly, his eyes heavy with sadness. "The possibility that even some of these deaths might have been prevented distresses me. And you're right. No one else should be allowed to die. Not because of their working conditions and certainly not from lack of support. This is the twenty-first century and we live in a first world country. People should not be dying due to stress and inadequate support on their job, and that's the end of it."

———————

Lachlan headed along Macquarie Street, away from the premier's office. The mid-morning Sydney streets were busy with noisy traffic and crowds of pedestrians he barely noticed. He felt like he'd gone a round or two with Danny Green, was dazed and a little confused, but all in all, he was satisfied with the outcome of his meeting.

It seemed like he had finally gotten through to the man who ran the state and was quietly hopeful some real change would come of it that would see long term benefits for him and his colleagues. It saddened him that Martin wouldn't benefit, but if it prevented other cops in the future from getting to that point of no return, then it was worth it.

His thoughts strayed to Ava. He wanted so much to talk to her. Though they'd attended the Griffin family funeral together, in the days afterwards, he'd put all of his focus on arranging media opportunities and fronting the press. Ava had returned to the city a few days earlier. It tore his heart apart to see her go, but there was nothing he could do. Her stint in the country was finished.

Making his way through Hyde Park, Lachlan crossed over Elizabeth Street and tugged out his phone. He hadn't seen Ava since she'd left, though he'd arrived in Sydney the day before. His hours had been spent prepping for, and giving interviews. And, he'd been nervous at the thought of approaching her again now that she was back on her home turf. Back where she belonged.

What if he had been nothing more than a passing diversion while she'd been playing country doctor? She'd turned his life upside down and all of it had been for the better. He couldn't bear the thought their time together might have come to an end.

He'd told her he loved her and she'd given him the same assurance, but that had been in Moree. Would she feel differently now that she'd returned to the city? He didn't know and the uncertainty was eating a hole in his gut. Now that his interview with the premier was over, he needed to see her and find out once and for all.

Dialing her cell number, he waited for her to answer and was equal parts relieved and nervous when she did.

"Hi, Lachlan. It's lovely to hear from you." She sounded nervous, too and the knowledge made him feel better.

"Hi. I'm in Sydney. I thought we might be able to meet somewhere. For a coffee, or even lunch. I haven't eaten since last night."

"Really? What happened to breakfast?"

"I had a meeting with the premier this morning. I was too nervous to eat. In fact, I've just left his office."

"That's great. I've been watching you on the TV. You don't look the least bit nervous."

"I'm glad. At least the whole world doesn't know," he joked.

"How did it go?"

"With the premier?"

"Yes. Did he give you a fair hearing?"

"Yes, in the end, I think I even managed to convince him about the seriousness and prevalence of the problem. He's agreed to look at it, possibly as a formal enquiry."

"That's a fantastic result, Lachlan! You must be so pleased."

"I am," he replied, but couldn't help but think of Martin and his family and how Lachlan's actions had come too late. The answer to the premier's question about why he hadn't stepped forward earlier, was complex. He vowed silently to take the time to sort it out.

"I have another patient due in a few minutes and my afternoon is fully booked, so unfortunately, I can't do coffee and I won't have time in between appointments to meet you for lunch, but how about dinner? Do you have any plans?"

Lachlan's heart skipped a beat and he swallowed a fresh lump of nerves. "D-Dinner sounds fine. Where would you like to meet?"

"How about you come over to my place? I don't live far from the city and I have a sensational view of the Harbour."

Lachlan's pulse lifted another notch. *Surely a woman who'd lost interest wouldn't invite him to her house?* "Sounds great," he managed.

"Good. I should be home by six. I'll text you the address. Do you like Thai food?"

"I love Thai."

"Great. I'll pick up some takeout on my way home. Does that sound all right?"

"That sounds perfect." He ended the call and couldn't stop grinning.

CHAPTER 20

Ava walked up the steps that led to her second floor condo and tried hard to quell her nerves. She hadn't seen Lachlan since she'd returned to Sydney. Should she kiss him hello, or simply offer her hand? Should she pretend their affair in Moree had never happened? She didn't know if their relationship was supposed to continue, or if it had been left behind in the bush.

Upon Phoebe's return to Moree, Ava had gone

over Phoebe's client files with her. Her friend had been relieved and grateful Ava had managed to keep the practice running smoothly. When Ava explained about Martin Griffin, Phoebe was only too happy to contact her father and request that he meet with Lachlan.

For Ava, the days before she returned to the city had passed in a blur. Lachlan was busy giving interviews to media outlets, despite an order from his boss to have nothing further to do with them. He'd told her he'd been advised, in no uncertain terms, that the police service had its own media unit whose job it was to deal with any interview requests. Ava couldn't help but admire him when he refused to be silenced.

She'd quietly and efficiently packed her bags and returned the key to her apartment. She'd stopped by his place to bid him a solemn farewell and had then caught the plane to Sydney. She hadn't spoken of the future or made any promises and he hadn't offered any in return. Disappointed and heartsick, she'd returned home.

But now he was in Sydney, and he'd called her, and she was about to see him again. Butterflies swarmed in her stomach.

"Hi, there."

The familiar, deep voice made her pulse jump. She looked up in time to see Lachlan standing there, holding the door open for her. He must have been waiting in the foyer near the bank of elevators, watching for her. The thought warmed her through and filled her with another rush of nerves.

"H-how are you?" she stammered and immediately blushed.

He smiled. "I'm great. It's good to see you."

He stepped forward and reached for the bags of takeout she carried in her hands and then pecked her on the cheek. Flustered, she managed to respond.

"Yes, thank you. It's… It's good to see you, too." Moving away, she went to the elevator and pressed the button.

"We could probably walk," she said to fill the silence. "I'm only on the second floor."

"It's a nice building," he said looking around at the carpeted foyer and freshly painted walls. "How long have you lived here?"

"Only a few years. I was broke when I finished college. It took me that long to save for the deposit."

She smiled and he laughed. His gaze lingered on her lips. All of a sudden, she couldn't breathe. Her heart pounded. Her mouth went dry. She stared at him hungrily, wanting to feel him close.

As if reading her mind, his eyes darkened with emotion and he moved closer until his suit pants brushed against her skirt. She swallowed a gasp.

Ding.

The sound of the elevator arriving startled her and she jumped away. More nervous than ever, she didn't know where to look. With her gaze trained forward, she walked straight into the elevator and turned and stared at the numbers above the door. Lachlan strode in behind her, carrying their dinner.

The aroma of the Thai food wafted toward her and her stomach rumbled. She blushed and giggled nervously and risked a glance in Lachlan's direction.

He grinned at her. "It sounds like you're as hungry as I am."

She stared at his mouth and then dropped her gaze lower to skim over his broad chest and narrow hips. He was dressed in a charcoal-gray suit and a pale blue business shirt. A navy-and-silver striped tie hung around his neck. He wore the clothes well and she was reminded of the firm muscles that lay hidden beneath. Once again, her breathing quickened.

"I-I missed lunch," she stammered, remembering she hadn't responded.

"I gathered," he murmured and then shot her a look so hot her pulse pounded.

Without a word, he dropped the takeout bags to the floor and pressed her up against the back wall of the elevator, holding her in place with his body. His lips came down on hers, fierce and urgent. Her glasses dug into his face, but she clung to his shoulders and kissed him back, loving the feel of him in her arms. She didn't even hear the elevator announce their arrival.

The doors slid open and she was left staring at her elderly neighbor who had been waiting outside the elevator. Mrs Christie's eyes were wide behind her thick-rimmed glasses and her mouth gaped open in surprise.

With frantic haste, Ava shoved Lachlan away and bent and hurriedly gathered up the takeout.

Pushing him out of the elevator, she kept her gaze trained on the carpet and mumbled a hasty greeting.

"Hi, Mrs Christie."

"Ava, it's nice to see you," her neighbor said, recovering from her shock. "You're home a little earlier than usual. And who is this?"

Ava came to a sudden halt. Keeping her back to her neighbor, she squeezed her eyes shut and begged silently for the woman to leave. "It's… It's no one, Mrs Christie. Have a good night." She took another step forward and then groaned under her breath when she heard Lachlan say, "I'm Lachlan Coleridge. I'm Ava's boyfriend."

Ava tensed and then relaxed. Had he just said he was her *boyfriend?* She grinned and almost did a little dance until she remembered where she was. Turning back to face the two people behind her, she walked back to where they stood.

"Mrs Christie, this is Lachlan. Lachlan, this is Mrs Christie."

Lachlan grinned at the old woman and took her hand, his eyes twinkling. "It's lovely to meet you, Mrs Christie."

A blush stole across the woman's wrinkled cheeks, but she offered him a pleased smile. "Oh, my! Aren't you a charmer! And sinfully good looking!" She winked at Ava. "I'd say this one's a keeper."

Now it was Ava's turn to blush. Heat crept up her neck. Unable to look at Lachlan, she kept her face turned toward her neighbor. "I think so, too," she whispered, loudly enough for Lachlan to hear.

She turned in time to see the light in his eyes flare brighter. He stared at her and she couldn't look away. It was only the sound of Mrs Christie clearing her throat that brought Ava back to her senses.

"It's nice to see you, Mrs Christie. Take care now." Not waiting for the woman's response, Ava turned tail and almost ran in the direction of her apartment.

Setting the food on the kitchen counter, Ava gave Lachlan a quick tour of her place. She was relieved she'd cleaned up before she left for work that morning. It wasn't that she was messy—just a little untidy. It didn't offend her to leave dirty dishes in the sink overnight or leave a bath towel on the floor. Okay, so she eventually got around to cleaning up, but what did it matter if things weren't done right away? She lived alone. There had been no one to complain. Until now.

Her body heated anew at the thought that she and Lachlan might resume their relationship. She wasn't quite sure how it would work, but the time away from him had proven to her that he was more important to her than her job, her condo and even her city life.

She grinned wryly. She must have the love bug pretty darn bad. A month ago, the thought of giving up her fast-paced lifestyle for the country would have given her a case of hives.

"What's so funny?" Lachlan murmured, coming up behind her and drawing her into his arms.

She stared up at him and memorized his

features: the tiny dark flecks in his green eyes; the fine wrinkles that lined his forehead; the thick auburn hair that had grown a little longer than he usually wore it; and the tiny scar on his chin that she still hadn't asked him about. There wasn't anything she didn't love about him and she hoped he felt the same.

"I missed you," she said softly and laid her palm against his cheek.

He turned his head and kissed her hand and her stomach did a flip. The simplest of actions and yet it had the power to turn her insides into a quivering mass of need. Her heart thumped, her breath came faster. She pressed herself against him. Reaching up, she brought his head down to hers and kissed him.

This time, their kiss was less frantic, as if they were satisfied they had all the time in the world. The night that had fallen outside the plate glass window was theirs to savor and enjoy.

"I thought you were hungry," Lachlan murmured against her lips, removing her glasses and tossing them in the direction of the couch.

"I am." She nipped at his chin. "Starving."

With her arms threading around behind his neck, she opened her mouth and kissed him like she could never get enough. His arms came around her and held her close. He matched her kiss for kiss.

His spicy cologne filled her senses and tickled her nose. She buried her face against the soft skin of his neck and inhaled. He smelled so warm and familiar. He felt like she was home.

Despite the fact her father had died when she was very young, she'd grown up feeling loved and secure. Lachlan made her feel the same way. She could hardly put it into words. She wanted to be with him forever, safe, protected and loved in his arms. She hardly dared to believe he felt like she did.

As if sensing her fragile mood, he lifted his head and stared down at her, his gaze probing. "Are you all right?"

She nodded, even as tears pricked her eyes. "Yes, I...I'm fine. I'm just really happy to see you. I didn't realize how hard it was going to be not seeing you every day, or nearly every day. I... I don't want to spend that much time away from you ever again."

"I don't want to be apart from you, either, but we live in different towns. On the way down here, I was thinking about ways we could make it work, but I'm a seven-hour drive from the city. It's even a two-hour flight."

She smiled, but it was shaky. "Not quite. The flight's an hour and forty-five minutes, to be exact. I know because I just did it."

Lachlan's expression remained serious. He moved away from her and went to sit on the couch. With apprehension sliding ominously through her veins, Ava forced herself forward. Reaching for her glasses, she put them back on and took a seat beside him.

"Talk to me, Lachlan."

He cursed quietly under his breath. "I want to be with you, Ava. I want it more than I want anything else, but I'm not cut out for a long distance relationship. It's going to be hard enough traveling to see my kids."

He drew in a deep breath and Ava stilled. "W-what are you saying?" she stammered, bracing herself against his answer.

He turned his gaze toward her. Her breath caught at the agony in his eyes.

"I don't want to lose you, Ava. Along with my children, you're the best thing that ever happened to me." He exhaled on a heavy sigh. "That's why I'm prepared to put in for a transfer and move back to the city. I want to do everything I can to make this work."

Ava reared back in surprise. It was the last thing she'd expected to hear. "But, you love living in the country!"

He took her hand and held her gaze. "I love being with you more."

Ava's heart filled so she thought it might burst right out of her chest. Tears filled her eyes, fogging her glasses. Letting go of her hand, he reached over and removed the offending eyewear again and tenderly wiped the moisture away.

"Why the tears?" he asked softly. "I thought you'd be happy."

"I am happy," she replied, offering him a wobbly smile. "They're happy tears."

He smiled back at her, his eyes full of love. "Oh, I see." He leaned over and gently brushed her lips with his.

Again and again, he tasted her mouth, as if memorizing its shape and form and feel and when his tongue sought entry, she eagerly let him in. Her arms came up around his neck and she kissed him with all the love and passion she held inside. Need built quickly. She was tense and tingly, aching for more.

"I want you, Lachlan," she murmured against his lips.

"I want you, too. Hell, it's been so long."

"Three whole days," she mumbled. "Way too long."

He growled low in his throat. "How about we take this into the bedroom? The view from the couch is great, but it's not exactly comfortable here."

Ava laughed. Her two-seater sofa was made of Italian leather and had cost her a bomb, but it was decidedly cramped with the two of them spread across it. She pulled gently out of Lachlan's embrace and levered herself up. Offering him her hand, she tugged him upright and then led him down the hall.

The queen-sized, four-poster bed was another extravagance she probably didn't need because most of the time she was alone in it, but she'd always loved the romantic nature of the gauzy fabric that hung off the frame. She also liked to be able to stretch and roll when she was in bed and the extra space allowed her to do that. And, the room was large enough that the bed certainly didn't seem out of place.

"Nice bed," Lachlan commented and then followed it with a wink and a cheeky grin. "Plenty of room."

Ava's cheeks heated, but she held his gaze. "Yes, well, I like to be comfortable."

"Oh, yes. It's very important to be comfortable. Now, come over here and let me see if I can make you...comfortable."

His voice was low and husky and emotion glinted in his eyes. Her pulse went into overdrive. She sauntered over, swaying her hips and was gratified to see desire flare brighter in his eyes.

With a feeling of womanly power surging through her veins, she eased off her suit jacket and tossed it over the back of the chaise. Her hands went to the buttons of her pale lavender, tailored blouse. Slowly, teasingly, she released each button until her shirt gaped open. With her gaze on his, she shrugged out of the garment and threw it in the direction of her jacket. Her breasts stood high and proud, filling the cups of her white lace bra.

Lachlan stood transfixed, his eyes dark with need. His fists were clenched like he was holding himself back. His chest rose and fell rapidly. Ava smiled, feeling all powerful and a little in awe at his reaction. It wasn't like he hadn't seen her naked, but somehow, the time apart made it feel like this was their first time.

She relished the feeling and held his gaze as her hands went around to the back of her skirt. Releasing the catch, she slid down the zipper and shimmied it slowly down over her hips. Stepping out of it, she twirled the skirt around her finger and gave him a flirty look before tossing it toward the growing pile of clothes.

Clad only in high heels, black stockings and her underwear, she sauntered toward him once again. This time, she came close enough that her breasts brushed against his shirt. She shivered at the impact and hoped she could see the striptease through to the end. Her own needs were becoming more and more urgent but she silently ordered herself to be patient. They had all night to love each other, to rediscover every erotic zone. There was no need to rush, no matter what her body screamed to her.

With that thought firmly in mind, she reached out and loosened his tie. The silk slid easily between her fingers. Without taking her eyes off him, she let it fall to the floor. She splayed her fingers across his broad chest, loving the feel of his hard muscles. Pushing his jacket off his shoulders, her hands went to the buttons of his shirt.

As slowly and precisely as she'd worked on hers, she eased his shirt buttons from their restraints and then tugged the fabric out of his suit pants. Spreading the shirt open, she looked her fill at the magnificence of his chest.

Broad and muscular and sprinkled with hair, he was a perfect specimen of a man. Her gaze drifted over him, across the wide expanse of smooth skin, to the flat planes of his belly and beyond. Unable to help herself, she touched him.

Sliding her hand over his smooth, heated skin, she flicked at his nipples with her fingernails and heard his sharp intake of breath. Moving lower, she slid her hand across his abdomen and then lower still, until her fingers were inside his pants.

His cock was hard and throbbing, heated to the touch. She fitted her hand around it and squeezed.

"Jesus," he groaned and closed his eyes as if the sight of her hand on his erection was too much.

"You feel rather...eager," she teased, squeezing him again.

"Minx," he muttered, with hooded eyes. "Your turn will come."

Ava's belly somersaulted at the velvet promise in his voice. Anticipation danced along her nerve endings. She removed her hand from his cock and focused on the belt around his waist. Releasing the black leather from the shiny silver buckle, she eased the belt through the belt loops and let it go. It hit the carpet with a soft thud. With her gaze fixed on his, she undid the button on his pants and slid the zipper down.

Once again, she reached under his underwear and found his thick cock. Her finger brushed across the tip and found warm moisture there. She spread it around and around his head, massaging as she went. He stared at her, his body tense, waiting for her to finish.

"You're driving me mad," he muttered, his voice now hoarse with need.

She smiled. "Good." With that, she kneeled before him.

Reaching up, she tugged at his loosened pants and, along with his underwear, dragged them all the way down. They pooled at his feet and he kicked them off, then stood there, naked except for his shoes and socks.

Licking her lips, she stared at his cock. It jutted out from his nest of dark hair, thick and proud and glistening. Still on her knees, she leaned forward and took him into her mouth. He groaned in relief and excitement and cupped the back of her head with his hands, holding her in place.

She sucked him hard and deep, taking as much of his length as she could. He groaned again and threw back his head, his eyes closed against the torment.

"Do you like that?" she murmured.

"Hell, yes. Too much," he groaned.

She swirled the tip of her tongue around his engorged head, tasting the fluid that gathered there. Her hand reached up to cup his balls, squeezing them gently. They were full and heavy and filled her hand. He shuddered against her touch.

Stepping back, he freed himself as his cock slid out of her mouth. "Enough. Get on the bed. It's your turn."

His gruff commands excited her, as did the determined look in his heated gaze. Anticipation shivered through her and she did as she was told. He followed her onto the four poster and pressed her back against the covers. Kneeling between her legs, with his cock stiff and hard, he leaned forward and unclasped her bra.

His erection slid along her stomach at the same time her breasts sprang free. He tossed the bra over his shoulder and then reached out to cup the soft mounds. Squeezing and massaging, he flicked her hard nipples with his thumbs. She gasped.

Desire raced through her and centered in the heated place between her thighs.

"And you thought you were the only one who got to tease," he rasped and then he bent and took one of her nipples in his mouth. He bit down gently and she gasped again as another surge of hot need found its mark.

Desire built up inside her, heavy and urgent and throbbing. She squirmed beneath him, desperate to have his cock.

"Please," she gasped. "I need you. I need you inside me. *Now.*"

To her chagrin, he looked down at her and chuckled. "Ah, not so smug, now, are you? You'll have my cock when I say so. You're going to be driven to the point of madness before I finish with you. Just like you did to me," he added with a satisfied smile.

Sliding slowly down her body, he came to a stop between her thighs. Her stockings were rolled down, one by one and tossed over the side of the bed. Next, his tongue swept over her lacy mound. Burying his face against her heat, he breathed in deeply of her scent.

She squirmed again. "Lachlan, please."

"*Shh,*" he demanded roughly. "You had your turn. Now, be quiet, while I have mine."

His voice brooked no argument, but she wasn't in the least bit scared. Instead, desire surged through her again, setting every nerve ending on fire.

He pulled aside the scrap of lace that covered her femininity. His finger traced her soft lips and then he tried to move his hand lower. The tiny panties restricted his access. With a muffled oath, he tore them off her and tossed them away.

She gasped in shock and excitement. Never had he treated her this way. She loved the feeling of being dominated, just as she'd dominated him earlier. With a sigh of relief, his hand cupped her bare mound and his tongue laved across her sensitive skin. Once again, his fingers moved lower.

He parted her lips and then bent his head and licked her from top to bottom. His tongue probed her entrance and pushed inside and then was replaced by a couple of his fingers. Moving rhythmically in and out, his tongue kept up the external pressure. She twisted her hips and cried out from the torment, but he refused to give her relief.

"Do you like that?" he rasped, mirroring the words she'd said to him. Beyond words, she could only moan her consent and still, he wasn't finished.

With her legs spread wide, he licked and sucked and nipped at her sensitive flesh. His fingers continued their wicked onslaught until she was mindless with desire.

"Lachlan, let's call it even," she gasped, her body white hot with need. "I can't take any more of this torture. I need you. Please, fuck me. Now."

The profanity shocked her, but Lachlan merely smiled. "You want me to fuck you?" he asked.

She stared up at him. "Yes."

Without another word, he rammed into her, filling her in a single hard thrust. Catching her breath, she clung to his shoulders, hanging onto him for dear life. She was already so close to the precipice, so close to exploding into a million pieces and falling mindlessly over the other side. His frantic thrusts continued and all of a sudden, she was there.

Toppling and spinning out of control, her body convulsed around his. Her fingernails dug into his skin, not easing until the last shudder had finished. Breathing hard, she opened her eyes and stared up at him in wonder.

His face was tense, his expression unfocused. His eyes were glazed with need. Teetering on the edge, he picked up speed, thrusting his hips hard against her. Moments later, he cried out in relief and collapsed in a heap against her.

His breath was harsh and hot in her ear. His heart thudded against her chest. She held him close and kissed his hair, exhausted and content. It was a long time afterward, wrapped in each other's arms that they had the energy to speak.

"You don't have to move to the city," she said, idling running her fingers up and down his arm. I'm happy to relocate to Moree. I enjoyed my time living there. It's a friendly community and closer to your kids."

He smiled down at her. "I love that you'd give up your life here for me, but it's not necessary. Kristy's going to make a home on the Central Coast, so it's closer for me to travel from Sydney to visit with my kids. I... I can't wait for you to meet them."

She pulled his head down for a soft kiss. "I hope they like me," she murmured.

"They're gonna love you," he promised.

"Are you sure you don't mind leaving the country?"

"Not at all. I enjoyed my time there and it's definitely a more relaxed lifestyle, but I don't mind living in the city. I was born here, after all. And I can spend more time with my mom. I'm sure she's been lonely since Dad died. Then there's Rohan—"

"And Sam," she interrupted with a smile.

"Of course. How could I forget? Their wedding was what brought us together."

"And aren't you glad they did!" she teased.

He kissed her again. This time, he lingered over her lips. "Absolutely."

Chapter 21

Dear Diary,

Did I ever imagine it might come to this? That there was nothing left for me, but the end of my family as I know it? I fear the answer is no, and yet, I am filled with equal parts terror and sad resignation. I realize now it's the only way. I've lived a lie for so many years, it's time I brought it to an end.

I might have scoffed at the hours of therapy, but they have helped me make my decision. I'm not beyond appreciating the irony. Therapy has brought me a measure of acceptance and peace. Now, I hang my head in shame.

Am I responsible for any of the tragic deaths that are now on everyone's lips? I want to protest any hint of liability. I want to shout my innocence from the rooftops, to anyone who can hear... And yet, I can't. I fear I am responsible. If not for all, at least, for some and the guilt is a heavy burden to bear.

I'm a cross-dressing, hypocritical, deceitful, middle-aged man. It is time I accepted the truth... I mourn the pain and anguish my actions will cause others, but my mind is made up. The truth will set me free.

Now all I need to do is find the courage to break the news to my wife. She isn't going to take my leaving well, but I refuse to live in the dark and shadows any longer. I've found my soulmate, the love of my life. He will help me through this transition. He's in a perfect position to do so. After all, he's been there, too...

Lachlan squeezed the last box into the back of his pickup. It was already loaded high. Even the backseats were full, but he'd managed to fit everything in. The moving van would be there within the hour to collect the furniture. The thought of leaving filled him with mixed emotions. He looked forward to a future with Ava, but he'd spent five years of his life in this town. He'd made strong friendships, he'd forged a career. He'd had a family.

A few days earlier, Becker had called him to tell him Elsie Irwin had retracted her statement, putting both Lachlan and Martin in the clear. Though Lachlan welcomed the news, it was bittersweet and the fact was, it no longer mattered. Martin was dead, along with his family. Life would never be the same again.

He looked around at the neat garden that bordered his family home. He'd listed it for sale. He and Kristy agreed it was for the best. They were both moving on, their lives headed in different directions. It saddened him to be bringing to an end the life he'd imagined would be his until he died, but he couldn't deny the joy and anticipation he felt at the thought of starting a new chapter with Ava.

The sound of his phone ringing broke into his thoughts and he collected it from where he'd left it on the front seat. Glancing at the screen, he noticed he'd missed three other calls from blocked numbers while he'd been going back and forth with boxes between his house and truck. He frowned and answered the phone.

"Lachlan Coleridge."

"Lachie, are you still in town? We need you at the station."

Lachlan frowned at the urgency in the voice of one of his former colleagues. "Mick, my resignation was effective three days ago. My time in Moree is done."

"I understand, Lachie, but we... We have a bit of a situation. We need your help."

"Where's Becker? Does he even know you're calling? He won't take too kindly to your invitation. He and I didn't exactly part on the friendliest of terms." Suddenly, Lachlan heard the howling of sirens. They didn't sound very far away.

"That's the thing," Mick was saying. "Becker's the reason for my call. He... He killed himself last night. Apparently, he left a note. His wife was working a night shift at the hospital. She left home at eleven last evening and arrived home a little after eight this morning. She found him."

"Shit," Lachlan muttered, shocked beyond

belief. *Becker was dead?* He'd committed *suicide?* Why? How?

The questions hammered away at his dazed mind. He simply couldn't take it all in.

"Please, Lachie. As the most senior officer on staff, we need you."

The quiet desperation in his colleague's voice finally broke through Lachlan's haze. He couldn't bring himself to remind the man he was no longer stationed at Moree.

"I'll be there as soon as I can," he promised. Ending the call, he swallowed a heavy sigh and closed the back of his car. It appeared he wouldn't be leaving for Sydney anytime soon.

Lachlan strode up the neat brick path that led to the house Becker shared with his wife and two young kids. Constable David Jacobs kept pace with him.

"The general duties officers who answered the emergency call told me the superintendent's death occurred in unusual circumstances," Jacobs said, a little too eagerly for Lachlan's liking. He shot the officer a hard look.

"Becker was the head of the Barwon Local Area Command. He committed suicide. Isn't that unusual enough?"

The constable blushed in embarrassment and Lachlan felt a surge of satisfaction. Good, the man ought to be embarrassed. No one's death was cause for innuendo and speculation, not even Becker's. Lachlan might not have liked the man, but it didn't mean he'd treat him with disrespect at a time like this.

Pushing past an officer who guarded the front door, he paused to ask the man about the location of the body.

"He's in the back shed, Detective Coleridge."

Lachlan nodded his thanks and kept walking through the house. Jacobs jogged to keep up. Two more constables stood by the back door and opened it as Lachlan approached. Once again, he nodded his thanks. He strode across the back porch and down a short flight of steps.

The yard was scattered with the usual assortment of kids' toys, a swing set, bicycles and dolls. The innocence of it tore at Lachlan's heart. Now two kids would grow up without a father. It didn't get sadder than that. It was bad enough for his own children that he was going to be their part-time Dad, but he was determined to be involved in their lives as much as he possibly could.

The shed loomed in front of him, the galvanized iron catching rays from the morning sun. Becker lived on a large block. The shed was large enough to house a bus. Lachlan wondered briefly why his former boss would need such a building and then dismissed the thought.

What did it matter what Becker had used it for in the past? It would be forever known as the place where he hung himself. The thought was sobering.

There were another two officers standing guard

outside the galvanized iron door that led to the inside of the shed. Blue-and-white checked police tape cordoned off the area. The officers acknowledged Lachlan and Jacobs in silence and stood aside to allow them to enter.

Far from being dark and gloomy, the inside of the shed was lit up like a football stadium at night. Lachlan blinked from the unexpected brightness. A forensic team was already set up, with high-powered spotlights illuminating every nook and cranny of the building. Their main focus was the body that still hung from a steel beam that ran the length of the shed. An old, rusted ladder stood less than a foot away from the corpse.

Lachlan moved closer, skirting around an assortment of vintage car bodies in various states of restoration and crates of what looked like miscellaneous car parts. *So, Becker had been a car restorer in his other life*. It was funny how little Lachlan knew about him outside the station.

Looking up, Lachlan got his first good view of the body and gasped in shock. Becker was clothed in a long flowing dress that looked like it might have come from his wife's closet, had she been a larger woman. The red silk fluttered in the light breeze that stole through the cracks in the walls. Red high-heel sandals adorned Becker's feet and matched the garish lipstick on his face.

Lachlan shook his head back and forth, trying to gather his thoughts. *Becker was a transvestite?* It certainly appeared that way. Just another hobby Lachlan had been ignorant of. Turning on his heel, he approached the forensic officer who held a digital camera in his hand.

"Are you finished with your pictures? Are we able to cut him down?"

"Yes. I've taken all I need. You're going to need help getting him down. He's not a lightweight, by anyone's estimation."

Lachlan nodded in grim assent. Like his shed, Becker had been an oversized man. Lachlan called out to Jacobs who moved over toward him, a slight grin on his face.

"I told you his death was a little unusual, didn't I?" Jacobs smirked, indicating the commander.

Anger stirred inside Lachlan. He might not have gotten on with Becker while he was alive and a lot of the time, he hadn't liked the man, but that didn't mean he'd think badly of him now, or allow others to make jokes at his expense.

"Enough!" he growled. "Have some respect!"

Jacobs' eyes widened in surprise, but he refrained from making any further comments and the sly look on his face disappeared.

"Forensics have what they need. Go and get a couple of the others. I need help to get him down," Lachlan said.

"Yes, Detective. Of course. I'll go and get someone to assist."

Jacobs scurried off in the direction of the exit. Lachlan glanced back up at Becker and sighed.

The man's face was blackened from lack of oxygen and his tongue hung out of his mouth, swollen and purple. It protruded from his face like some gruesome caricature of a hanging victim out of an old cowboys and Indians movie. The skirt of the dress was stained and smelled of urine and feces. In his dying moments, the superintendent had obviously lost control of his bladder and his bowels.

The desperation he must have been feeling to drive himself to something like this did Lachlan's head in. It was the same as Martin. *How did a man get to this?* At least Becker hadn't taken his family with him, but that wouldn't ease their suffering. Both of his children were under ten. How could they understand how their father had come to make such a decision? How would *anyone* understand?

And then there was the cross-dressing thing. *What was that all about?* Had it had anything to do with his suicide? Unless Becker had explained himself in the note he'd left, they'd probably never find out.

The desperate sadness of the awful tragedy hit Lachlan full force. He gasped, winded, and bent over, trying to drag air into his lungs. One of the forensics officers glanced over at him, but said nothing. The other officer ignored him and continued to pack up their gear.

The door to the shed opened again and Jacobs came back in, followed by two of the officers from the house. Quietly, Lachlan gave the men orders to climb up the ladder and cut the body loose. In silence, they donned gloves and went about the gruesome task. Lachlan stayed on the ground with one of the other officers and held Becker steady while the other two went to work.

As the rope gave way, Lachlan took the weight of the body, grunting with the strain. His recently healed collarbone protested, but he steadfastly ignored the pain. They lowered Becker down carefully, then laid him on the ground. A black bra peeked out from the opening of the dress and the skirt rode high to reveal black, lacy stockings. Lachlan turned away, unable to look any longer.

"Where are the morgue guys? Has someone notified them?" He threw the question in Jacobs' direction. The constable appeared to know more than anyone else.

"Yes," Jacobs replied. "They should be here any minute."

"Send them in when they arrive. Tell them he's right to go."

"No problem, Detective. I'll see that it's done."

Lachlan nodded grimly, his lips compressed. Despite what he'd seen, the worst was yet to come. He still had Becker's wife to deal with. Swallowing a sigh, he turned on his heel and left.

———

Ava glanced at her watch. Her last appointment for the day seemed to be dragging on forever. She knew her desire to bring her workday to an end had more to do with Lachlan arriving that evening from Moree rather than the monologue of complaints that were coming from the young woman who sat in the chair opposite Ava's desk. Still, time was passing painfully slow.

She'd expected to hear from him by now. He'd been hoping to get away from Moree mid-morning, at the latest. She'd left a couple of messages on his phone, but she had yet to speak with him. *Maybe he was out of range?* There were spots along the country roads he needed to travel to get to the city where cell phone signals were weak or non-existent. Or, perhaps he had the music up and hadn't heard the phone ring over the noise? She could imagine him nodding along to the tunes on his iPod. He'd recently confessed he loved listening to songs from the 80s.

As if she'd conjured him up, her phone vibrated inside the top drawer of her desk. She glanced at her patient who appeared engrossed in the sound of her own voice and surreptitiously opened the drawer. Checking the screen, her heart skipped a beat and then she cursed silently. It was Lachlan. She'd have to let the call go through to voicemail. At least she now knew he was back in phone range and had received her messages.

Twenty minutes later, Ava ushered her last patient out and eagerly returned to her office. Tugging open the desk drawer, she snatched up the phone and dialed Lachlan's number. It rang out for so long, she was sure he wasn't going to answer and then finally, he did.

"Ava, I'm sorry. I... I should have left you a message, but I wanted to tell you myself."

His voice was grim. Foreboding surged through her veins. *He'd changed his mind. He wasn't coming. He was going back to his wife...* She gritted her teeth and forced herself to get a grip.

There was no way he'd go back to Kristy. He loved *her*—Ava. He'd told her so. She focused on keeping her voice neutral.

"Tell me what?"

"I... I'm still in Moree."

The sense of foreboding increased, but she forced herself to remain calm. "Oh, I thought you were arriving in Sydney today."

"I was. I intended to leave as soon as I'd given directions to the movers, but...something's come up."

"Right," she said, doing her best to keep calm.

"I'm not sure what you're thinking, but the reason has nothing to do with us. I want to be with you more than anything else, but right now, I just can't."

The dread in her belly eased slightly. She let go of the breath she'd held. "Talk to me, Lachlan. Tell me what happened."

"It's... It's the superintendent. Nigel Becker. He... He hung himself last night... Or maybe early this morning. We're not yet sure of the exact time."

Ava gasped. Shock rendered her momentarily speechless. *Nigel Becker? Her patient?* He'd committed *suicide?* No, Lachlan must be mistaken. Nigel struggled to deal with work stresses, like most police officers, but the last time she'd seen him, he appeared to have accepted Nigella would always be a part of him and was at peace with himself and the way he lived his life. It couldn't be the same Nigel Becker.

And yet, she knew in her heart, it was. It had to be. Moree was only a town of about ten thousand people, including the surrounding areas. While Nigel hadn't told her he was the superintendent, she was aware he was in law enforcement. There couldn't possibly be two of them.

"Ava? Are you all right?"

The concern in Lachlan's voice brought her back to reality with a rush. She realized she hadn't responded and hurried to reply.

"Yes, yes. I... I'm fine. I'm just a little shocked. First Martin and now your superintendent. What about his family? His wife and children?"

"How do you know he had a wife and children? I didn't realize you'd met."

Ava thought fast and then realized a dead man probably didn't have any need for confidentiality. Besides, she was confident Lachlan would keep it to himself.

"He was a patient of Phoebe's. I saw him a few times while she was away."

Surprise laced Lachlan's voice. "He was receiving *counseling*?"

"Yes."

There was a moment of silence and then Lachlan spoke again, this time a little more slowly. "I guess you know about the cross-dressing thing, then."

Surprise and confusion made Ava frown. How would Lachlan know about a thing like that? Nigel had told her the only person who knew was his wife.

"What cross-dressing thing?" she asked, buying time.

"Apparently, he liked to dress up in women's

clothing. You know, like a transvestite. We found him wearing a dress and makeup and he had on women's underwear. We interviewed his wife. She denied having any knowledge of her husband's predilections and said she didn't recognize the clothing. They were several sizes larger than what she wore. We suspect he purchased the items himself."

Ava listened to what Lachlan was saying and wanted to shout out a denial. How could Nigel's wife tell the police she'd known nothing? She'd known all about his obsession. She'd threatened to divorce him and prevent him from having contact with his children. At least, that's what Nigel had said.

Troubled, Ava continued to listen to Lachlan explain how he was going to be caught up in Moree for a few more days, at least until an acting superintendent could be appointed.

Her horror at what happened continued to grow and swell inside her until she could no longer hold it back.

"Did he leave a note?" she blurted, interrupting Lachlan mid-sentence.

"Yes, he did. It says words to the effect that he was disgusted with himself and his secret and it was best for all concerned if he put an end to his life. We also found a few diary entries that appeared to have been torn out of a book. They seemed to support the fact he was depressed and bordering on suicidal."

"No," Ava breathed in desperation. "I don't believe it."

"We're all finding it hard to believe."

"No, I mean, he was receiving counseling and of course, we discussed how he liked to dress up in women's clothes, but he wasn't depressed about it. Uncomfortable and embarrassed, perhaps, but I would never have determined he was suicidal. I saw him not long before I returned to Sydney. He was upset that his wife couldn't seem to accept his alternate lifestyle, but—"

"What did you say?"

"I said we talked about how his wife was angry about his...hobby. They'd argued about it. She'd threatened to leave."

"Hang on a minute. Are you sure?"

Lachlan sounded tense. His words were clipped. Ava could understand why. "Of course I'm sure. Our conversation only happened a couple of weeks ago."

"Fuck."

The quiet oath sounded heavy with dread and disbelief. Ava bit her lip, wishing there was some way she could reassure him, but knowing there wasn't. She'd spoken the truth. He needed to dig a little deeper and make sure things had happened as they'd assumed, that this wasn't a clever plot to conceal a horrible crime.

"This is going to take longer than I anticipated," he muttered a few moments later.

Ava nodded and then said, "Take all the time you need. I'll be here waiting."

"Thank you," he breathed and she heard the relief and gratitude in his voice.

"Anytime."

CHAPTER 22

Lachlan filled his lungs to capacity and then blew out his breath on a heavy sigh. Audrey Becker waited for him in one of the interview rooms. He could tell she'd been surprised when he'd asked her to come down to the station to answer a few more questions, but she'd eventually shrugged and arrived at the appointed time. He wasn't sure what he was looking for, but after Ava's bombshell, he owed it to Becker to find out.

Opening the door to the interview room, he walked in and took a seat opposite Becker's wife. She glanced up and smiled. She was a pretty woman, small and petite and looked at least fifteen years younger than the superintendent. Lachlan wondered about their story; how they'd gotten together. Opening a notebook to a fresh page, he pulled a pen out of his pocket and began.

"Mrs Becker, let me tell you again how sorry I am for your loss. It must have come as a shock to you."

"Yes, it did, Detective. I had no idea. I mean, I was aware Nigel was getting counseling, and though I don't put much stock in that kind of thing, I truly believed it was helping. I can only assume the pressures of the job got to him. I'm sure you know what I mean. Police officers see way too much of the most awful things there are to see and nobody understands, nobody knows what to say."

A tear formed in her eye and she patted it away with a dainty, lace-edged handkerchief. "Nigel used to try and talk to me about it in the early days, but to tell you the truth, I couldn't handle it. I couldn't handle hearing about all those awful things. It was the reason I suggested he get some counseling." Her voice caught on a sob. "I thought it was *helping* him! He seemed to be getting better!"

Lachlan forced himself to remain unaffected by her display of emotion, even though it was difficult to sit back passively and witness her pain. After giving her a few moments to collect herself, he spoke again.

"Mrs Becker, when I talked to you at the house, you told me you knew nothing of your husband's penchant for women's clothing. Do you remember that?"

She blinked and stared up at him. "Yes."

"But, that's not the truth, is it, Mrs Becker. You did know about it. In fact, you and Nigel argued about it not so long ago. Isn't that right?"

She lowered her gaze and stared at the scarred Formica table that stood between them. Fresh tears welled up in her eyes and trickled down her cheeks. A long moment later, she nodded.

Lachlan sat forward in his seat and pitched his voice low. "Why did you lie to me, Mrs Becker?"

The woman gasped on a loud sob and buried her face in her hands. "I'm sorry, Detective! I'm sorry! I was distraught, and embarrassed. I didn't know what to say!" She lifted her head and stared at him, her eyes red with tears.

"My husband was the commander of the Barwon district. He was responsible for close to thirty officers in a town that has its problems. At night, in the privacy of his home, or our shed, he liked to dress like a woman. It was disgusting! It was shameful! How could you expect me to own up to knowing something like that? It didn't make any difference. It certainly wasn't going to bring Nigel back!"

Her sobs increased in volume and pressure and Lachlan clenched his jaw against her pain. She was right. He wasn't sure he'd have admitted to knowing such a shameful family secret, either.

His gaze raked over her again. Even if she'd had sufficient motivation, there was no way she was strong enough to pull the hanging off. Becker had weighed more than two hundred pounds. It had taken four men to cut him down. No, she couldn't be responsible for her husband's death. It was time to reassure her and let her go home and grieve in private.

"I'm sorry, Mrs Becker. I know how hard this is for you. I didn't want to upset you. I'm just doing my job."

She raised her head and looked at him, her pretty skin blotchy and red from her tears, but she smiled at him kindly.

"I understand, Detective. I was married to a policeman for nearly a decade. I know all about how your job works."

He nodded, grateful for her understanding. Pushing away from the table, he helped her to her feet.

"Thank you for coming in, Mrs Becker. I appreciate it. Do you have someone to drive you home? I'm happy to organize a ride."

"No, thank you. I... I came here with a friend. I asked him to wait for me outside. He's keeping an eye on the kids."

At the reminder of Becker's two young children, Lachlan's gut twisted with dread. It would be a long, hard road for them to come to terms with their father's death, if ever. He was glad he'd spared his own kids that kind of pain.

Showing the woman out, he thanked her once again. She nodded and left the station. She didn't look back.

Lachlan dragged himself wearily back to his desk and collapsed into his chair. It had been a long and tiring couple of days. He wanted to find a hot shower and then sleep the sleep of the dead, but first, he had to call Ava. He missed her.

The phone dialed out and he waited for her to answer.

"Good morning, Lachlan. How are you?"

She sounded quiet and subdued, as if testing out his mood. The night before, he'd been so busy, he'd barely had a minute to speak with her.

"I'm fine," he replied. "You'll be pleased to know it's over."

"Becker's investigation?"

"Yes."

"What happened?"

"I just interviewed Audrey Becker. I'm satisfied she had nothing to do with his death. It's going to be ruled a suicide, as we suspected from the outset."

"Oh, well, I guess that's good. At least you can be satisfied you know the truth."

"Yes. Now all I want to do is finish up my report and sign off. I'm going to take a shower and catch a few hours' sleep at the station and then I'll hit the road. I hope to be in Sydney by this evening."

"That sounds wonderful."

He heard the excitement and happiness in her voice and couldn't help but smile. Just the thought of being back by her side brought comfort to his battered soul.

"I love you," he said.

"I love you, too. I'll see you soon."

He swallowed the lump of emotion that lodged itself in his throat and managed to reply. "I'm counting down the hours."

EPILOGUE

With every step that took Audrey Becker further away from the police station, her heart lightened incrementally. By the time she reached the car where Edward and her children waited, her face was wreathed in smiles. At last, it was over. Time to put it behind them. Time to get on with their lives.

Edward opened the door on the driver's side and climbed out of the car. He looked at her and grinned.

"I take it you have good news?" he chuckled.

In deference to the children seated in the car, she pitched her voice low. "Yes, you would have been proud of me. I played the role of grieving widow like I'd been born to do it."

"And they fell for it?"

Her smile widened and she winked at him. "Of course. What did you expect? I'm a woman of many talents, as you know quite well..."

Edward whooped and hollered and swung her up in his arms. His large frame carried her easily as he turned them around in a joyous circle. Their laughter melded together, until the sound of it became one. Coming to a stop, he slid her slowly down the front of him until her feet once again touched the ground.

She felt the bulge of his erection against her stomach and her eyes widened in delight. Bringing her hand up, she caressed his cock through the fabric of his pants.

"It looks like you might need a little attention before we get on the road," she murmured, squeezing him once again.

He chuckled and cupped her bottom in his large hands and pressed her up against him. "It's nice of you to notice," he growled low in her ear.

Standing on tiptoe, she dragged his head down and swiped her tongue across his lips. "I *always* notice."

"Yes, you do, honey," he replied and swatted her on the ass. "And that's what I love about you."

NOTE TO READERS

I do hope you have enjoyed reading Ava and Lachlan's story. If you've enjoyed this book, please feel free to leave a review for The Final Bullet at Goodreads and your favorite digital retailer. Every review is very much appreciated.

If you would like to receive news on upcoming stories, release dates, book launches and other snippets, please feel free to sign up for my newsletter. You can do this by visiting my website at www.christaylorauthor.com.au and clicking on the "Subscribe to my Newsletter" link on the right.

The Debt Collector is the next book in the Sydney Harbour Hospital Series. Here's a sneak peek:

Hannah Langdon loves working with the dead. As an embalmer at the Max Grace Funeral Home in the inner city Sydney suburb of Balmain, she is proud of her work and considers it an honor and a privilege to prepare someone for their final resting place.

But lately, there have been an alarming number of her co-workers who have been killed in horrible accidents. The fact that these people live on the fringes of Sydney society and have no one to mourn them doesn't ease Hannah's turbulent state of mind. By chance, she reconnects with a man from her past, a man she'd rather forget.

Doctor Jared Black is now a highly respected surgeon who works in the reputable Sydney Harbour Hospital, but she remembers him only as the seventeen-year-old drunk driver who killed her high school boyfriend. Now Jared's twin has gone missing and Hannah wants to know why. After all, the last time she saw him was at the Max Grace Funeral Home...

What is happening to the people employed at the funeral home? Hannah can't help but think she might be next...

The Debt Collector will be released on 26 June, 2016 and is available for pre-order from your favorite digital retailer.

About the Author

Chris Taylor grew up on a farm in north-west New South Wales, Australia. She always had a thirst for stories and recalls writing her first book at the ripe old age of eight. Always a lover of romance and happily-ever-afters, a career in criminal law sparked her interest in intrigue and suspense. For Chris to be able to combine romance with suspense in her books is a dream come true.

Chris is married to Linden and is the mother of five children. If not behind her computer, you can find her doing the school run, taxiing children to swimming lessons, football, ballet and cricket. In her spare time, Chris loves to read her favorite authors who include Richard North Patterson, Sandra Brown, Kathleen E Woodiwiss and Jude Devereaux.

You can find out more about Chris and sign up for her newsletter at her website:

http://www.christaylorauthor.com.au